THE TOWER PRINCESS

SHONNA SLAYTON

AMARETTO PRESS

ALSO BY SHONNA SLAYTON

FAIRY TALES

Cinderella's Dress

Cinderella's Shoes

Spindle

Snow White's Mirror (coming soon)

HISTORICAL

Liz and Nellie

PROLOGUE

*J*n a land, far, far away where the winters are bitter and the springs are wet, there is a kingdom called Morlaix. Once a famous land where merchants traveled to trade for salve and balsams made from the fabled rowan trees, the land is almost forgotten today.

Morlaix Kingdom was once strong and united. In that lush, green land, two boys grew up together as best friends. Did I say grew up? I meant, competed. After all, one was Anglo-Saxon. The other, Viking.

"Bet I can climb the castle wall without getting caught by the constable."

"Bet I can shoot my arrow through the cook's hat and pin it to that post."

Problem was, they both wanted the same thing when they grew up: the crown.

"When I'm king, I'll expand my territory in all directions—as far as I can ride. I'll let you till my fields."

"When I'm king, I'll build the grandest castle around and let you serve my bread."

"You'll never be king; your head is too fat."

"You'll never be king; you can't shoot straight."

Boys grow into pages. Pages into squires. Squires into knights. One knight was tall with chiseled chin and quick reflexes. One knight was short with cunning mind and piercing eyes.

Finally, all their betting and arguing came down to one final war. The knights fought valiantly, side by side, to defend the ailing Morlaix king—their king who was desperately ill and dying without an heir.

The battle was won but the strongest two knights, well, they were not done.

"Who's got the fat head, now?"

"Look how straight my shot was, eh?"

All through town the knights did battle, ignoring the towns-people they did seek to govern, smashing the very town they did wish to own. About to destroy the life-giving center of the Isle of Morlaix.

"You will relinquish to me."

"You will hand over your sword and muck out my stables."

They knocked each other off their horses and continued fighting fist to fist for both the upper hand and for the kingdom.

"You will lose in hand combat. My reflexes are quicker."

"My mind is fast. Hand combat is my best skill."

Finally, the fight came to a standstill underneath the Tree of Morlaix. My tree. And that is how I got involved. The tree must not be hurt no matter the ego of the knight.

"Stop your bickering.

Your biting.

Your belly wagging."

Swinging nimbly out of the tree, I planted my two small feet between the growling, frothing knights.

They stopped and stared. Likely surprised to see me. I am the stuff of legends and tales and bedtime stories in this land.

"Who are you?"

"What are you?"

Maintaining a menacing stare to make up for my small stature, I proclaimed, "King of the Woodlings." I expected them to bow. Most do.

Blank looks.

Bawk! In their ignorance, they were the same. I uttered a deep growl that began as distant thunder and quickly multiplied to an earthquake. The shaking earth caught their attention and brought them to their knees.

> "WOODLINGS ARE THE MAGICAL CREATURES WHO PLAY
> UNDERNEATH THE FORESTS ON THE ISLANDS OF
>   MORLAIX."

With eyebrows raised, the two knights, still on their knees, awkwardly bowed.

I have a little bit of magic, not a lot. Enough to make people wonder about me. And take a rest from fighting to listen to my poems.

> "I SEE YOU TWO MEN, FULL OF SASS,
> HAVE FOUND YOURSELVES AT QUITE AN IMPASSE.
> BOTH OF YOU WANT TO BE KING,
> RISING WHEN KING RORICK SINGS HIS FINAL SING.
> YET, YOUR SKILLS ARE EQUAL IN EVERY WAY.
> YOUR FIGHT WILL GO ON AND ON, FOREVER BEYOND
>   A DAY.
> PERCHANCE WHEN ONLY ONE OF YOU REMAIN,
> T'WON'T MATTER ANYWAY—THERE'LL BE NOTHING LEFT
>   TO GAIN."

At the end of this speech I made the two knights turn around and witness their selfish battle through the village.

They had dueled through the very heart of the marketplace. And, being autumn, and the harvest fully in, the marketplace was rather packed. They had smashed through piles of pumpkins, leaving trails of stringy orange innards strewn about the stalls. Exploded hay bales littered the ground. Columns of dark smoke smudged the sunset in the distance and marked the knights' path of destruction through the metalworking corridor. As they stood observing, a decorative gourd that had been flung onto a rooftop rolled down and shattered, breaking the silence.

The sound seemed to release an angry craftsman—a plump fellow with a pumpkin smashed on his head. He took a step forward, shouting impolite things while jabbing his finger at the knights. After speaking his mind, he flung pumpkin guts on each one, dulling the shine on their shining armor.

> "ALL THIS DISASTER CREATED WITHOUT AN ENEMY
>   IN SIGHT.
> WOULDN'T YOU SAY—FOR THESE VILLAGERS—IT WAS AN
>   UNFAIR FIGHT?"

The two knights managed to hang their heads and look ashamed, even though they were not. Their brains were already whirling, trying to come up with new ways to gain the crown.

Thus, I negotiated a peace treaty between Jorvik the Large and Simon of the House of Waterton. They each took half the kingdom. Exactly half.

"Half? But that is not whole."

"Half? That is only part of what I want."

> "THERE IS ONLY ONE WAY TO SOLVE THIS FINE RIDDLE.
> THE TOWN MUST BE FIRMLY SPLIT DOWN THE MIDDLE.
> HALF TO EACH OTHER, AND WITH A DIVIDING WALL
> THAT IS MY DECISION. THIS IS MY CALL."

We built a wall right then, splitting the town into North Morlaix and South Morlaix (for the reigning king did, after all, sing his last sing.) The wall traveled from where the water laps the base of the sea rocks, to where the thick forests choke the shore, through the fields and villages, across the moat, until it split the very center of the castle. Half for Jorvik and half for Simon. The stables, the drawbridge, the moat. Dividing everything into North and South Morlaix. Eighteen feet high, six feet across, the Dividing Wall separated the land for two new rulers, friends no longer.

North Morlaix was mainly Viking and South Morlaix mostly Anglo Saxon.

As for the peace treaty, it was to last as long as each knight held the throne. They could never again attack each other, or outside forces would take over and neither would win. But if they would allow, love could conquer all.

THE KINGS' CONTESTS

After the wall went up, King Jorvik and King Simon set about to build their families and their armies. They decided if they could not attack one another, surely, their children could. They each took a bride. Jorvik from among the strongest damsels. Simon from the wise.

BY PROCLAMATION OF THE KING OF NORTH MORLAIX: A CONTEST. TO FIND THE DAMSEL OF GREATEST STRENGTH. IN FIVE DAYS' TIME. A TOURNAMENT.

The winning damsel was built like a fighting horse. She could carry the knight's charger five paces. She could throw a boulder from the top of the castle keep and hit the ocean. Her name was Ingrid, which means "hero's daughter." She was exactly what Jorvik was looking for in a wife.

Not to be outdone, Simon also held a contest.

BY PROCLAMATION OF THE KING OF SOUTH MORLAIX: A CONTEST. TO FIND THE DAMSEL OF GREATEST INTELLIGENCE. IN FIVE DAYS' TIME. A TEST.

Simon's bride would come from amongst the most scholarly. He devised a series of puzzles and riddles to be solved. The damsel who could solve them all would become his wife. The winning damsel not only solved all the riddles, but also made up her own that Simon himself could not solve. Her name was Margaret, which means "pearl." She was truly precious to Simon.

Jorvik wanted to produce a strong heir, Simon, a cunning one.

Jorvik's wife was fertile and bore him seven sons shoulder to shoulder. Delighted in his growing army, he directed their training exercises next to the Dividing Wall in the castle court-yard. He had them growl and grunt and throw heavy objects to make sure their strength could be heard.

Simon's wife was barren. She used all her cunning to study herbs and balsams to help her bear a son. As the ivy climbed its way up the wall, time slipped by and Simon had no heir. He suffered through years of hearing the army train next door. With no children of his own, Simon poured all his energies into training his own knights from the populace of South Morlaix. He knew as soon as his old friend Jorvik stepped down from the throne, the sons of North Morlaix would scale the wall to attack. He must be ready.

King Jorvik watched his sons train each morning. He was proud of their strength and skills. The only fly in his mead was that to win the entire kingdom, he would have to abdicate his throne to one of his seven sons. He was not ready to do so. The eldest was eager to step forward as the new king. Daily he stalked back and forth before the Dividing Wall like the caged panther he had once brought home from a trip to Africa.

The second, third, and remaining sons trained only because they enjoyed the exercise. They knew their older brother would take over the throne.

"You did not make the bulls-eye. Try again," commanded the eldest son, Herrick, cracking the small whip he carried with him.

"I was close enough. If t'were a man he'd be dead already." The second son threw down his bow. "I'm going fishing." He stalked off, taking youngest sons numbers six and seven with him. The boys were not yet teens and were much more interested in catching supper than in practicing under Herrick the Panther's critical eye.

A BOY AND GIRL ARE BORN

Then one day there was the unmistakable cry of an infant from the South. The Panther stopped in his tracks, cocking his head. This cry was coming from the castle, not from a village brat.

Royal trumpets sounded.

The Panther's lip curled in a smile that looked more like a grimace. "Finally, my competition has arrived." He reached back into his quiver, pulled out an arrow, and shot into the Dividing Wall. "Until we meet."

∾

IT WAS TRUE. A son was finally born to Simon and Maggie. There was great celebration. With an heir at last, Simon pinned his every hope on the healthy eight-pound creature. He named the baby boy Manny, meaning "powerful warrior."

"How long I have waited for you," whispered King Simon.

Unfortunately, Queen Maggie, exhausted from the difficult nine months of carrying the child and after a strenuous labor, lived only hours after her bright boy was born. On that final day, her skin turned pallid and the bed sheets became soaked with perspiration. Her fever would not come down and no one knew what to do, least of all King Simon. He paced at her footboard while she held the sprawling infant.

"Manny, dear," she said to the baby. "My time with you is short. I must give you a lifetime of love while I can." She kissed his little baby nose. "You will never remember me. But my prayer for you is to unite the kingdoms the way they once were and bring peace to the land." She kissed his little baby fingers. With trembling hand, she removed her jeweled cross necklace and laid it on the boy. She looked at Simon with pleading eyes. "Don't let him forget me," she whispered. "I want him to know how much I wanted him." She kissed his little baby toes.

Then Maggie died holding Manny in her arms, the king holding them both.

A ruddy nursemaid removed the squawking infant from his mother's arms and gave him to the king. Choking back his tears, he brought the infant to the window to show the waiting citizens their prince.

While holding the babe in view of the citizenry, he unfurled the child's banner. The people whooped and hollered. They knew the stakes of the divided kingdom. Did they not hear the next-door army practicing every day? The prince was their hope as well.

Then, with a cry of despair, the king unfurled the black banner of death. The cheering and dancing stopped. The people stood and stared. No! Their beloved queen? It could not be. Yet there were the two banners side by side. One signifying life, the other death.

The king knew he should speak. The people needed his strength and his wisdom. But he had nothing to say. He backed away from the window until the people couldn't even see his shadow.

Not knowing what to do, the people sat on the ground and waited. King Simon didn't know what to do either. For the moment, he did not care that he was king over only half a kingdom. For just a moment he thought only of his family and what he had lost. But then, something inside him shifted. Realigned his thinking. He had to preserve what he had left.

He knew the Panther stalked at the wall. He felt his enemy's restlessness grow every day. He knew his son would be in grave danger. The Panther would have no heart for a baby. Could he make a double funeral? Would it be convincing? Then he could send his son into hiding—away from his family to be raised as a commoner.

Wishing he had his wife's wise counsel, he collapsed into a chair. He knew now, more than ever, what a pearl he had in Maggie.

While he was mulling over these thoughts, the nursemaid approached him, wringing her hands.

"I 'ave a sister, newly widowed. She bore a babe yestreen and 'as no way to care for 'em. Bring 'er into the castle to raise her son like he wos the prince. A decoy, as it may."

The king stared unblinking at the nursemaid. Could he put someone else's babe at risk? He was shamed for even thinking it.

"'T'would be her 'onor to serve the king in this way," said the nursemaid, sensing the king's concerns. "'Tis for the safety of the prince."

What the king didn't know was that the nursemaid and her sister were conniving, greedy women. The nursemaid herself did not wish to leave the luxury of the castle, and she had been looking for an opportunity to bring her sister in to share the wealth. It was not the kingdom's best interests she was concerned with, rather, her own. And what she was sensing was not the king's feelings, but opportunity. Once the king went along with her plan, he would be hard pressed to restore the real prince. The entire kingdom would recognize the nursemaid's nephew, Nigel, as the prince of South Morlaix.

"And where would my boy go?" asked the stricken king, studying the baby, marveling at his tiny ears. Grief flooded his mind and he had a hard time putting thoughts together.

Smiling wide, the nurse revealed her crooked teeth. "Thar be a fine tailor and his wife in town. They 'ave not been able to 'ave children, much like yerself. He wonts an apprentice. They would be most agreeable. And 'is wife would be sure to hide the true nature of the wee babe." She stroked the prince's cheek.

The king nodded, relieved that he wouldn't have to send his son away. He could watch him grow up. But what kind of relationship would they have? Could he risk not letting his son know he was the prince until he had grown into a man? Simon pressed his hand to his temple to stop the throbbing. Then the babe awoke, screwed up his face, and let loose a piercing wail. The king wished he could scream too. Instead, he handed the child to the nursemaid with all the ideas.

~

NOT LONG AFTER, in North Morlaix, the cry of the eighth child born to Jorvik's wife rang out. This time, a girl.

The king stared at the babe. He was so used to having sons that he felt a bit awkward. His wife, too was a little shocked.

"It's…a girl?" The king set down the sword he had brought with him. He had given each of his seven sons a sword at their birth. *What did one give a girl? A shield mayhap?*

"We can't call her Thorwald like we planned," he said.

Ingrid laughed.

Jorvik had never heard his wife laugh before. Once she started, she couldn't stop. Her mirth was catchy and soon Jorvik also broke out in joyful noise. The child's birth was the beginning of other changes in North Morlaix.

After much debate and suggestions from every member of the family and the court, the babe was named Gressa, meaning "pearl." This made the old nursemaid raise an eyebrow, but she kept her tongue silent.

No one stepped into the castle without a quick look in on Gressa. Presents piled up. Fancy linens and imported silks. Gold jewelry and precious gems. Not to mention grain and chickens from the townsfolk.

Ingrid kept company with plaiters to learn how to entwine Gressa's hair when she grew a lock or two. The princes of North Morlaix came to coo and make funny faces at the baby. In all, Gressa brought out a softer side of her family. In everyone except the Panther.

THE CRY THAT CHANGED EVERYTHING

At first, the king and queen rejoiced over their daughter. It was like they had never had a child before, the way they doted on her. One day, when they were strolling in the garden, they heard a baby cry on the other side of the wall.

In King Simon's private garden.

In response, their baby girl cried and reached for the wall, as if to comfort the child on the other side.

The hearts of the king and queen grew cold. The young prince of their enemy. A boy on one side, a girl on the other. Too many kingdoms had been lost over forbidden love. They decided then, that the two must never meet. King Jorvik had a lock installed on the princess's room in the tallest tower.

The Panther observed what happened in the garden of North Morlaix.

"My father's response is weak," he seethed. "He allows a coal to burn." Then, planting stories filled with fear and uncertainty, he convinced his father that the princess must be protected from all harm.

What he really meant was that his own future was to be protected at the cost of his sister's freedom.

King Simon, realizing the implications of destined love, also took measures. He handed back his true son to the tailor's wife and told her never to bring him secretly to the castle again. His son would not be killed by his rival's son, nor beguiled by their daughter.

From my home in the ancient rowan tree I watch it all. Those knights—turned kings—think they have outsmarted me. They don't know everything.

I left a hole in the wall.

CHAPTER 1

*M*anny Taylor struggled up the ramps from the unloading docks in South Morlaix with arms laden down by leathers and furs. A shipload for his father, the tailor, had come in from Copello early that morning and Manny had insisted on carrying double his share. His hands had already been made strong from tailoring, but he needed arms fit for the glory of arm wrestling at the castle gate.

"These look like furs from our forests," Hoxham said, grunting in disgust. The older apprentice resembled a dandelion puff—skinny and tall with a shock of blond hair sticking out in all directions.

"Likely they are," Manny replied. "Sold on the mainland, and then resold back to us for a price."

"Tis not fair they have more forest than we."

Manny grunted. Poor Hoxham kept a long list of complaints about the injustices of living on the south side of the Dividing Wall. The North had better water, better trees, better houses, better craftsmen. All this knowledge, yet Hoxham had never stepped foot in North Morlaix.

"But we have more fields. More food," Manny countered. He, too, had lived in South Morlaix all his life. The coastline provided an abundance of fish, the fields were plentiful with wheat, and the villagers were a friendly lot who looked out for each other.

"I'd rather have more meat, meself."

Manny shrugged. "At least you don't have to suffer through a North Morlaixan winter."

Hoxham rolled his eyes. "Whoever made up that joke isn't the least bit funny. There ain't no difference between their winter and ours."

"I think that's the joke, my friend." Manny chuckled.

"It's still not fun—" Hoxham collided with someone rushing in the opposite direction. They knocked each other to the ground with leathers landing in clumps all around. In a flash, Hoxham was up, fists at the ready. He'd lived in the streets as a castle rat before Manny's father had taken him in as an apprentice and was always quick to fight.

Amidst the leathers lay a portly fellow, struggling to rise while spouting insults back at Hoxham.

Prince Nigel. Manny groaned. *Not again.*

Face red with rage and exertion, the downed prince pushed his stout figure off the ground and took a swipe at Hoxham's head. "Oaf! Look where you're going."

Hoxham easily ducked and was about to take the prince from behind in a headlock when Manny leaped between them and received an elbow to the eye.

Manny grabbed onto Hoxham's arm and deftly flipped him to the ground, pressing his boot to his friend's collarbone. He nodded politely at Nigel.

"Fine spring day, Prince Nigel. What brings you to the docks?" Manny grimaced as he pressed his foot harder into his friend to keep him down.

Nigel glanced up at the tallest tower on other side of the wall dividing North and South Morlaix. The rooms where the Tower Princess was rumored to be confined.

"She's not lookin' at you," Hoxham said before Manny could mash his face into the dirt.

Nigel scowled but looked away from the tower. "Sir Fletcher arrives today for the land granting ceremony. I'm here to welcome him," Nigel said in his attempt at sounding superior. He replaced his hat, the one with an overly large purple plume, onto his princely head.

Knowingly or not, Nigel emphasized *land granting ceremony*. The one thing Manny desired but could never have if he remained a simple tailor. His own estate. Had the prince known Manny's ambitions, he would have gone out of his way to rub it in.

The prince scowled at Hoxham, still struggling under Manny's grip. "One word from me and the dungeon floor will be the only land you see." He spat in the dirt by Hoxham's nose before speaking to Manny. "Try to keep your dog under control." As he walked by, Nigel cuffed Manny on the side of the head.

Manny's head snapped back, but he showed no sign of reacting to the pain. Ever since they were kids, Manny had been the castle target until Hoxham came along. And once Nigel had targeted someone, it was like giving royal permission for every other bully to take a shot. Maybe that was why he felt so beholden to the scruffy boy.

Biting his lip, Manny pressed down with all his might as Hoxham strained against his grip. "Not now," Manny insisted. "I'll get him in archery practice."

Once the prince was safely out of view, Manny let his friend go.

Hoxham sprung up, hands balled into tight fists. "I don't need your protection. Our prince is worthless. North Morlaix has the better prince, too." He kicked at the leathers Manny was piling up.

"I wouldn't call the Panther the better prince. Maybe the more dangerous."

"I wish the pestilence on him." Hoxham cursed but accepted the pile of leathers Manny shoved at him.

"You do not. No one wishes to see that evil return to the kingdom."

Hoxham shrugged and fell silent. But Manny could tell by the way his friend was clenching his hands that his fight with the prince was not over.

Manny had planned to even the score with a well-placed arrow accidentally-on-purpose shot through Prince Nigel's outrageous hat, but didn't have the opportunity. Archery practice was called off to allow the squires and knights to attend the ceremony. Since Manny was neither squire, nor knight, simply a volunteer to help protect the land he loved, no one told him.

However, finding himself alone at the field and with his bow at the ready, he fired off a quiver full of arrows. With each pull back, the bow stretched taught, straining his muscles. The twang and thump of the arrows hitting their mark was soul-satisfying, so much more so than sewing a leather for an ungrateful merchant.

He really should be back at the shop instead of practicing on his own. The shop that was crammed from floor to ceiling with linen and wool, leathers, and the odd piece of silk in readiness for tournament season. He shot another arrow. *Zing.*

The shop that battered his ears with the noisy chatter of the apprentices rising ever more loudly over the constant hum of his mother's spinning wheel at the back or the clackety-clack of his father's loom. Another arrow zoomed into the target.

The shop that stifled his senses as if he were wrapped in wool and sewing near a blazing fireplace in the heat of summer. *Zip. Zip. Zip.* He was out of arrows.

A quick glance at the sun told him he had indulged too long in practice. With his guilt caught up to him, he retrieved all his arrows and headed back to the shop. But not via the most direct route. Instead, he circled past the castle keep, ears open to catch the land announcements.

Most knights wanted flat land for raising crops. The land on the island was limited and the choicest plots were already gone. But there was some land, he had heard, beyond the forest and bordering the sea, that was too rocky for planting grain. This was the land he dreamed of. Though a modest dream, it was out of reach to someone of his station.

The doors to the castle were closed, as were the windows. All except the one around the corner, in the back. If he were quiet, and the king spoke loud enough...

"You there!"

Manny squinted up unto the parapet. A guard was aiming an arrow at him.

"Step away from the keep and be gone with you."

"Right." Manny held up both hands while backing away, keeping them far away from his own weaponry. He lowered them once he rounded the corner into the open space before the market.

One day, he would be inside that ceremony. He would gladly take the land that no one else wanted. And once he had been given his plot of land, he would find a way to plant rowan trees. He would bring South Morlaix back to its former riches, when people from around the world traded for the famous rowan balsams. He nodded to the guard, who was still watching, before double-timing it to the shop.

CHAPTER 2

On the other side of the wall, the only daughter of the king and queen of North Morlaix fussed with her embroidery. With an angry tug, Gressa pulled a tangled thread through the fabric, ripping a hole in the center of a tree in her picture.

"Argh!" She threw the fabric—hoop, needle, and all—across the tower room. Her long gold-red braid fell forward, brushing her arm. She flung her hair back and huffed.

Teacher and nursemaid, Old Anne, set aside her own handiwork. A spinster, she was thin, gray-haired, and with deep blue eyes. Her stiff joints meant she couldn't move very fast, but she more than made up for her physical limitations with her quick mind.

"Tsk," Old Anne said quietly as she shuffled over to the handiwork and examined it. "I will show you how to fix the hole, but we best try it when you are of a better humor."

"My legs cramp sitting here in this small room. Why must I be a prisoner when I am a princess?" Gressa sprang from the window seat and marched around the room, which wasn't as small as she let on. The Dividing Wall that split the castle in two did not touch her room, though it did render a back staircase all but useless. "My brothers are free to roam where they want. Axell is in Copello. Varin tends a farm outside the gate. Jutland goes hunting every day, and the rest tag along with whoever they want. 'Tis not fair."

Old Anne glanced out the window, setting her lips firm. "One day, you will be free. Do not lose heart." Her eyes brightened. "Shall I ask if you can take a daily turn about the grounds?"

"Daily? I can't imagine anyone agreeing to that."

"Leave it to me."

Taking a turn was not much better than being confined to the tower. The rare time she was allowed outside, she had to walk with a chaperon and follow a prescribed path that kept her as far from the Dividing Wall and as many people as possible. And, more often than not, Herrick's black gaze followed her every move.

What she craved was the sun on her face and fresh air in her lungs.

"Ask about the garden again. Just a small patch for my herbs. I would rather tend that in the morning and take a turn in the after-noon. That doesn't seem like too much to ask." Noting Old Anne's expression, she added, "Please, if I may."

The sorry plants lined up against the window needed to be planted in the ground where they stood a better chance at survival. She hadn't found the right balance of sun and water for them in the clay pots, and expected them to start dying off one by one if she didn't release them into the wild soon. Healthy speci-mens were needed if she were to experiment with the healing recipes in the newest book her brother Axell had sent from Copello.

Axell was her conspirator. He didn't like that she spent so much time in the tower either. Whenever possible he sent her things that would draw her outside. Just when she'd run out of ideas, he'd send her something new to ask Old Anne about.

As a young girl, she had the run of the castle. When she walked among the stalls on market days with her mother, the townspeople sprinkled her with gifts, so glad they were for a princess. But ever since she had grown tall and added curves to her silhouette, she'd been tucked away in the tower.

Old Anne was hidden away with her, and the nursemaid didn't seem to mind, no matter how surly Gressa got. Yes, Gressa was grateful for the company, but she sensed that other girls didn't live like she did. She overheard the servants talk about going out into the countryside, or down to the sea at the base of the castle to swim. Gressa had never swam in her entire life. Or maybe she did when she was little and had forgotten.

"Do I know how to swim?" she asked Old Anne.

"We took you when you were a wee thing, but the waves scared you. Your mother thought they should keep you in the water until you got over your fear, but your father scooped you up and brought you home to eat sweets. You never went farther than knee-deep after that."

"Hmm." Gressa suspected she knew which parent Old Anne agreed with.

She leaned out through the open window as far as she dared. Her chambers in the tallest tower gave her a tiny, tiny view of where the knights of South Morlaix conducted their exercises. If her brother ever found out she spent hours watching the knights from the rival kingdom, surely, he would move her to a room closer to the dungeon.

Daily, she positioned herself at the corner of the window, pretending to need the light for her embroidery. Every time Old Anne's back was turned Gressa would give up any pretense of handiwork and sit and watch the young men exercise.

The cursed prince was usually in the practice field. Laziest thing she ever saw. Last in all the races, could barely hit a target, and cared more about his doublet than wrestling. For someone destined to meet her brother in battle, he wasn't trying very hard. So much for looking to South Morlaix for her rescue.

Gressa had already asked Axell about the princes in Copello, but he said they were all spoken for. His tone implied not to press him further. Who would want to rescue a princess they'd never seen or spoken to?

But there was one young man who showed promise. He was tall and with hair the color of beach sand. Quick with the bow and arrow, he always out-performed the others. But more than that, he was kind. They were too far away for her to read facial expressions or hear what they talked about, but from her tower she'd become a student in body language. You could tell a lot by the tilt of a head or a shift in a torso.

The prince stood the way she expected him to, based on the descriptions she'd overheard about the haughty boy. Feet shoulder-width apart, arms crossed, chin high, looking down on the others.

Old Anne had told her that King Simon of the South was a kind man. She couldn't understand why the prince was not more like his father, unless he was so scared of the Panther that he'd already given up.

The kind boy, on the other hand, was always in motion. He was the first to start a task, often the winner of a race, and frequently joked with those around him. Would that he be a noble and maybe, just maybe, they could have a future together. She imagined sending him a letter tied to a starling and having him storm the castle, taking her far away from Herrick the Horrid.

The boy from South Morlaix was, of course, the root of the problems she had with her embroidery. Today he was the only squire at practice and it was like a gift to her to watch him and only him. But when she lost sight of him, it was like her dream had also disappeared and her confinement closed back in on her. She didn't think she could take one more day, let alone years of living under Herrick's restrictions. And there was no use talking to her mother or father. The entire kingdom was bent on preparing Herrick for the Great War.

She snorted. Based on what she had seen of the prince of South Morlaix, it would be a short war. By the time war came, she needed to be ready with her healing balsams, if not for her own people, then for those over the wall.

"Did you say something, my pearl?" Old Anne stood expectantly.

Gressa shook her head, still staring out the window. No, she was just dying inside, that's all. There was nothing Old Anne could do.

CHAPTER 3

*J*ust as Manny had suspected. A pile of jerkins was cut and waiting for him. He glanced over at the other's tables. Half as much work as he had. He'd be sitting here late into the night. Again.

As he sat down and placed a worn thimble on his finger, his mother called him over. She was at the loom preparing the warp threads for a brown woolen piece. She wore a simple crafter's dress of green and a large apron tied at her waist. Her hair was pulled back by a polka dot handkerchief like it had been every day of his life.

"How was practice today?" she asked.

"Fine."

She lowered her voice. "Any trouble from Nigel?"

Manny looked to see if Hoxham was in the room before answering. He wasn't. "Not at practice, but he and Hoxham had a bit of a row when we brought the leathers around this morning. The prince was in a hurry to meet Sir Fletcher." Manny tried to keep his voice casual as he spun the thimble on his finger. "The land-granting ceremony was today."

His mother stopped arranging the threads, her hands hovering over the loom. She cleared her throat and continued her work.

"How nice for the knights. The plots are getting smaller each year, I hear."

Hoxham would have said that the North Morlaix knights received bigger land grants, too. But that was only because the king in the north had to pay fewer men for their loyalty. What with all the sons he had, the land could stay within the family. Their king in the south only had the one son.

Manny shrugged, not masking his face which surely revealed frustration. His mother knew what he wanted, but she would never talk about it. Always changed the subject every time he brought it up. His future wasn't in the shop, no matter how diligently they trained him.

His mother placed her hand on his elbow. "What is it, dear?"

"Nothing. I have a lot of work to do."

"Yes, we all do. You don't get out of work because you are practicing extra with the squires." She eyed him thoughtfully. "Perhaps after tournament season your father and I could—" She stopped talking and made room for Father to take up position on the stool. He held the large shuttle with the bobbin already wound. His large frame looked bulky and awkward perched the way he was, but despite his sausage-like fingers, his stitches were the finest in the land.

"Best get back to work," Father said, scratching his beard and setting his face in a gentle rebuke.

Manny waited to see if Mother would finish her thought, but she didn't. He had hoped she was going to say they would release him from the shop so he could train full time, but that would never happen. They barely let him do what he was doing now.

His parents had had a huge fight when he first asked if he could train with the squires. In fact, that was the only fight between them he'd ever heard. They must have had disagreements over the years as other couples he'd seen. But this particular row came in the middle of the night and caused the air to fill with such thick tension that Manny's head hurt.

"We must allow this! It's at the king's invitation." That was his mother's voice.

"Bah, the king!" answered Father. "He doesn't know what he wants. Never has."

Manny sat up groggily in his loft bed. His father never spoke so harshly about Good King Simon. The king had been nothing but kind to them, extending his favor by patronizing their shop more than any other. It was because of him that they were so prosperous.

Earlier that day the constable had come to the Saturday School to talk to the village boys. He said that the king was making a generous offer to allow some of the unsponsored boys to train. Since most boys were already taking Saturdays off from helping the family business for their schooling—at the king's insistence—it seemed likely that none would be granted permission. But the constable had talked of future opportunities, including land. That's when Manny stopped listening and started planning. He begged his parents to let him go. They said they would discuss it.

"We have no choice. You know that. It wasn't a question. It was a command. He could make things difficult for us." Mother's voice was shrill. Panicked even.

Why would Good King Simon want to harm their family? The constable said it was a generous opportunity.

"He wouldn't dare. We know too much."

Father's voice was full of venom. They had ceased arguing between themselves and were focused on the king. What secret could they know about the king?

There was a pause and then the conversation took on a new tone. "We could leave. Take passage to Copello and never come back," Mother said.

Manny held his breath. Leave? But South Morlaix was his home. There was no better land anywhere, he was sure.

The silence grew, building like the storm clouds over the sea. Manny rested his head on his pillow and almost fell back asleep before he heard his father's final answer.

"We stay. Manny can train."

And that was the last his parents spoke on the subject. Manny joined the squires during their training, and when the young men served in the castle, he continued to work at the shop. Which was where he was for the rest of the day now. He forced himself to his work bench to take up a needle. As he sat down, the two young apprentices brought on to help during the tournament season stopped their conversation. They'd obviously been talking about him.

This wasn't unusual. Being the son of the owners and the only boy given permission to attend both the Saturday school and also the training, Manny was left out of most of the shop talk. He didn't care. That much.

One day it wouldn't matter anymore. He'd either be a hero and earn his reward, or he would leave.

CHAPTER 4

*G*ressa packed the freshly tilled dirt around her struggling herb plants. "There you go, my sweet woodruff," she said. "Grow strong here in the shade." She sat back on her heels, admiring the neat rows of seedlings transplanted from the pots in her room. At least now they had a chance of surviving outside with the common graces of the sun and the rain.

"And what does that one do?" asked Old Anne. "I'm not familiar with it."

She was pointing to a cluster of deep green leaves with flowers just beginning to bud. Gressa stood and planted her hands on her hips. "According to Axell's book, this one works well for an upset stomach and for healing wounds. However, what the book recommends most is to dry it and place it in our beds. Its common name is bedstraw. It's supposed to keep the fleas away."

"Och! If it does that, we should plant more of it! Let it grow all over the Dividing Wall instead of the ivy. We'll hand it out to everyone at Whitsunday before the warm weather calls the little critters awake."

Gressa laughed. "I best not go near that wall or Herrick would have my head. He has memorized every nook and cranny and would notice the tiniest change in it before I had even thought it through." She crossed her arms. "However did you convince him to let me into the garden? Of all my requests, he's never granted me this one before. It puts me too close to the wall." She eyed the tall rock structure. It was said the king of the woodlings made it with his magic, and that was why no one could tear it down.

A smile played on Old Anne's lips. "Your brother isn't here. I asked your father while he was going over some business with Siguard, and Siguard backed me up. It seems he and Axell have been corresponding about you."

"You dears." Gressa swatted Old Anne's arm. "When does Herrick return and what else can we ask my father before then?"

"One must be prudent in these matters. Do not overreach."

How was an hour spent gardening overreaching? Asking to go over the wall to talk to the boy next door might be overreaching. Exciting, tempting, and stomach-churning, but not likely to ever happen.

"Siguard said rumors have spread to other lands that the North Morlaix princess remains hidden away for reasons that she is unmarriageable, and that did not sit well with your father."

"Unmarriageable? Is that what they're saying about me?" Gressa plunked down on the stone bench near a koi pond and fiddled with her necklace, an heirloom from King Rorick's reign. She watched the fish lazily wiggle their tails.

They don't even know me. But how could they when they haven't had the chance?

"I will take your advice," she said simply. "I can more easily endure my tower knowing I may escape to the gardens every morning." All she needed was to get her elbows out and prove to her family that whatever they were afraid of was not going to happen to her.

"Perhaps not every morn'. Only the ones when your eldest brother is not here."

"What?" Gressa frowned. She figured if her father declared it, it would stand. He was still the king. "How far away did Herrick go?"

"No one outside the personal servants in the castle knows he is gone. I don't know whether he be back soon or whether he be back late."

Gressa squinted up at Old Anne. "Sounds mysterious. And like my brother is up to no good. Do you know his task?"

"Continuing your father's search for rowan trees, mayhap?"

"My brother?" Gressa scoffed. "You really think he'd do something that would benefit everyone else more than himself? Never. He cares nothing for the rowan trees. He thinks father is foolish for trying to restore them to our land. Each time father goes on one of his fruitless trips, Herrick uses the time to gather the noblemen closer to himself."

"How do you know this?" Old Anne's voice was sharper than normal.

"I see things outside the window when we are working. Don't you?" Gressa said sweetly. She almost gave away her secret. "If father doesn't watch out, Herrick will have his kingdom before he's ready to give it up."

"Well, I don't know about that, but restoring the rowan trees would benefit whichever side of the kingdom does it first. It would be in Herrick's best interests as well."

"Whichever side? We are not two halves, we are two separate kingdoms."

"Yes, mistress. You've never known it to be different, but I remember the way it was before the Dividing Wall went up."

"Yes, and rowan trees are like fairy tales to my generation. I'm sorry, Old Anne, but Herrick is our future, and although he plans to unite the two kingdoms, it won't be for their benefit." She nodded to the south. "I've never known anyone to be so selfish as him. I feel like I should warn them, but I'm sure they already know."

"Herrick has grown up with pressure and expectations on him that none of the rest of you have had. It has affected him a certain way."

"No one is around to overhear you. You may speak freely. I

can't be the only one who thinks of him like this. He seems to have the entire family under a spell. Just because he's the oldest is no reason to put him in charge."

Not answering, Old Anne sat beside Gressa. Together they watched the fish swim round and round. The poor things were trapped as much as Gressa was.

"Why can't he be more like Axell? Not that he has to bring me presents all the time. That's not what I mean. But Axell notices people." She splayed her hands toward her freshly planted herbs. "Who else would send me a book on healing herbs? Not only does it give me something to do in the tower, but if I learn how to use all these, I can be a help to the kingdom."

She fingered the gold pomander hanging from a long chain around her neck. The pomander was another gift from Axell when he first left North Morlaix to receive his knight training in Copello. A clever contraption, each segment could be peeled back like an apple wedge, revealing a tiny compartment for storing herbs for medicine. She had filled it with lavender, sage, and rosemary. The rowan wedge was empty, of course.

"That's Axell's way," said Old Anne, with a hint of pride in her voice.

"And it's not only me. I see you wearing a new kerchief."

Old Anne patted her head covering, a sea-blue color like the women in town liked to wear. She smiled.

"He spends his own coin on it, too," said Gressa, her words building steam. "Herrick is a mean crow. Axell is lovely songbird. Herrick is bitterroot. Axell is a morning glory." She thought for another analogy. "Herrick is the rain. Axell is the sun."

Old Anne grunted. "Herrick is heir apparent. Axell is a knight-in-training."

Gressa picked at the dirt under her fingernails. "Herrick hates me. Axell loves me."

CHAPTER 5

The knights held a footrace through the forest after an intense morning of training. Manny was hoping to see the great Sir Fletcher perform, but apparently, he was in conference with the king all week.

For the footrace, the competing knights ran across the drawbridge, onto the rugged dirt path, and then back again. There were bragging rights to be earned for the fastest record. The king's timekeeper used both a sun dial and a sand timer to record the speed. King Simon's record still held from the days when he was a young knight and raced against his rival, Jorvik. They say that Sir Fletcher could beat it, but he never ran the race when it was timed.

Today, the knights went first, then the squires. After a long practice session, Manny was hot, dripping with sweat, and with every muscle in his arms and legs worked until the point of exhaustion. Still, he held himself firmly in the middle of the pack as they crossed over the drawbridge.

All of them would be forced to spread out when the trail narrowed in the forest. Manny would have to be near the lead of the main pack if he were to keep his position to the end. Being strong and having endurance weren't the only ways to win a race; you also needed strategy.

Prince Nigel wasn't even trying to keep up. He jogged at a leisurely rate with a third group made up of one boy who was recovering from a leg injury, and a handful of hangers-on who only wanted to impress the prince. When Manny's gaze met Nigel's, the prince doffed an imaginary hat at him.

Manny turned back around and clenched his jaw as he ran. Didn't that sorry prince feel the eyes of the Panther boring in on him? If he were the prince, he would spend day and night in training. He would pour over battle plans and come up with new ways to defend his kingdom and keep his people safe. The only thing that Nigel seemed to pour over was the cook's weekly menu.

The path narrowed and the runners were squeezed into running single file as they entered the blessed coolness of the forest. Manny picked up the pace, still not going full out. Soon it would be time to leave the pack behind and join the two front runners, Bruce and Charlemagne, who were fighting hard to keep the lead.

His thoughts for the future kept time with his steps and the gentle thump, thump of the chain around his neck. After performing some wonderful feat of honor, he would be granted his land. Then he would embark on an expedition to find a forest or grove, or even a single rowan tree with saplings to bring back to Morlaix. He couldn't understand why Good King Simon hadn't already tried this.

A punch in the gut brought Manny back to the present. *Oof.* Right where the stitch was starting to form from running. Manny bent over, and nearly tripped on a rut, but he fought through the pain and kept going. He hadn't noticed that one of Nigel's gang had crossed through the forest and hidden behind a tree, waiting for him. A dirty trick. Manny should have been more alert.

Coming out of the forest, he had to pass another of Nigel's

gang who had slowed down and was waiting. Manny tried to leave a wide berth, but the boy pivoted with surprising quickness and shoved Manny into the runner behind him. They both went down, rolling out of the forest in a spectacular display of flying rocks and dirt.

Sir Gordon, who was overseeing the race, didn't notice the shove, or if he did, he wasn't calling it out. Instead, he yelled, "Manny, you just earned yourself tack duty."

Nigel's crew exchanged smiles as they ran by, kicking up pine needles in Manny's face.

Determined, Manny leaped up and charged after them. He may not win today, but he could at least beat the prince. Never mind that he would have counseled Hoxham to let it go because he would only make it worse. It was the principle of the matter. He easily caught up with the prince and company, as if they were waiting for him. But he dodged and weaved through them, keeping an eye on wayward fists and feet.

The other runners had all slowed down to watch the theatrics, allowing him time to catch them too. By the time he could see the drawbridge, Manny was directly behind the two lead runners. The group of knights were finished and catching their breaths at the finish line near the guardhouse. They too had sensed something happening outside the forest and had gathered to watch.

Time to sprint. Manny pulled from his reserves and shot out to overtake Charlemagne and Bruce. He dodged to the right as he went by them. Just as he suspected. Bruce made a move to trip him up and instead went sprawling himself on the ground. Manny grinned at the noise behind him. You never could trust Bruce during a race.

He and Charlemagne huffed side by side, crossing the line together.

"You almost had me that time, tailor-boy!" said Charlemagne, clapping Manny on the back. "I don't know anyone as stubborn as you."

"I think you mean determined," Manny said, breathing hard. They waved and parted company. The squires were expected to serve lunch in the great hall while he was expected back at the shop.

The courtyard in front of the castle keep was quiet at this time of day. The preparations in the great hall kept many folks busy, and the shopkeepers took the time for their own lunches. The baker was standing by the door to the kitchen, supervising a delivery of flour, and a few straggling children were running home for their lunches.

He continued on his way, stepping into a swarm of gnats. He waved them aside, but felt a sting like a needle prick. Ouch. A spot of blood appeared near his thumb. What was that? He sucked on his hand. Must have been a mosquito.

As he turned to go down the street to his shop, he felt a breath of hot air on his neck. His reflexes were still alert from training, and he whipped around, expecting Bruce or Charlemagne to have snuck up on him. There was no one.

He almost missed the shadow slinking near the Dividing Wall. He blinked and it was gone like a will 'o the wisp floating over the sea at twilight. The little hairs on the back of his neck prickled his skin. He looked around to see if anyone else had seen it.

Over yonder by the kitchen door, the king's baker shouted at an apprentice who had dropped a sack sending out billows of flour clouds. At the stall closest to the wall, a candle-maker had left his lunch on the table to barter with a sharp-tongued woman. But not a one of them was looking at the wall.

There had been a shadow, hadn't there? Cautiously, Manny went to investigate.

What he saw made the blood drain from his face. Behind the climbing ivy was a gap in the stones of the Dividing Wall. A definite crack. And it was large enough for a body to squeeze through undetected.

His hand instantly reached for the dagger in his leather boot. Had the Panther finally broken through to spy on them? Or worse, was his army about to attack the people of South Morlaix without warning?

For years Hoxham had been drilling it into anyone who would listen that South Morlaix was doomed. He said it was only a matter of time before the Panther was let loose. From all accounts, both kings were healthy and the treaty intact. But if Hoxham were right, and the Panther was coming for the king's son, well, the knights of South Morlaix would have to protect the young prince. For surely, Nigel couldn't defend himself against a goose.

Manny took a deep breath and a quick survey of the land. Here was his chance to prove he was more than a tailor's son. The knights were in the keep, and only a handful of guards stationed at the sea wall. If he could save the kingdom, his parents would see his life was meant for more than sewing tunics and dresses. Perhaps he could leapfrog his plans and go straight from volunteer squire to rewarded landowner.

He clenched his dagger and inched through the crack, scraping the stones as he squeezed through. He'd find out what was going on and then report to the king. If he was fast and clever, he may even be able to capture the Panther himself.

The air was old and musty, like the air down in his mother's root cellar. The way was like a tunnel, angled to the right. Three steps in and the passageway went dark. A chill set in as the tall walls blocked the sun. He cocked his head, listening for the scrape of a boot on rock, a suppressed sneeze, or even the creak of leather that would give away an impending attack, but it was as silent as grass growing. Dare he continue and go all the way into North Morlaix? He'd come this far. He would just look around, then scoot back home.

When he emerged from the wall, everything looked startling white as his eyes adjusted to the sudden light. He ducked back into the passage, heart pounding. He pressed his back against the wall, praying that no one had seen him. He strained his ears for shouts warning of an intruder or pounding feet coming his way. Again, all was silent. Strange. He expected to at least hear the typical castle sounds: a blacksmith's hammer, a baby crying, the knights of North Morlaix shouting threats over the wall.

Curious, he leaned his head out a fraction, and found he was not in North Morlaix as he expected. Wide-eyed, he stepped out into an empty, grass-filled open space with a large tree all abloom in white blossoms in the very center with a bubbling stream at its base. Stunned, Manny about dropped his dagger. What was this place?

Surrounded by the wall, the land seemed neither North Morlaix nor South Morlaix. Keeping his back against the Dividing Wall, Manny circled the small expanse, hopping over the brook twice, and came upon no other break in the wall but the one through which he entered. Even the brook rose up out of the wall at one end and dove back under at the other end.

Where was the shadow he had seen? The one that led him here? He peered deep into the branches of the tree, the only hiding place in the meadow. There. A movement.

A rush of starlings flew out of the greenery. With lightening reflexes, Manny dropped his dagger to grab at the bow strapped to his back.

Pausing only a moment to take aim, he shot and landed his supper. Three birds with one arrow. Two for the king's cook and the third for his mother. As long as he kept the cook in fresh fowl, the man allowed Manny a share in the spoils instead of accusing him of poaching the king's land.

With another arrow poised, Manny stalked around the tree, looking for the shadow he had seen. He left himself in a vulnerable position, but saw no other way to coax out the enemy. He let fly a number of arrows, none of them hitting a mark. Curious.

His shoulders relaxed as he studied his surroundings. No feat of honor for him today, only the discovery of a secret place.

The sun was no longer straight up in the sky. It was time to go. He gathered up his dagger and prey and returned to his side of the Dividing Wall. Mother would be glad to have meat on the table tonight.

Back in South Morlaix, he rearranged the ivy to cover up the opening and marked the spot with a round rock. He would be back. Whistling, he swung his birds by their legs as he brought them to the castle kitchen. Maybe the cook would reward him for the birds with an extra sweet cake.

CHAPTER 6

The smoke from the blacksmith's fires hung low, making the air outside Gressa's chambers nearly as oppressive as the air inside. But who was she to complain? It was far better to be out of her tower than in it.

Despite Gressa's misgivings about Old Anne being able to convince both her father and brother to allow her more freedom, the nursemaid had managed to secure permission for a daily short trip to the garden as well as an afternoon turn about the grounds. Dear Old Anne.

The herbs had taken to their new home and were stretching their leaves to the sun, drinking in the rain. The pleasure Gressa gained from watching them thrive surprised her. It was a small victory for her, but meaningful, because for the first time she felt like she might have a purpose in the kingdom.

The townspeople were not used to seeing the Tower Princess and so, surprised, they curtsied and bowed at her as she walked by. A little boy, nudged by his mother, stumbled forward and handed her a sweet cake.

She bent down and tweaked his nose. "Why, thank you, sir. I can tell this will be the best sweet cake I've ever tasted," she said.

The boy turned red and hid behind his mother's skirts. The

mother beamed. Gressa was about to speak to her when a disturbance in the marketplace caused everyone to stop and look for the
source.

It was Gressa's eldest brother, Herrick, riding his tall war horse
through the busy lane, followed by his two most loyal knights.
The townsfolk leapt out of his path and crowded up against the
stalls to get out of his way. He took nary a glance to the left nor
right, not even acknowledging the people. After the horse stepped
on an old man's toe, Herrick proceeded to brush past a table laden
with pippins, sending an avalanche of apples to the ground.

Gressa watched, agape. If he were purposely trying to rattle
the shop keepers, he could not have done a better job. But he
didn't even seem to notice. His nose was upturned too high to see
anything.

As he left the crafts area, his foot sticking out from the stirrup
grazed a pole holding up a display of crockery. The old woman
tending the stall leaned forward, overreaching as she tried to right
the collection of pots. She stumbled and fell in the dirt with a cry
of pain.

The young man in the next stall raised a hand as if about to go
to her aid, but with his gaze back on Herrick, he remained in his
stall. It looked like no one would go to the woman's aid until
Herrick was out of sight.

With a grim look at her brother, Gressa rushed forward and
knelt down in the dust beside her. "Are you all right, mistress?
May I help you stand?"

"My wrist." She cradled her right hand against her stomach. It
was already beginning to swell and turn a mixture of red and
purple.

"Oh, dear. You may have sprained it. I certainly hope it isn't
broken or you won't be able to make such fine crocks." Gressa
looked pleadingly at Old Anne. "Might I purchase some of these
for my dowry chest?"

She did not have free access to her own money, though she did
have a beaded purse in the shape of a frog, empty but for a hand-

kerchief and some rocks which, to make a point, she carried with
her. Her father didn't think women-folk needed any money. Then,
for Anne's ears only, she whispered, "Enough so she may eat
whilst her wrist heals."

Old Anne nodded. "I will put in your request."

"You should see the healer, mistress. Do not delay." Gressa
lifted the golden pomander from around her neck and looked for
an herb to give the potter woman.

The woman shook her head. "I have a small bit of a rowan
lotion. It will be enough."

Gressa's eyes widened, but she held her voice in check. "Very
good, then. I hope to see you at your stall the next time I pass
this way."

"Thank you, princess." The woman bowed her head until
Gressa had walked on.

"Rowan lotion!" exclaimed Gressa once they were out of
earshot. "Not even mother has rowan lotion."

"Yes, your mother used her supply liberally. No one expected
all the rowan trees to die and especially so quickly after the wall
went up."

Gressa felt a slight tickle on her neck, followed by a sharp
pain. Ouch. She slapped at the spot.

"What is it?" asked Old Anne.

"I think I got bitten," said Gressa. "Is there a mark?" She held
her hair back.

"Only a red mark where you hit. Oh, wait. I see a little pin
prick of red. Black fly, maybe?"

Old Anne continued their leisurely pace close to the Dividing
Wall, but Gressa, her mind filled with thoughts of rowan lotion,
fell behind. If her father would allow her to work with the town
healer, she might be of help to the kingdom. She could learn to
use her herbs to make healing balms. With a brother such as
Herrick, there was good need for healing.

Old Anne's shadow fell across the ivy growing up the
Dividing Wall and Gressa realized how far behind she'd fallen.

"Wait for me," she called and ran to catch up. It looked like Old Anne had tucked herself in a clump of the ivy. How unlike the nursemaid to show a playful side.

With quiet footsteps, Gressa sneaked forward and lunged at the shadow, hoping to give Old Anne a fright. The Dividing Wall fell way and Gressa tumbled forward, landing in a mound of soft green grass. She looked behind and the Dividing Wall was sealed as if there had never been an opening at all. The castle, the villagers, Old Anne, all gone, swallowed up behind an impenetrable brick wall. She held her breath. She was in South Morlaix!

She couldn't look. She jumped to her feet and pounded the place in the wall where she could have sworn she fell through. Her heart stopped as she pushed at the bricks. Solid. Unmovable.

"Old Anne?" she whispered. "Old Anne?" Her voice caught in a sob. She pounded at the immovable rocks. She had to return to her side of the wall before she was seen by the South Morlaixans. Who knew what they would do to her?

Crossing the wall could be seen as a breaking of the treaty. She could plunge both kingdoms immediately into war. Herrick would be thrilled. Her father would never forgive her.

She cleared her throat and tried again. "Old Anne!" Her cries stopped at the wall. She clawed and scraped at the rock until her fingernails came away chipped and broken.

Slowly, gently, a single starling song filtered its way into her thinking, coaxing her to turn away from the wall. As she followed the sound, her gaze led across a meadow to the base of a wide tree that was more flower than tree, with all its white blooms bursting forth. Next to the tree flowed a trickling brook with water clear to the bottom and a bed lined with rounded stones. There were no people anywhere.

What was this place? Surely not South Morlaix. She knew from using her spy glasses that they had no stretch of open grass like this within the castle grounds.

Yet not North Morlaix either. They were bursting from edge to edge with buildings and townsfolk. There was no open space like this until you got well past the village. A secret meadow?

She threw her arms back, lifted her face to the blue sky and spun and spun until she fell, dizzy to the ground. She stared up at the blue sky. What was this place? It was the perfect hideaway for a princess. That is, if she could find a way in and out.

She jumped to her feet, reminded that she had to find the opening. To be trapped here would be worse than in her tower. At least in her tower she had regular meals and Old Anne to keep her company. Old Anne! Old Anne would be frantic by now.

Gressa had to find her own way out if she were to keep this meadow a secret. Her own secret meadow, imagine that?

She ran back to where she had fallen in and began to search for an opening. This wall was filled with secrets. She glanced back into the meadow, wondering if the king of the woodlings had heard her wish for freedom and granted this to her. "Thank you," she called out, in case he was listening.

When she turned around, she noticed a narrow passage in the wall. "Where did you come from?" she whispered. As she slipped back through the wall, she tapped it twice, her promise that she would return soon.

Then she was back in the crowded marketplace, the noise of the people a welcome sound in her ears. Now, to find Old Anne.

Not two steps later, Herrick caught her arm in a tight grip. Heart racing, she lifted her gaze to him. His eyes bore into her in that cold, hard way of his, making her shiver despite the warmth the sun had baked into her arms.

"Where have you been? Your nursemaid has been looking all over for you." His voice was a low growl. "I knew this was a bad idea. Get back to your tower." He flung her arm forward toward the castle. "Reduced to looking for sniveling brats," he complained, striding away like a sea storm retreating back into the ocean.

Gressa shivered. Herrick was exactly the reason she needed a place between the walls.

She was still fuming when she entered her chambers. "I'm sorry," she said automatically, but not sincerely.

Old Anne stood at the window with a thoughtful expression, looking toward South Morlaix. She didn't look angry or worried.

"Herrick said you were looking for me?" Gressa asked, as if being off on her own were a usual occurrence.

Old Anne turned from the light. "Yes, we best get more work done on our embroidery." Her mouth formed a tilted smile. "Since we were interrupted earlier in the day."

She adjusted the two seats by the window to best catch the afternoon sun.

Gressa, still buoyed by her time in the meadow, bounced into her chair. "Have you had a nice afternoon?" Gressa tested the nursemaid, wanting to see how long Old Anne could resist asking where she had been and what she had been doing.

"Yes, mistress. I had an interesting turn about the castle grounds. Through the gardens, past the merchants and ending at the baker's door for a bun." She picked up her needlework and began her tiny stitches. "Walked it twice, in case I missed something." She glanced up.

"Sounds lovely." Gressa scooped up her hoop and needle. Her stomach growled. She regretted missing the stop at the baker's.

Ingrid flung open the door. "There you are, child." She stormed into the room, her presence filling the space. "Where were you? Herrick saw Old Anne walking by herself this afternoon. Alone! We had the entire village looking for you. It was like you disappeared into the walls."

Gressa kept her face as stoic as her brother Siguard the friar did when reading the Old Testament. Her mother had no idea how close she had come to guessing the truth. She straightened her spine in an effort to appear indignant. After all, her brothers were given way more freedom than she was.

"Old Anne's walk was like a footrace this afternoon. Don't know what her hurry was. I wanted to take my time and enjoy the fresh air since my chambers are stale with all of us breathing the

same air over and over and over. As you can see, I'm right here."
She spread her hands to emphasize her point. "I didn't disappear
anywhere. And no harm came to me. I wish you all wouldn't
hover so. You never do over the boys."

Gressa made the mistake of looking at Old Anne. Her look
read: *Walking too fast, indeed!* Gressa's face flamed to be caught in
a lie.

Ingrid shook her head. "Gressa, Gressa, Gressa. The boys are
different. They're trained in combat. You...you...well, we tried."

Gressa felt a surge of anger and her eyes flashed. She remembered the humiliating combat sessions. Her brothers were merci-
less before Ingrid gave up and let Old Anne begin teaching her
more princess-like ways. Gressa reached into her tall leather boot
and wrapped her hand around her dagger. With a shot as fast and
clean as a hummingbird's flight, she flung the blade inches past
her mother's head and into the bedpost behind her. "I can take
care of myself."

She smiled smugly, wondering if she had impressed her
mother with her hidden talent, the only skill in training she'd
been good at.

Old Anne stood, her mouth gaping, and her hands up, first
turning toward Ingrid and then toward Gressa as if trying to stop
what had already transpired.

Ingrid's mouth dropped open, then as quickly as Gressa had
flung the blade, flew forward and slapped Gressa across the
cheek. She turned without saying a word and marched out of the
room, slamming the heavy oak door behind her.

Stunned, Gressa pressed her hand to her stinging face. That
was not the reaction she expected. She stared at the closed door.

"You might think of another way to please your mum besides
grazing her with a knife." Old Anne held out Gressa's embroidery. "A little handiwork will help calm your temper."

CHAPTER 7

a full month had passed before Manny was able to return to the meadow. What with training for the king and working for his father, he had little time for remembering his own name let alone solving a mystery. Even now he would have to be quick, as he was expected at the shop immediately after training.

He just needed a moment to make sure what he had seen was real and not a waking dream he'd had. Besides, there was so little opportunity to be alone in the village, and today he needed a sanctuary. Sir Gordon was overly harsh on him again at practice. Nigel could do whatever he wanted, but Manny couldn't sneeze without getting extra laps or tack duty. It was obvious to him that Sir Gordon was trying to win points with the prince.

It wasn't only practice that was weighing on him, but also work in the shop was nonstop. The annual tournament was three months away and everyone in town who could afford it wanted a new doublet, matching canions for the legs, or a larger neck ruff.

Manny flexed his hands which ached from continuous, repetitive work. The leather was stiff and took a firm grip and strength to sew. The work wasn't all bad. It made his competitors complain he was breaking their hand bones during arm wrestling.

The opening was around here somewhere. He adjusted his quiver while looking for the rock he used to mark the hole in the wall. Where was it? He scanned the Dividing Wall but couldn't find the opening. It was like it had never existed.

He walked the length of the wall looking for any hint of the passage. Not a hole, a gap, or even a crack. Confused, he paced his steps, sure of where he had been last time. Nothing. He even dragged his hand along the wall, feeling for the opening.

"Hey Manny, better watch it or we'll start calling you the Panther like that crazy prince on the other side," said Hoxham.

Startled, Manny spun around to see his friend watching, loaded down with packages from the tailor shop. "Funny, Hoxham. You're a real court jester."

"You coming to the shop?"

"Be there in a minute. Need to walk off the exercises first." He rotated his arm to emphasize his stretching. "You should train with us. It'd be good for you."

Hoxham hefted up his bundle to rub his scrawny belly. "I know what's good for me and it ain't training to get myself killed. I'm off to make some deliveries. Might take me all day if I do the job proper."

Manny waved him away. His friend would never learn the trade for his focus was oft on other pleasures. It was a wonder his father kept him. Charity work, he supposed. Hoxham still had that castle rat manner about him, despite the years he'd been working an honest job.

Manny stopped and leaned casually against the wall. He glanced right and left while pretending to pick a flea off his tunic. He pressed the wall here and there, with his heel, his elbow, his head. Nothing gave way.

Surely, he hadn't invented the meadow between the walls. His mother had roasted the fowl he hunted. Even now his mouth watered at the thought of the juicy meat.

He waited until he was sure no one was looking before beginning his search again. He pressed and there it was. A narrow gap like it had been there since the beginning of time, leading to the tunnel-like passage.

Quickly, Manny stepped in. He glanced behind to see if anyone noticed, but the wall had sealed up again as he walked through. He pressed against the stones behind him, but the way was sealed tight. He wasn't getting back to South Morlaix. Adrenaline shot through him and he automatically pulled out his dagger. If this was a trap, he was now the rabbit caught inside.

The only way to go was forward, and with each step in, the wall re-formed behind him. He didn't remember the wall sealing up like that last time he was there. But, then again, he hadn't looked. Would there still be an empty field this time, or an ambush? He steeled his nerves, preparing for the worst.

He walked cautiously through the narrow tunnel, half hoping the field was empty and half hoping for a chance to become a hero. He drew closer to the light, body flattened against the stones, and then cautiously peeked into the meadow.

It was exactly as he had left it—empty—except for one peculiar change. Past the tree and near the back of the enclosure was a rust-colored tent. A poorly constructed lean-to, really.

This was it. He was going to find out who created this space. Manny crept up silently on the dwelling, raising his dagger to the attack position, straining his ears until they began to ring at the silence. The structure billowed with each burst of wind, looking like a breathing being. Who could have built it? Someone from North or South Morlaix? Maybe the shadow he had seen that led him to the opening.

He squinted through the cracks of the shelter but there was no movement inside. He couldn't help it, but his heart started to pound like when he was a child and found himself lost in the village after the curfew bell. What kind of knight would he make if he couldn't stay calm in an open meadow with no sign of an attacker? He had the element of surprise on his side.

The wind gusted, and then someone was standing before him.

He moved to thrust when he realized it was only a cloth doorway that had flapped outward in the wind. Relieved, he let out a quick breath and caught the edge of the fabric with the next gust of wind.

He looked inside and, finding the place empty, he entered. The structure shook and shuddered with each new wave of wind. The colors were all tainted an orange hue as the light filtered through the rust-colored cloth. Manny had never seen the like of these fancy things except inside the castle of King Simon: a quill and ink, some sort of musical instrument, a wax tablet, and a horn book of all things. Not a cache of weapons as a knight would collect.

He picked up the horn book. *Pater Noster, qui es in caelis.* He smiled. The Lord's Prayer in Latin. For not the first time he was glad of his basic education. The parchment was covered with transparent horn to protect the writing. Similar to what he learned on, only this book had jewels embedded in the handle. And the wooden frame had strange markings on it. Runes, perhaps?

Some of his suspicions were confirmed. These items belonged to someone of Viking descent, most likely a North Morlaixer. *A magician who moved the wall at will?*

Manny rushed out of the shelter. He had to find a way to get back to South Morlaix and warn the constable, even if it meant losing this secret place. The security of the Kingdom was at stake.

"Oof." He crashed into someone, taking them both down to the ground. In a shot, Manny had rolled over and pounced, his dagger pulled. Maybe he could knock the man out long enough that he could make a run for South Morlaix. He raised his arm, about to strike with the butt of the knife.

Only, the intruder wasn't a he. The intruder was a she. A she with big green eyes that stole his breath. A she with a smattering of freckles across her pretty nose.

"Who are you?" he asked gruffly, adrenaline still pumping through his body.

She frowned and turned her head away from the dagger.

"Answer me or," he paused. "Or, I'll..."

"Stab me?" she finished. She spoke with a light accent he had only heard once previously when on a rare trip to Copello for his father.

He tightened his grip on the damsel. "A North Morlaixan. Are you a spy?"

"Do I look a spy?"

Manny had to admit if she were a spy she would make a good one. Who would suspect such a finely dressed girl? And those eyes, they were bewitching.

"A magician?" His voice squeaked, betraying his confusion.

She laughed. *Laughed.* Was he that non-threatening, or was it that she was confident?

"Don't magicians deal in tricks? I know no tricks." Her gaze searched his like she was trying to decide something.

"How many boys have hair the color of the beach like yours?"

What an odd question. He shifted his weight so as not to crush her and slipped the dagger back into his boot. He was unsure of what to do next. The girl had answered his questions with more questions. And her demeanor, though startled, was more mocking than afraid. Would she make a run for it if he released her?

While he was debating all this, the girl suddenly twisted and writhed, and before he knew it, she was on her feet and running for the wall. Her fine skirts billowed out behind her and her braided gold-red hair bounced with each step. When she got to the opposite Dividing Wall, she began searching it.

"At least I know from whence you come," he called. She was a confirmed North Morlaixer if her first instinct was to run for that wall.

The girl turned long enough to give him a disgruntled look before resuming her escape.

Manny took his time walking up to her, testing a theory. If her side of the wall worked like his, she wouldn't find an opening when someone was watching. When he was a few paces away, he could hear her muttering to the wall.

"Are you going to tell me who you are and what you are doing in South Morlaix?" He had decided on the spot to stake a claim for King Simon.

She turned, placing her back to the wall. Looking exasperated, she crossed her arms and examined him up and down, as if measuring his status. Her jaw set. "This isn't South Morlaix. It's *between* the Dividing Wall. Besides, it is I who should be asking you. What right have you to be here?"

Manny was taken aback. Most girls he knew either giggled in his presence or kept their gaze on their shoes. His mother told him it was because he was handsome. Hoxham said it was on account of his big nose.

"The name's Manny." He figured he could give that much away since she had given up where she came from.

"What were you doing in my shelter, Manny?"

Manny looked over his shoulder at the falling-apart tent. "Your shelter, eh?"

She narrowed her eyes. "Answer me."

Manny laughed outright. He couldn't help himself.

"What's wrong with my shelter? It's a very fine one." Her face showed uncertainty.

"I was in that shelter and was afraid the wind would knock it over. The thing shakes like a squire facing his first joust."

The girl tried to hide a smile but failed miserably.

Manny grinned.

She stepped forward with a slight curtsy. "I'm Gressa. I thought I was the only one who visits this place, so I made a shelter to keep things here."

"So, you're from North Morlaix?"

She nodded, then tilted her head, squinting as she looked up at him. "And you are from South Morlaix." It wasn't a question.

"Yes." There was no point in trying to deny it. Where else could he have come from?

"How did you get in?" she asked.

Manny shrugged. "I found a crack in the wall and came to check it out in case—" He stopped himself before he mentioned the Panther. He shouldn't let a North Morlaixer know what the South Morlaixers thought of their crown prince. "Well, I was curious to see what was here."

Gressa glanced at the sun. Her face clouded over and she went back to searching the wall. "I need to get back before...I need to go. Can you help me find the exit?" She pointed at the wall. "My uh, doorway seems to have disappeared. It does that sometimes."

Manny decided to try his theory. Instead of helping to look, he turned his back.

"Did you find it yet?"

No answer.

He turned back around. The girl was no longer there. He smiled. He at least knew one more thing about the Dividing Wall. He should have asked this Gressa how she got in. And if others knew the secret way as well.

It wouldn't do to have a passel of North Morlaixers flooding the meadow and figuring out the secret of the wall. At least, not before he unlocked its secrets.

He touched the spot where Gressa disappeared, holding it firm in his memory. Both the girl and the location.

Then he sprinted to his side of the wall. Next time, he would test the opening on North Morlaix's side. If Gressa could get through, maybe he could, too. *And do what?* Attack the Panther himself?

CHAPTER 8

*G*ressa hurried through town, through the busy kitchen
where Herrick never stepped foot, up the servant's stairs,
and slipped back to her chambers unnoticed. Her room
was empty. *Perfect.* She had to know for sure about the boy.

She lunged for the spy glass under her mattress. Her brother
Axell had given it to her on her fourteenth birthday. When no one
was looking, he had slipped it to her wrapped in a blue and
purple scarf under the table. He told her it contained rock-crystal
lenses that would help her see things. Intrigued from both his
secretive manner and the prospect of what the lenses could help
her see, she decided not to tell anyone, even Old Anne, and kept it
hidden. The spy glass made far-away things look close enough
to touch.

Several days after Axell had given her the spy glass, she
learned Herrick had put a peddler in the public stocks for failing
to deliver a package to him. He had ordered it special from the
Trickster, a traveling performer who also traded in unusual
objects. Axell's wink across the dinner table worried her. If the spy
glass was intended for Herrick, and he found it in Gressa's chambers, she couldn't imagine what he would do. In fear, she almost
destroyed the lens one night when Old Anne's snores were loud

enough to cover the sound of breaking quartz. But then she looked through it one last time—at the moon. Such a sight she had never seen before. She couldn't destroy this wonderful tool. Neither could she get caught with it.

She took the spy glass now and dashed to the window to see if she could glimpse the boy leaving the Dividing Wall. Another top section in the palisade had crumbled away in a rainstorm two days ago, giving her a narrow window into the marketplace across the Dividing Wall. She had a suspicion about the boy. The way he moved in the meadow suggested he was the boy she had seen training with the knights of South Morlaix. The kind boy.

Was she too late? It was difficult to judge where he might come out, as her view was so restricted—but there. Up the street sped a boy wearing a green tunic and brown trousers. Yes, it was the same one who had surprised her in the meadow. Too quickly he was out of her view, but she had seen enough.

She grinned. It was him. But then, why was he so uncivil with her? That's not how she imagined their first meeting would be. Holding a knife to her throat? Although, as soon as he realized she was a girl, he put the weapon away. And he did think she was a spy, so he was defending his kingdom which was honorable of him.

Still, a linger of doubt held on. What if he wasn't as nice as she had imagined? What if the South Morlaixans were as terrible as Herrick said they were? She'd never met one, so it was entirely possible she'd dreamed up that they were the same as her.

She had to find a way to knock down more of the wall so she could see the people of South Morlaix better. Watching them was so much more interesting than what happened within the confines of her chambers. And, she was curious about their lives. If history had been different, the people on the other side of the wall would be living amongst her people. All as one.

A shuffling sound in the hallway brought Gressa back to the present. She stashed the glass under her mattress and picked up her needlepoint, pretending she had been hard at work.

Old Anne entered with a tray of drink and biscuits which she set down on a little serving table beside the bed.

"Enjoying the fresh air today?" asked Old Anne.

Gressa stared at her. Had the nursemaid seen her? She thought Old Anne nearsighted, the way she had to look at everything close up. Surely the old woman did not witness her mad dash through the courtyard and up the stairs. Unless she had been in the kitchen when Gressa dashed through. There had been so many servants up to their elbows in dough and cutting root vegetables that she hadn't paid attention.

Old Anne pointed to the window. "'Tis a lovely spring day out today, yes? A sweet breeze blows in on the wind."

Gressa let out a breath of relief. Of course, Old Anne was referring to the open window under which she was working her embroidery. The open window where she was pretending she had spent the day on her stitching.

As of late they had forged some kind of unspoken deal that Old Anne would allow her a certain amount of time alone. Old Anne was her very best ally, but she was still accountable to the king. How far would Old Anne go to help the princess if it meant betraying the king?

"Yes," Gressa said, continuing the ruse. "I've been enjoying sitting right here and working on the Battle of Five and Two." It was partly true. She had made a stitch, and she did enjoy sitting near the window.

Old Anne bent down and peered at the work. "Not much accomplished, I see. Too busy staring at the Dividing Wall?"

Gressa startled at Old Anne's tone of voice. It sounded like a rebuke. So unlike Old Anne's gentle ways.

As Old Anne straightened, her whisper warmed Gressa's ear, "The walls have eyes and ears. You best be careful."

Gressa stared agape at Old Anne. What an odd thing to say.

Old Anne returned to the serving tray and poured the drink. She offered it to Gressa. "Buttermilk?"

"What do you mean?"

"I thought you might be thirsty."

Gressa frowned. Old Anne knew it wasn't drink Gressa was asking about.

Old Anne set down the glass. In a low voice she said, "Are you quite sure you want to pursue your current course of action, mistress? If you're caught, the consequences will be certain. For both of us."

The meaning of her words sunk in. Of course, if Gressa were caught, Old Anne would be held accountable as well. Probably receive worse punishment, as she wasn't family. "I wasn't thinking—" Gressa started.

"Don't fear for me, child. I'm an old woman and I've been waiting a long time. Some things are worth the risk."

"What do you know?" Gressa asked, touching Old Anne's arm.

"There are workings beyond us two. I know not yet what role we play. Have we the courage to do our part?" Her eyes watered, out of fear or joy, Gressa couldn't tell. "You are my priority, my pearl. I would wish no harm come to you, but this is no way for a young girl to live, pardon my place." Her tone was harsh, but Gressa could tell it was a relief for her nursemaid to speak up.

"You are the bravest person I know," Gressa said. "But what are you talking about?"

"Do you want things to change in this kingdom?" Old Anne asked.

When Gressa nodded she said, "Then be alert. Be ready. And if you need my help, ask for it."

Gressa set her lips. She knew Old Anne was on her side, but that was why she hadn't spoken about the meadow earlier. She sensed she shouldn't risk Old Anne's loyalty by making her keep secrets. At least the nursemaid could honestly say she didn't know anything. She may suspect, but that's not the same as knowing. No, Gressa would put no one else at risk. If she acted foolishly, it would be on her own so no one else got hurt.

CHAPTER 9

*M*anny eyed Hoxham, who had kicked back from his work bench, hands clasped behind his head and looking the perfection of ease. Manny himself had spent his fair share of time daydreaming this past week. The girl he had met in the meadow was even more distracting than finding out there was a magical space between the walls. He envisioned her staring up at him with those large green eyes, hearing her lightly accented voice. He felt himself blushing just thinking about her.

He shook his head. No. He wasn't going to let a girl distract him. He'd not be another boy with big plans who meets a girl and ends up with a big family. There'd be plenty of time for that later.

However, the look Hoxham had was not that of a love-sick fool. It was hard to read and could be anything from Hoxham finally planning his revenge on Nigel, or planning to run away. Whatever the meaning, his look worried Manny.

"What are you so smug about?" Manny tied a knot then cut his thread.

He didn't know why he cared so much about the apprentice. There were plenty of castle rats needing compassion. Maybe it was because Hoxham was the first he'd noticed. He still remembered the day he'd seen the boy, all skin and bones getting chased away from the castle trash, clinging tightly to an apple core. The core, of all things. Manny sometimes threw away as much as half an apple.

A smile danced on Hoxham's face. "You'll see. Big changes are coming."

"What? Is my father finally going to sack you for slacking on the job?" Manny teased good-naturedly while folding a jerkin. He added it to the pile for his mother to embroider. She had stepped out to help Father place an order with a visiting nobleman and his wife who were staying in the keep with King Simon.

Hoxham sat up, glancing at the door. "You're the court jester, ain't you?" He stood and looked out the window toward the Dividing Wall. "You wouldn't understand even if I told you." He leaned out the open window and took a deep breath. "I can smell it on the wind."

Manny guffawed. "You're smelling the butcher's leftovers. I can smell that from here."

Hoxham turned from the window, his face red. The angry blush rose up between his white blond hairs at the top of his head.

What did I say?

"You think you're so smart because you took those classes and they let you train with the knights. The volume of Hoxham's voice rose as he talked, causing the two young apprentices, Howard and Mace, looked up from tidying their benches for the night.

"Don't be jealous." Manny tried to keep his tone light, but Hoxham had picked at an old wound. Once Hoxham got something in his head, you couldn't reason with him, and he'd decided long ago he couldn't have the life that Manny did, and that Manny shouldn't have it either. It was envy, pure and simple, and they kept circling back to it. "You could have gone to class, too."

"Right. Like I can afford to take time off work to learn something as useless as reading. Admit it. You're spoiled. You get everything handed to you. Even the king shows your family favor. If you'd have had my life you'd be dead by now, you're so soft. And I keep telling you, bettering yourself ain't no use. I've seen the princes of the north. We're no match for them. You best learn to grovel so that when they come they might spare your life."

Manny tried not to react. Hoxham was so scared of the North that he had no ambition. He spent his days waiting for the world to end, endless talking instead of action to make it better. But after meeting the girl in the meadow, Manny had renewed hope that South Morlaix would make it. A girl as sweet as she, there had to be more like her in the north. People who would stand up to a bad ruler.

"When did you ever see the princes?" he said.

Hoxham lifted his chin. "In your life of ease, you've forgotten that I'm a castle rat. I can go anywhere because no one notices me. I've seen and done a lot more than you ever have."

Manny flexed his callused hands. A life of ease? He looked around the shop. Howard and Mace dropped their heads, putting the last of their tools away. Everyone would go home for the night, but he'd be back with his parents after supper to enjoy his life of ease.

"We see in the dark, unlike the guards," Hoxham paused and, as if realizing they had the attention of the room, bent to whisper in Manny's ear. "I've stolen passage on a cargo ship to Copello. Some of them princes were there, on the docks. Any of 'em had more fight in their pinky finger than Nigel will ever have. You know it's true."

After all his parents had done for Hoxham, after all *he* had done, Hoxham still didn't get it. Manny frowned while he waited for the young apprentices to leave. After the door shut, he continued the conversation.

"You aren't a castle rat anymore. You are an apprentice. You have a future."

Hoxham turned his back to Manny. "Once a castle rat, always a castle rat."

Manny was about to argue further when his parents walked

in. His father was grinning as he dropped a large sack of fabric onto the cutting table, so it must have been a profitable trip. His mother was licking her fingers.

"Manny," she said. "You must find more starlings for dinner. Cook has shown me a new way to make a most delicious roast. He said the birds you brought him were the best he has tasted in all his years and you should bring him more, and more often."

"Sure, Mother. I'd be happy to." *Happy to go back to the meadow with permission.* He could even say he was on the king's business. He grinned with the thought, but then noticed Hoxham scowling at him.

"Er, Hoxham?" The apprentice had returned to his seat to pack up his tools. "I could teach you to use the bow if you want." Not that he would ever show Hoxham his secret meadow. They could still go hunting in the forest.

Hoxham jumped up, slamming his stool against the wall. He brushed past them all, not saying goodbye. The family exchanged looks. He knew his parents could sense something had happened in their absence, but he didn't want to embarrass Hoxham in front of them if this was another of his passing moods.

If Hoxham would only change his attitude and *try* something for once, he could lift himself out of being a castle rat. No one could do it for him.

CHAPTER 10

a ngry voices outside Gressa's door caught her attention. She hopped off her bed where she had been sorting through her jewelry box and pressed her ear to the door, eager for news outside of her tower.

"You really think it wise to allow her this when she has behaved so irresponsibly these past few weeks?" The deep, grating voice was Herrick's, punctuated by the clinking of his keys.

Gressa's stomach dropped. What was Herrick doing in her tower? He'd never come this close to her sanctuary before. It had been the one place she didn't have to worry about running in to him. Well, now that she had the meadow, it wasn't the only place.

A terse reply followed. "I do. Gressa is growing up. We can't keep her locked up in her tower." Her voice went down a notch. "Do you know they call her the Tower Princess? Like in a fairy tale? There is more Viking in her than we realize. She ought to have a debut of sorts. The people should see their princess in her royal position, not just taking a turn now and then in the market-place like we are airing her out."

Gressa caught her breath. Was that a hint of pride in her mother's voice? She lunged for her window seat and took out her embroidery lest they catch her eavesdropping and she lose whatever status she had gained.

Old Anne was not in the room, as she had already gone down to the kitchen to bring up the midday meal. When the door opened, Gressa pretended to be intent on her handiwork.

"Put the tray on the table. I'll eat in a moment, once I've finished this row."

"It's me, Gressa."

She looked up to see her mother holding her lunch tray. There was no one behind her.

"Starting tonight, I want you in the great hall for all meals."

"Truly, Mother?" Normally, she was usually only invited for birthdays and holidays.

She wanted to ask about Herrick's position on the matter, but feared he was lurking. After all, it was his doing that kept her away from dining in the great hall on a daily basis.

Ingrid set the tray down and then gently stroked Gressa's hair. "You aren't a child anymore. It's time for you to take your place in this kingdom. You've spent years learning the ways of a princess. And, you've shown that you are cunning with a blade." Ingrid frowned, but her eyes softened, giving away her true feelings.

Herrick, apparently listening in the hallway after all, stepped into the doorway and Gressa jumped in surprise.

"This is against my wishes," he said. "Know that I will be watching you. You are not to bring shame to this family." With a final glare, he strode off, his steel-tipped boots echoing in the hallway.

Gressa flinched at the sound before relaxing as each step took her brother farther away from her. Of all her kin, he was the most insufferable. He had never said a kind word to her. Ever.

"Why is he like that, Mother?"

Ingrid sighed. "He feels the weight of the future. Always has. Your other brothers are free to pursue their own pleasures, while Herrick prepares to become king. We all need to find our own way. He chooses a barren and rocky path." She stared out the window, as if contemplating the future. "Strong Viking blood courses through his veins. Hopefully his heart is not so hard that it destroys him. A king needs a heart that knows when to be soft."

"Mother?" Gressa had never heard her mother talk this way before. Father would say she was going daft in the head. That, of course, Vikings are to be hard and strong, not soft and weak.

Ingrid waved her hands in front of her expansive chest, like she was waving away the last few moments. "Never mind. Let's look at your wardrobe. Has Old Anne been taking care of your clothing needs?" She rifled through Gressa's beautiful frocks.

Old Anne indeed had been taking care of her. Though why the Tower Princess needed such clothing she had no idea.

"These look fine. Banquet season is upon us and we will be having many persons of great importance dining with us. Let's keep our eyes and ears open for potential matches, shall we? You need a castle of your own where you can spread your wings." She gazed out the window. "Away from here. Such a strange place this is where the walls can be so oppressive."

Gressa's eyes opened wide. Who was this woman standing before her? Mother was speaking confidences that Gressa had never imagined she harbored. Perhaps they were more alike than she realized.

Ingrid laughed. "Like I said, you are no longer a child. I was not much older than you when King Jorvik held his contest for a bride. Let's find someone close by, though, shall we?" Ingrid looked intently at Gressa. "We used to spend much time together when you were young. Lately..." She rubbed her temples. "Well, I fear I have missed out on your growing up. I should like you to be near me." Ingrid turned to go. "One of my children ought to give me grandchildren while I am young enough to witness it. Those brothers of yours are too busy either planning war or going fishing. Not a one seems ready to find a bride."

Ingrid was true to her word. Not only was Gressa welcomed in the great hall every evening, but she sat on the dais with her family in a place of prominence. Herrick scowled at her the entire time, making her nervous enough to spill her drink and drop her bread on the floor.

Of course, Gressa had never gone hungry in the past. Her food trays were always filled with more than she could eat, but to see the food brought in and laid out on the great banquet tables was a sight to take in, especially on days they had visitors. Roasted pig, peacock, plates of seasoned eel, pies, and baked pretzels.

And the dogs! She didn't know whether she liked the mutts or was scared to death of them. In the marketplace, she tried to stay away from the creatures. But here, while they were eagerly licking up the crumbs, they seemed rather cute. All except for Herrick's dog who, with a terse growl, took whatever he wanted from the other dogs. Like with Herrick, no creature stood in his way.

After every meal, there was entertainment of some kind. A traveling minstrel. An acrobatics troupe. Even a painter name Zeke. He stayed for several days and painted Gressa's portrait.

Tomorrow, there was to be a trickster of some kind. A man who could make things disappear and reappear at will. One who dealt in herbs and knew how to command the elements to make a great spectacle.

The entire castle was thrown into preparations for this great event, so Gressa was hoping for an opportunity to slip away to the Dividing Wall. With her invitation to join the residents of the castle for meals, she had lost some privacy as she became the novelty everyone was waiting for.

After the mid-day meal, Gressa saw her chance and eased out the front door, barely missing Herrick's attention. She bolted around the nearest corner and pressed herself against the keep. He passed by, tracking her into the marketplace.

Ha, ha! He didn't see her. She would be the one to track behind him until she could go between the walls.

Her mother's renewed interest in her was also keeping her busy and she hadn't time to visit the meadow in days. She was curious to see if the boy had come back. Of course, she shouldn't be curious; she should be on guard. He *was* a South Morlaixer, an

enemy of her kingdom. She would be a fool to trust him uncondi-
tionally. He might try to take her hostage or...or worse.

She watched Herrick's head bob away through the throng of
shoppers. No, the boy on the other side was not her biggest threat.
She lived with "worse" already. She was willing to take a chance
to see what would happen.

CHAPTER 11

*M*anny sat in the shade of the tree washing the blood off his arrows when *she* appeared in the meadow. *Finally.* He'd visited several times since their first encounter, but she was never there, and the items in her tent remained unmoved. If it weren't for the tent, he might think he'd made her up.

He had been purposely taking longer than necessary to clean up from his hunting in the hopes that she might visit the meadow today. Her red-gold braids sparkled in the sun, much like the gold threads in her dress. The fabric was expensive, like the kind Mother had just brought in to make the noblewoman's dress. The girl, Gressa, made her way over to him cautiously, her eyes fixed on the weapons.

Oh, of course, some girls were squeamish when it came to killing their food. He shook off the water and placed his arrows back in the quiver. When her eyes transferred to the pile of dead starlings, he quickly gathered them up and put them in the bag Cook had given him.

Suddenly tongue-tied, Manny stood and awkwardly bowed. He immediately felt foolish and his face warmed. "Good afternoon."

She smiled and revealed straight, white teeth and a cute

dimple in her right cheek. The teeth and the dress revealed her noble heritage. Maybe it was good that he bowed.

"Do you come here often to hunt?" she asked in that lilting accent of hers. "This is the king's property. You could be jailed for what you have done." She lifted her chin and studied him.

Manny cocked his head before answering. She didn't sound like she was accusing him of wrongdoing. "I have the king's permission."

She opened her mouth to speak, but looked confused and said nothing.

"Good King Simon of South Morlaix," he explained. "Perhaps you've heard of him?" He made his voice sound light and playful. He was trying to tease her, but that wasn't how she took it. Her mouth formed into a tight line.

"Yes, of course I've heard of him."

Changing tactics, Manny took the opportunity to ferret out information about North Morlaix. "What do people in the north say about King Simon? Do they call him good?"

She shook her head. "I don't know what they call him. He isn't our king. If it were not for him, our kingdom would be one."

Manny crossed his arms. It bothered him that she would attack King Simon when it was Jorvik who'd raised the Panther to prepare for war. "You mean if it were not for *your* king the kingdom would be one."

Gressa clenched her hands into fists and took a step closer to him. "I have heard that your people are impossible. I see that the rumors are true."

"And I've heard that your people are stubborn." Manny took a matching step toward the girl. If she would defend the wicked king maybe he was wrong about her. How could the people be so deceived on the other side of the wall? They were now inches away from each other, both as angry as hornets whose nests had been disturbed.

"Steadfast is the word," said Gressa, "because we are in the right. It was Simon who would not admit that King Jorvik had been appointed next in line to the throne. It was Jorvik who won the Battle of Five and Two. It was he who King Rorick had been grooming to take the throne." Her nostrils flared, her passion acute.

"Is that what they teach you in the north? Lies, all of it. It was King Simon who was being trained to resume the throne. And if it hadn't been for his cleverness, the Battle of Five and Two would have gone to Copello or Lundy or one of the others. As for the Two in that battle, that was all Jorvik's doing. If he didn't keep the fight going, the battle would have ended with the five kingdoms." Manny stopped talking when he finally realized the look on Gressa's face was a mix of anger, frustration, and...and disappointment. "I'm sorry. I didn't mean to offend you. It appears that we have learned different histories of the same event."

Gressa raised her eyebrows and let out a deep breath. "It appears." She took a few steps back. She unclenched her hands, and then smoothed her skirt.

There was no way for Manny to backtrack. He would get no tactical information from the girl now that her guard was up. "So," he said, changing the subject, "what do you think about our meadow? What do you think it is?" He swatted at another swarm of gnats, then remembering the last time one bit him, he moved away from them.

She used her hand as a sun visor as she looked from brook to tree to open meadow. "I don't know what to make of it. It's a surprise for sure. I don't think anyone else has found it." She appeared just as glad to move on to another topic. She took off her shoes and stepped on the rounded rocks until she was in the middle of the stream. "What do you make of it?"

"I haven't finished my opinion, yet." *About the meadow or about you.* "I should like to conduct some experiments to find out what else it can do besides magically opening a door now and then."

"It is magical, isn't it?" She breathed in deep. "Whatever this place is, it is a gift. I would never be allowed to do this back home." She lifted her skirts to her knees and plunked her feet into the icy water.

Manny laughed. "Nor I. There isn't the time."

"What do you *do* over there?" She squished up her nose while squinting at him.

Several thoughts raced through his mind at once. The first being how cute she looked. The next about how he appeared to her. What to tell a nobleman's daughter? A North Morlaixan's nobleman's daughter! Admit that he was only a tailor's son? Brag about being a volunteer squire? While she might be impressed, he would open himself up for revealing the kind of information he wanted from her.

She put her hands on her hips. "Fine, don't tell me. I'll guess." She studied him, starting at the top of his head and working her way to his bow and quiver stuffed with arrows.

She tapped her dainty finger on her pink lips. "You speak as if you are educated. You are skilled with a bow." Her mouth twisted into a crooked smile. "And fast with a dagger as I recall."

She stepped out of the water and walked around him. "Your clothes are well made, yet not expensive." Eyebrows raised, she formed a knowing look. "You are a squire from Copello. Your father is a new landowner and you are the first in the family to train."

Manny tipped his head but didn't answer. He went over the tree and wrapped his hands around a strong branch. He pulled chin ups for several counts before pausing at the top, muscles flexed. "You wear a finely tailored frock, yet not one near as nice as the tailor in South Morlaix could make. Your skin is delicate, so you don't go out in the sun often. You show great loyalty to your king, likely a result of an over-zealous tutor." He resumed pull-ups. *Expensive cloth, sheltered girl, loyal to Jorvik.* Manny's mouth went dry. He could very well be looking at the princess herself. He dropped down. What was the penalty of a lad from South Morlaix talking to the tower princess?

A cloud passed over the sun, casting a temporary shadow.

"You...you like fine things." He nodded to her shelter, thinking of the items inside. He cleared his throat. "Your father must be a fine merchant man. Perhaps involved in the trade of pelts." He rushed the last conclusion, hoping she wasn't the princess.

She tipped her head and smiled. "Neither of us is correct about the other, are we?"

Manny swallowed. "We should probably spend more time together so we can learn." *What was he saying*? He was just blurting out what he was thinking. If this girl was princess or spy, he would give away anything secret she asked for. He was supposed to be getting information from her, not turning into a mooning fool.

"I'm not allowed out much. My family is afraid of something. Something that happened when I was a child."

"You're out now."

She laughed. "Yes. Maybe this is what they were afraid of." She looked around the meadow. "Maybe there's an old legend about a girl being trapped within the walls and they were afraid it would be me."

"Well, you're not trapped and I'm not a dragon planning to eat you for a sacrifice, in case they've heard that old story, too. Guess you're okay then."

"Yes." Her eyelashes fluttered down and she looked so vulnerable. It was a brief unguarded moment she'd shown him. She was either very good at playing a spy, or she was simply a girl in trouble. The tower princess who didn't want to be in her tower anymore. Manny was determined to learn which.

"If you're in trouble, I'd help you," he said, giving her an opening. Would she trust him enough to tell him who she really was?

"I believe you would, mysterious stranger."

"Not a stranger anymore. We've met already and exchanged names. I'd say we are becoming friends." He held out his hand to shake hers. An unusual gesture between male and female, but he wanted to press upon her that he could give her strength.

She hesitated before reaching out. "It's nice to have a friend, Manny," she said, her face turning a delightful shade of pink. "But I must go. I can never stay for long."

Manny crossed his arms in triumph as she ran back to her side. She may have disarmed him with her freckles and big, round eyes, but he was pretty sure he'd seen her melt a little at his touch. Struck with an idea, he entered Gressa's tent where he sought out her wax tablet and, grinning, left a message.

CHAPTER 12

*M*anny hurried to the shop, hoping the other apprentices wouldn't notice how late he was. When he came in late they would often use the opportunity to hide his needle or put honey on his seat. Little reminders that they knew he was getting away with something none of them could get away with. Apparently, they didn't notice how late he stayed to get his share done.

He had stayed too long in the meadow. He told himself it was so he could learn more about North Morlaix, but it was really to learn more about Gressa. And when he had tried to get through the wall, there was no opening for the longest time.

He needn't have worried about being missed. The shop, normally alive with the click-clack of the loom and the low murmur of voices, was closed. The door locked. People on the street rushed by, casting worried glances at the building.

"Why is the shop closed?" he asked a man herding a pig along the cobblestones.

The man pointed to the upper floor as he shuffled by.

The shops on this street were two stories, with the shopkeepers' homes built out larger on the second floor, creating an awning over the shops, which helped keep the walkways dry in the spring. When Manny looked up, he saw that his door was barred and the sign of the pestilence—a crude X—was painted in red onto the lintel. His knees buckled and he grabbed the wall to steady himself. Surely this was a mistake. His parents never got sick. The last time the pestilence swept through the town, this entire street had been spared.

"Hello?" he called out from the street. With the house barred, he couldn't go up to knock on the door.

There was a rustling of the cloth covering the window, and his father's grave face looked down on him. His dark curly hair was unkempt and his beard and mustache barely hid his frown.

"Do not come any closer, lad. Your mother has come down with the pestilence and no one may go in or out."

Manny could feel his face draining of blood. *Impossible.* "Is she all right?" He asked the question even though pestilence almost guaranteed death.

"Today she is."

"Can't I see her?"

His dad shook his head.

Manny thought about the last thing he said to his mom. "Have any eggs?" He wished he'd have said "I love you." But how can a person know when it's the last time they'll talk to someone?

"Tell her, that, um, you know. I hope she'll get better." He didn't want to think of death. Of saying anything that sounded final.

"I will."

"And you?" Manny rubbed his forehead. "Are you—"

His dad looked down and shook his head, no. "Someone has to care for her." He cleared his throat. "Take over the shop. You know what to do. There's a bedroll in there. Not too comfortable, but 'tis only temporary." He cleared his throat again. "Bad time for this to happen what with the tourney and everything. You'll be working from dawn 'til dusk."

Manny nodded. "Right then. See you later. Me and Hoxham will take care of everything."

His dad gave a low growl. "Keep an eye on Hoxham. Something shifty about that boy."

Manny was startled. "Really? You've never said anything before."

"Never a need before."

"All right. Don't worry about a thing. Just take care of mum."

The curtain fell back in place and Manny left his folks with his heart heavy. The Great Pestilence. No one had had that for years. Maybe all Mother needed was for the king's physician to examine her. Perhaps the king would send the doctor for a bloodletting.

Even though it was past time for an audience with King Simon, Manny went straight to the castle. His family had served the king well all these years. Their service and loyalty should account for something.

The bailiff recognized Manny and asked him to wait in the great hall. A large, multi-purpose room, the great hall was the place for eating, for entertainment, for dancing. Even though the room had been twice the size before the wall had divided the castle, there was still plenty of room for the king and his court. The floors were recently covered with fresh straw and lavender, and the oversized wooden tables washed down and ready for the morning meal.

Manny paced the room while he waited. He planned to throw himself on the mercy of the king. Beg if he had to.

Giant portraits of the King's family lined the Dividing Wall running through the castle, as if to claim the wall as their own and erase the history. The life-like work was the hand of Zether the painter's, great work. He was hired the first year of the king's reign to redecorate Simon's half of the castle. Manny had never looked at the pictures closely but was amused to see how all the relatives resembled King Simon. Firm jaw, piercing eyes, wide forehead, black curls, and proud. The only model Zether had had was the king himself, so he recreated Simon's lineage as best he could, changing eye color, eye shape, or nose. But they all looked like slightly-off versions of King Simon. Supposedly, Zeke, the painter in North Morlaix was a more skilled artisan.

At the end of the great hall was a reflective glass. It was as tall as Manny and he could see his whole self in it. He blinked. Maybe it was being in this room surrounded by version after version of King Simon, but looking in the glass, even *he* looked like King Simon. It was as if Zether the painter had fashioned a younger King Simon but with a differently shaped mouth and blond hair. Manny examined his face from different angles. A little bit like King Simon. Must be the South Morlaixan chin.

The echo of expensive boots reverberated in the great hall. Manny spun around to face the King. His countenance was gentle, like he already knew why Manny was there.

Manny bowed. With his head still lowered he made his request, "My mother has fallen ill. Father thinks it is the pestilence. May you send your physician to see if, perhaps, the sickness might be something else? Something that he could cure?"

"Manny."

Something in the king's voice made Manny straighten and look up.

"I have already sent my physician. He applied the leeches, but only as a precaution. He left your father with a balsam to give her to ease her suffering." He opened his hands wide. "I have done all I can do."

Manny was honored the king had already acted. *Good King Simon.*

"Thank you, sire." It was more than he expected. Now all that was left to do was to wait and see what would become of his parents.

"Your mother has lived a good life. As long as any of us hope to live." The king took a deep breath. "She is proud of you. I hear how she speaks of your many talents."

Manny offered the king a nod, his countenance downcast. He tried to look more pleasant, being in the presence of the king, but all he could think of was his sick mother who likely had only days to live. It was as if all the sunshine of the day had been collected and thrown into the deepest part of the sea. He bowed before turning to leave.

"Do you have a place to sleep until the danger is past?" asked the king.

For a minute, Manny thought King Simon was going to offer him a room in the castle. But the king was probably only being kind. Maybe he was going to offer the stable to him.

"Yes, sire. I will stay in the shop."

"If you need anything else, you may come and ask it. You, your parents…it is the least I can do." Again, it looked like the king was going to say more, but he didn't.

Manny left the castle with his hopes buried in the sea with the sunshine. The physician had declared his mother sick with the pestilence. That was it, then.

When Manny entered the courtyard, Hoxham strolled by and clapped him on the back. "Ho, there. Why the sour face? T'was a fine spring day today." He jingled the coins in his pockets. "That washer girl smiled when I winked at her. I think she's takin' a shine to me. If only her mother did not keep such an eagle eye on her."

Hoxham always seemed to have a pocketful of coins to jingle. His father's warning took on extra meaning as he studied his friend. "Where have you been today?"

"Oh, out and about, making deliveries for your father."

Manny frowned. He had never noticed how vague his friend could be at times. "And where is *out* or *about*?"

"Yonder hill and yonder dale, of course." Hoxham clapped him on the back again. "Enough about me. Pray tell what you are doing leaving the castle? Another tête-à-tête with the King?"

"You don't know?" Hoxham must have been goofing off all day. "My mother has fallen ill with the pestilence. I asked for an audience with the king to request his personal healer examine her on the chance that it was another illness."

"Ill?" Hoxham, with look of disgust, took a step back from

Manny. "You do not feel faint, as well, do you? You and I share much, but the pestilence I do not wish to share with any."

Manny shook his head. "I haven't been home much lately with the added work at the shop and my training with the visiting knights." Manny copied Hoxham's manner of speech. "And with visits to yonder and dale, I have missed out on the quarantine."

"Who is caring—?" Hoxham started then his mouth dropped. "Not your father? What is to become of the shop?"

"You are going to help me. There is much work to be done between now and the Tournament. The new apprentices need supervising." Manny knew not to look for comfort from Hoxham, but he hoped for some support. After all his parents had done for the castle rat.

"Aw!" Hoxham made a face. "I hate work. You know that. I'm a bit of a slacker." He picked up a small pebble and tossed it into the middle of a group of girls gathered around the well. They spun around and glared at him.

"Yes, but you're all I've got." He realized this was true. The young apprentices who were brought in to help with the simpler tasks could not be trusted with much. The thought made his heart sink.

Hoxham examined his fingernails. "How did she become ill?"

"I don't know. Father didn't say."

"Was she near the king's cook?"

Manny shook his head. "I don't think so." Sometimes they traded recipes. But he always delivered any fowl he caught to the cook himself. "What does that have to do with color of the sky?"

Hoxham shrugged. "Sorry 'bout your ma. You can count on me to help out at the shop 'till she gets better."

"They don't expect her to get better."

CHAPTER 13

*M*anny rubbed his eyes. His fingers were sore and his legs restless. He needed a break but there was too much sewing to do. Besides, working helped to keep his mind off of his dying mother. He stood at the doorway and measured where the sun was. The smells wafting past his door confirmed it was nearing the dinner hour. His stomach grumbled in agreement.

He took the bit of bread and cheese he had and closed up shop. There was enough light remaining in the day that he could retreat into the meadow between the walls and forget about the pile of fabric waiting to be stitched. And maybe talk to that girl again. He'd already sent the younger boys home and Hoxham had been gone for hours.

From the street, Manny called up to the house. "Father? Can you come to the window?"

The cloth covering opened and an eye peeked out. "Yes, Manny. How is the shop today?"

He splayed his sore, red fingers. "My hands are getting the worst of it. And my legs have protested enough that I am going for a walk."

"Good. And is Hoxham much help?"

Manny shrugged. It had been a long day and his patience worn thin. He was annoyed that he always had to stick up for his friend. Hoxham was getting harder and harder to stick up for. "I sent him out to work some measurements for a rich merchant. Hasn't come back yet. He seems to do best on errands that let him wander."

His father nodded. "You are wise for one so young. Send him here tomorrow so I can work on those designs for you."

Manny looked hopeful. "So, you are feeling...fine?"

"Aye. Fit as I ever was, but your mother is worse. She's not got much longer." He glanced into the house. "Perhaps you could come in quickly and talk to her. Just stay back near the door. Make sure no one sees you."

Manny looked around. The street was in a rare state of empty, so no one would see him breaking the quarantine. Most had gone inside, busy with their dinners and ignorant that his world was collapsing.

He took the stairs two at a time and slipped inside.

His father had a lamp burning, casting flickering orange light in the dim room. The scent of burning oil from the rush light mixed with the fetid smell of illness. Mother lay in the bed, covered up to her chin with a blanket, her eyes closed.

"Is she awake?" Manny licked his lips. His throat closed in, dry.

"She was a minute ago. Talk to her." His big, burly dad spoke so gently that it about did Manny in.

"Mother?"

Her eyelids fluttered but stayed closed.

"It's me. Manny."

She turned her head in his direction. "Manny?" she whispered.

"Yes, Mother."

"You're a good lad." Her breathing was labored. "So happy... to have you... as my son all these years."

Manny tried to swallow down the lump forming in his throat. His mother looked nothing like the woman he had seen a few days past, smiling and spinning her spindle. This woman was sunken into the bed, with dark splotches on her skin, like a burned-out piece of leather. The disease was progressing quickly.

No words would form in his mouth. He looked at his father for help.

His dad sat at the small wood table with his head in his hands, his shoulders sagged. A bowl of dinner left uneaten and shoved to the side. *Had he been eating anything?* Manny realized the toll this must be taking on his father. Not only draining his energy, but his spirit. He should send for the friar to have a talk with him.

He focused back on his mother. "I'm very busy at the shop," Manny said instead of all he was thinking. He looked down at his hands. He'd started hours before the sun rose, as he couldn't sleep. The tallow candles had been terrible to work by, but his eyes were burning anyway. He flexed his cramped fingers again, worried they might seize on him if he didn't keep them moving.

"Good," she whispered. Her eyes fluttered again and opened. "I wanted to see...you...one last...time."

Manny lifted his arms. "Here I am." He smiled for her, feeling awkward. What do you say to your mother who is dying? "I miss you." It was all he could get out without breaking.

"I know, Manny." She closed her eyes again and her breathing took on a steady up and down flow of sleep. He turned to go then she spoke again.

"Manny, you were born for greatness. When the time comes, be ready. Be courageous. Your life...won't always be...the shop. We kept you safe as long as....I've loved you as much as any mother could love a son." Her eyes fluttered open for a moment so she could hold his gaze. Then she closed her eyes again.

She knew him well. Though he had never shared his plans for fear of hurting his parents' feelings, she knew. An image of the girl in the meadow flickered across his mind. He wished his mother could meet her.

His father spoke. "You better go now." He stood at the

window with the curtain pulled back an inch. "The lane is empty."

Manny hung back. He knew he should go, but he couldn't just yet. He wanted to reach out and hug her one last time. "Good-bye, Mother. I love you." On impulse, he rushed forward and squeezed her hand.

She turned her head and smiled, her gaze following him to the door.

What had he done?

Outside, he ran straight to the Dividing Wall. He found the opening immediately as if the wall was waiting for him, and he rushed into the meadow. He'd never been in the meadow so late. The sun was setting, already below the height of the wall, creating shadows he could hide in.

The brook gurgled in the quiet night, calling Manny closer. He followed the sound and plunged his hands into the cold water. He shivered as the liquid flowed over his skin. What would his father do if he came down with the pestilence, too? He'd lose his wife and only son all in one week. Manny shouldn't have touched his mother, and in the morning, he would know if he had the pestilence.

He stumbled to the tent, grateful for Gressa's shelter between the walls. It shuddered in the wind, but the rug on the bottom was soft and she'd made a lounge out of silk pillows. He sunk into them and then noticed the wax tablet held a response to his question: Can I trust you?

Yes. And I you?

Collapsing on the pillows, he whispered, "Gressa, I'm sorry. Please don't come near me," and fell asleep.

CHAPTER 14

*G*ressa woke with a start in the darkness. She'd had a dream that the beautiful tree in the meadow burned with fire. The dream was so vivid that her pulse still raced and her room seemed to be filled with the sweet smell of smoke. As she slowly came to her senses, she realized Cook had started up the fires for the day. He used a wood that smelled of baking ham and always made her mouth water.

She tried to fall back asleep, nestling into her feather pillow, but images of flames tearing into the branches assaulted her each time she closed her eyes. It was no use. She wouldn't feel at peace until she saw the tree for herself and made sure it was untouched.

The sky was just beginning to show the faintest blush of morning through her tower windows. As Gressa's eyes adjusted in the darkness, she flopped over the edge of the bed to see if Old Anne was still asleep on her pallet. The nursemaid made a large bump in the middle of the bed, lying on her side.

Gressa bit her lip, wondering if she could slip out and back again before Old Anne awoke. Only one way to find out.

She tiptoed to her wardrobe and quietly pulled out a shift and a robe with a wide hood. A disguise wouldn't hide her activities from Old Anne, but it might help her sneak past any early-rising villagers. She'd never been so daring going to the meadow before.

At the door, she looked back. Old Anne rolled over and resettled in a new position.

Gressa remembered her determination to not take advantage or put her nursemaid in danger. Before leaving, she took out her embroidery and placed it on her seat. Hopefully Old Anne would take it as a signal that Gressa was accounted for and would be back soon. No need to tell the entire household she was missing again.

By the time Gressa exited the castle, it was later than she expected, as the world had gone from shades of gray to pale color. The aroma of bacon and wheat cakes and coffee floated out of chimneys and made her stomach grumble. She'd avoided the kitchen because that was the busiest place in the castle in the mornings, but she wished she could have swiped something to eat on the way out.

The pale skies were clear of any signs of a big fire, with only individual wisps of smoke rising out of private homes. But if the wall hid the meadow space between, wouldn't it also hide the sky between? Could it do that? It was all so strange.

When one of her brother's men stormed down the street in his practice gear, she instinctively cowered near a closed stall, hood pulled low. She'd forgotten Herrick's men headed out to the fields early to train.

She waited until the man was out of sight and then ran. A swarm of gnats hovered near the special place in the wall, which was open like it was waiting for her, as if needing her to hurry. She darted in and glanced back as she always did—half out of reflex to make sure no one had seen her or followed her in, and half out of wonder that the gap always sealed behind her.

For a moment, she leaned against the wall and breathed and took in the sight before her.

There was the tree.

Untouched by fire, its branches spread out over the meadow

and the brook. Immediately, the tension and worry from her dream drained away. The tree was safe, so was she, and the meadow was as peaceful as always.

She walked toward the tree, intending on patting its trunk, but paused when snores emanated from her shelter. Her heart skipped a beat, and then she giggled. That boy Manny must have found her poorly-built shelter comfortable if he'd camped out in it.

But what if it wasn't him?

He'd never stayed overnight before, at least, not that he'd shared. Perhaps the wall opened to others as well? Just because neither of them had met anyone else there didn't mean someone hadn't stumbled across the magic opening like they had.

She chided herself for not bringing her little dagger, but the boots she had grabbed in the dark were new and stiff and without a special pocket for the weapon.

Cautiously, she peeked through the gaps between the orange fabric and the wooden poles, for once thankful she didn't know how to construct a more secure structure. Not that she would ever admit it to Manny.

Hair the color of the beach rested on her pillows. *Good.* Manny was curled up cute as a puppy, but with his mouth open and snoring as loudly as any of her brothers. His last snore was so loud that he spurted and sputtered, then rubbed his eyes.

Gressa jumped back, not wanting to be caught staring at him when he woke up. She retreated to the wall before coming forward again, this time singing a friendly tune. She also didn't want to sneak up on him and fall victim to his quick reflexes again.

The young man appeared in the doorway. He looked pale and drawn but then smiled a goofy grin when he saw her.

She stopped humming and smiled back.

"Hello," she said, lowering her eyes, suddenly shy.

He yawned and stretched his arms wide. "What was that song you were singing?"

She shrugged. "I don't know what it's called. Something Old Anne used to sing when I was little. A North Morlaixan children's song, I suppose."

"Hmm."

"Hmm what?"

"Nothing, really. I know that song, too. I thought it was a South Morlaixan song."

"Maybe it's both. Did you mother sing it to you when you were growing up?"

Manny's face clouded over and he pointed toward the south. "I should leave."

"Did I say something wrong?"

He shook his head, eyebrows raised, looking worried that he had offended her. "No, it's not what you said. My mother is very ill. I should stay close to home." He looked around helplessly. "I just needed a break, you know?"

Gressa sucked in a breath. "Oh, I'm so sorry." She lifted her hand, wanting to hug him or at least pat his arm, but he looked away at that moment and she crossed her arms. "We have a physician. And there's a traveler coming tonight. He is known for a great many healing balsams that he brings from afar."

The boy shook his head. "The pestilence."

No. She tried to keep the look of horror off her face. He needn't say more. She'd heard about the pestilence, though they'd never had it in North Morlaix. Years ago, it had started in Copello and was carried over on the ships to the south, which imports more goods than the North. When her father heard of it, he closed the ports and they waited it out, using their stockpiles of supplies. Herrick's mad insistence on preparing for war was good for something, as they were able to stave off starvation while waiting for the pestilence to pass. South Morlaix had not been so fortunate. If the pandemic was starting all over again, what were they to do? She had to warn her father immediately.

"You can't go back, then." She looked uneasily at her side of the wall. "I can try to sneak you in. Or you could stay here and I'll bring you food."

Manny shook his head. "I need to help where I can. I was too young to do much the last time it came round, but this time there are things I can do." He squinted his eyes. "Would it be terrible if I asked you to stay away from here until it's passed? The starlings seem to love it here, and we might need them for food if the farm workers succumb to the disease. And the more time I'm able to sequester myself here, the better chance I have of not getting it myself. I don't want to put you at risk."

"Of course. I'll be careful," she said automatically, wanting to do anything she could for him. "But there are things I can do, too."

"I know, you're quite talented," he said, reaching for the wax tablet. Tiny footprints, like fairy feet marched around the boarder and danced around their words.

Gressa gasped. "I didn't do that." She took the tablet and traced her fingers over it. "The printing, yes, but not the design. You didn't either?"

"Not me."

"Who do you think—" Gressa cocked her head. There was a far-off scraping sound. A pounding, and more scraping.

"Do you hear that?" She set down the wax tablet.

Manny nodded.

Together, they followed the noise to where she knew the breach in the North Morlaix wall to be. A shiver went down her back. *Herrick.* Who else would dare to harm the wall? He must have seen her leave the castle, or one of his men noticed her near the wall. She had led him directly to her secret place.

"You all right?" Manny reached out and steadied her.

Gressa didn't even realize she was swaying. Surely attacking the wall was a breach of the peace treaty? Father let Herrick do many a thing, but never to harm the wall. They weren't to touch it.

Manny pressed his ear against the wall. "Metal against stone," he whispered.

The scraping stopped.

Gressa strained her ears for more sounds, but there was nothing.

Manny wiped his hands on his apron. A tailor's apron. "So, that's it, then." He walked backwards toward the wall at South Morlaix. "See you...later?"

She nodded. "Take care of yourself."

Then he turned and sprinted for the wall.

She turned away so the wall would open for him. What a clever wall they had to help them keep their secret. When it was silent for too long, she looked—and was alone in the meadow. How long would the pestilence last this time, and would she ever see Manny again?

CHAPTER 15

*G*ressa waited at the wall until the gap opened up, knowing it would allow her to leave undetected, but not knowing if Herrick would be waiting nearby. He may never be able to see her actually emerge from the wall, but he could see enough to ask questions and tighten her restrictions again.

When the passage opened, she slipped through and lunged for the closest shop, a cheese and sausage place. Fortunately, the patient shopkeeper was busy with a stout woman wanting to sample everything before she made her selection. Gressa's mouth watered at the smell of sage and rosemary. If she didn't need to keep her eye out for Herrick, she would have joined in on the tasting.

One, two, three, four.... Gressa counted silently while she scoured the crowd for her brother. Finally, she worked up the nerve to venture into the narrow street. There was no sign of her eldest brother but that didn't stop her from jumping out of her skin whenever she saw a man fitting his build and coloring.

It wasn't likely he'd be out here mingling with the common people, but he did have a knack for ferreting out trouble. Or causing it. If she kept sneaking off to the meadow, there was bound to be a confrontation some time. Until then, she'd do her best to be careful, but she couldn't stop going to the meadow. Especially now, since she'd already decided she was going to help Manny, and by extension, the people of South Morlaix.

Her knowledge of herbs was limited, but it was all she had. That, and access to the court physician. She could make subtle inquiries on what to do and then use that knowledge to make a difference.

As she raced to the great hall, it dawned on her that if the shops were open, that meant she had missed breakfast. The people were used to her not being at meals, so hopefully her empty chair went unnoticed, or Old Anne was able to cover for her. But where would her father be at this time of day? If he was with his advisers, she'd not be able to talk to him for hours. She didn't know what else he did with his time.

She chanced to look down the narrow alley behind butcher's row and saw her brother talking intently with a tall, bearded man dressed in brown and orange robes like fire. He and the stranger stood beside a well-seasoned traveling cart, guarded by a fear-some-looking dog. Only the dog noticed her, and she quickly ducked her head while slipping into a family group walking by. Once inside the castle proper, she let out a shaky breath and strolled up to her room like she'd just come in from the garden. Old Anne would know what to do next.

Gressa poked her head around the doorway of her room to see breakfast on a tray near the window, Old Anne working on her needlepoint.

"Bless you," said Gressa, stepping inside. "You were asleep when I woke. I didn't mean to be gone so long."

"I hope you won't give me reason not to trust you," said Old Anne, peering over the top of her glasses. She needed the lenses to see close-up work.

"Old Anne, the opposite," she said with passion. "More and more I'm realizing my world has been too small, leading to desires too small. A walk outside. A garden. A storehouse of healing herbs and knowledge."

She didn't know how to put her yearnings to words. The meadow was a gift and she needed to find out why it was given to her. And how Manny, a commoner from South Morlaix fit into it. *Is she to save his mother's life?* Was it that simple, or was she to do more?

"We have all believed you to have great purpose in your life. If you are also beginning to feel it, then the time is close."

Old Anne's words startled Gressa. What a curious thing to say. They would have to come back to this conversation, but first she had to get the port closed. "I have an important message for father. How would I go about finding him? Or, better, yet, could you deliver it for me so he doesn't ask me how I found out?" She leaned on the back of Old Anne's chair, placing her chin on the woman's head.

"And how am I supposed to have found out this secret information if he asks?"

"You'll think of something. You have to tell him the pestilence has returned to South Morlaix. We should close the port immediately like last time."

Old Anne set down her handiwork and moved so she could see Gressa's face. "How do you know what is happening on the other side of the wall?" She didn't sound concerned in the least, as if she didn't believe the words Gressa was saying.

"My source is reliable," she said, raising her chin. Shouldn't she be believed for the words themselves? As a child, she made up fantastical stories, but she'd grown out of her childish ways. She hadn't told a story about the woodlings living in the forests and playing pranks in ages.

"What evidence am I to give him? I can't waltz into the presence of the king with such a demand and no evidence."

How would they relate the information without giving away that Gressa had been in contact with someone from the south?

"Has the south raised their banner?" Old Anne asked. "The

last time the pestilence spread, each town affected raised a black flag to warn travelers not to enter."

Gressa ran to the window. The only black flag she could see was the tattered and frayed corner of the death banner which still hung from one of the towers. The sight of it always made her think the southern king was a man who never got over the death of his wife. She hoped the rest of their castle wasn't draped in black. What a depressing sight for the villagers to see every day.

"I don't see one from this view, but that doesn't mean it's not there."

"I believe it is unnecessary for you to expose yourself in this way. If the plague has returned, we will know it soon enough."

"What if they're being quiet about it, hoping that we all catch it and die?"

Old Anne sucked in her lips. "I don't think they would do that. But if it would make you feel better, I know someone." She held up her hand. "Don't ask questions. I'll send a message and see what is going on over there."

Old Anne knows someone? Who could she know in South Morlaix? Can she pass through the walls, too? Does she go all the way into South Morlaix?

"I can see your imagination has taken off." Old Anne waggled her finger at Gressa. "It's not as exciting as you think it is. The master of a friend of mine in Copello trades with the south. There'll be talk in the household if the pestilence has returned. She'll hear things. But I tell you, news like this spreads quickly. If you know about it today, it is highly likely your father knew yesterday."

"Oh." Old Anne was probably right. But if Gressa didn't have to worry about being found out, she could have been the one to sound the alarm and rescue her people. Then the tower princess would be known for something besides sitting in her tower.

Gressa spent the rest of her day looking out the window for signs of any panic in the south. The small glimpses she could catch showed people carrying on as usual. The same as on her own side of the wall. Could it be Manny was mistaken? But he'd looked so forlorn. Perhaps his mother was the first to come down with it, and the authorities were waiting to see if it was a true epidemic before sounding any alarms. No news at the noontime meal, but her father wasn't there. Like Old Anne said, he may already be working on the problem.

Finally, it was time for dinner. No sooner had Gressa taken her place at the dais than all the candles but those surrounding the dais were blown out at once. A hush fell over the crowd. There was a sizzle and a pop, then the room exploded in a bright orange light.

The people gasped and strained their necks, looking for the source of wonder. As an acrid smoke spread throughout the room, the great trickster appeared as if from nowhere. He was the tall, bearded man she'd seen talking with Herrick earlier in the day, and his robes of fire looked like they were on fire with the smoke swirling around him.

"Tonight, you will see things you have never seen before." His voice was deep and edged with mystery. "For your safety, everyone stay where you are. Do not attempt to come any closer."

His deep voice rumbled across the crowd, sending shivers down Gressa's spine. She'd missed out on entertainment like this her whole life.

Sensing being watched herself, she turned in the direction of the feeling. Herrick's eyes fixed steadily on her instead of the performance.

She was flummoxed for the rest of the night. She couldn't shake the feeling Herrick was watching her, yet she wouldn't allow herself to look again. She concentrated on the performance. There were disappearing balls and floating objects and magical hoops that passed through each other. It would have been a delightful show if she could have relaxed enough to enjoy it.

Then the trickster drew the night to a close. "I have traveled to a great many exotic places and found many wondrous items to heal any of your diseases. If any of you have need of lotions or potions, tinctures or balsams, my cart is right outside. I shall be here on the morrow as well."

A balsam for Manny's mother.

Gressa made a move to follow the people out the great hall, but Old Anne stopped her. With a hand on Gressa's arm and her eyes watching Herrick, she said, "You best retire."

"But—" Gressa wanted to say that tomorrow might be too late. Manny's mother needed help now. But with Old Anne's firm insistence and Herrick's unrelenting stare, Gressa conceded. "All right."

She would wait for Old Anne to fall asleep, and then slip away to the trickster herself. It was better that way, anyway.

CHAPTER 16

*M*anny wanted to stay in the meadow with Gressa, but he couldn't, not with the way things were back home. He wondered so many things about her and the meadow, and why it opened up for the two of them, but seemingly no one else. What did that mean? Were they expected to do something, and if so, who was directing them and why?

He went straight to his house. Such a familiar sight, the wooden beams at crisscross to each other, the gingerbread trim his mother was so proud of, carved by her own father as a wedding present.

"Father!" he called out. People walking by on the street made a great show of walking far around him. No one wanted to risk contamination.

The curtains rustled, and his father peered out, more disheveled than yesterday.

"No change," he said.

"And you?"

"Tired. But that is all."

Manny scanned the street to see how many more homes had been affected. None of the others bore the red X. "How many others have fallen ill?"

Father shook his head. "None that I know of, but then again, no one but you is talking to me."

His face was blank, but his eyes communicated all Manny needed to know. Their family would be blamed for the epidemic, shunned for the rest of their lives if it was a particularly bad run. It was quite possible that no one would collect their garments they were diligently crafting, and that meant no one would pay. The shop would fold within a matter of weeks.

"I'll check in again after I close the shop." They would continue as always until something changed.

"Make sure you get Sir Fletcher's jerkin done today. I forgot to tell you I'd pulled it aside to work on it personally. It's the large one on my bench."

"Sir Fletcher?" Manny's voice rose. "He would come by the shop?"

"Not likely. If anything, he'll send his squire to fetch it. If he hasn't already heard." Father glanced inside.

"Right." Outsiders might learn that someone in town had the pestilence, but not know who they were and still come to pay for their goods. But were there enough of them to keep the store afloat? Mother always handled that side of the business.

Which one was Sir Fletcher's squire? Manny had seen the man several times since he'd arrived, but he must be keeping the squire busy running errands, for he'd never seen them together. Not that Manny had been paying such close attention.

"Are you listening?" Father said.

Manny shielded his eyes from the sun. No, he'd been thinking about how he was going to impress Sir Fletcher's squire when he came in, so that later he might get an introduction.

"Take your time with it, even if it sets you behind on the others. This one's an important one to get right."

"Yes, Father. I'll work on it first thing."

The others had gathered outside the shop waiting for Manny to unlock the door. They'd been trying to look nonchalant, as if they weren't listening in on Manny's conversation with his father above them. The two younger apprentices had taken to playing a game of chance using rocks in the dirt.

Manny swept the stones away from the entrance. Even though he doubted they'd have any customers, it was still a matter of pride to have a tidy entrance. After Manny opened the door, they all shuffled into the dark room. Hoxham opened the windows and the morning sunlight took away some of the gloom.

Silently they pulled up their stools and began work. The two younger boys kept exchanging glances, until at last Howard spoke up.

"Are they sure it's the pestilence, then?" he asked. He stuck out his tongue has he carefully cut out a sleeve.

"'Course it is." Hoxham dropped his needle. "What else could it be?" He patted around until his fingers found the sharp end. "Ouch!" He uttered an oath.

What else could it be, indeed. Manny knew nothing of the healing arts other than the land of Morlaix used to have a special balsam made from the rowan trees. People said if they still had that, the pestilence would never have killed so many.

"But no one else has got it, have they then?" Mace said, backing up Howard. "By now, Manny's da should have it, and surely..." He looked at Manny as if searching for the tell-tale bruising. He swallowed. "...the others down the street."

"You don't know nothing," Hoxham said. "Quit flapping your jaw in front of Manny here. Show some respect." He got up and whacked them both on the backs of their heads.

"It's okay," Manny said. "I wonder about the same things. We'll find out in due course. Meanwhile we continue on as best we can." He meant to give them a reassuring smile, but his face felt stiff.

He found the jerkin for Sir Fletcher right where his dad said it would be. It was large, indicating it was made for a strong man. He threw himself into the work.

The room was oddly silent with the loom sitting idle. Normally the boys would want to chat with the owners gone, but

Hoxham's glares kept them to themselves. With no interruptions, and focused work, they made good progress.

At the end of the long day, Manny waited for the boys to leave, then he confronted Hoxham. "What do you think is going on? Is it the pestilence or something else?"

"How should I know?" He said it loudly, as if offended.

Manny didn't want to voice that Hoxham was a castle rat and seemed to know everything that happened before it happened. He was trying to get his friend out of that mentality. So instead, he simply raised an eyebrow to indicate he was calling his friend's bluff.

Hoxham scowled. "So far as I can tell, your ma's the only one with it. But it's got to be the pestilence. Got all symptoms, doesn't she? If it walks like a duck, quacks like a duck, it's a duck."

Hoxham was overly insistent, like he wanted the pestilence to be back. Was his life so terrible that he would wish a disease to flood the town? To what end? Add excitement or end his supposed suffering? While Manny did his best to understand his friend, sometimes he just couldn't. Who would want massive suffering?

CHAPTER 17

*L*ater that night Gressa lay in bed, ears straining to hear the start of Old Anne's gentle snores. There. In and out. In and out.

Gressa slipped out her door and down the cold stairs from her tower. She wore her favorite silk slippers to keep her movements silent, regretting how dirty they would become on her night adventure. With no candle to light her way, she fumbled a bit, almost tripping when she misjudged the stairs. She didn't know who would be awake at this time of night so she dared not use a flame. She walked with caution, though she wanted to run through the halls. What if the trickster had already left?

She needn't have worried. The trickster was at his cart, still in his brown and orange robes, closing his boxes and chests, illuminated by the tiniest of flames. He was shadows among the shadows and Gressa had a feeling that even during the day he moved in the darkness, from alley to alley to closet and dungeon.

She shivered, and pressed closer to the wall. He was getting ready to leave. She needed to do what she came to do, and quickly. Steeling her resolve, she darted out from the castle.

A low growl made her stop midway to the cart, balancing on

one leg. The dog, lean and wild, which had been nestled in the shadows stood and stepped toward her, teeth barred.

Without turning around, the man said, "Panther, be patient. The potion you seek takes time. I told you I'd have it in the morning. You should have been more specific the first time."

Gressa cleared her throat. *Imagine being mistaken for her brother. What potion could he possibly want from the trickster? If it was something to make his army stronger, he didn't need it.*

The trickster turned from his work. "Oh, 'tis only a wee lass coming from the castle door. Stand down," he said to the dog. Then to Gressa he said, "Come forth. What is it that brings you out in secret? A love potion? A tincture to make you the most beautiful in the land?"

His voice, almost kind, drew her in. He was a performer, but underneath, only a man. She'd heard he'd lost his wife and son in a flood and restless, traveled the land. He might have compassion.

Gressa stepped forward, and as she did, more of the man's features came into view. A pock-marked face above the beard showed signs of childhood illness. A survivor. Yes, he would understand her need.

"I have a friend whose mother is sick with the pestilence. Might you have something for her?"

The man looked closely at Gressa and recognition dawned.

"You are the king's daughter?"

"Yes." Gressa looked behind her, afraid she might find Herrick coming out to do business with the trickster.

He shook his head, a wry smile forming on his lips. "The pestilence, you say? I didn't know the pestilence had come to North Morlaix. I thought it was only in the South."

Gressa felt the blood drain from her face. Two thoughts rushed through her mind. The first was that he confirmed what no one else could. The pestilence was in the south. Second, was that she shouldn't have come. He probably didn't have anything and now he would tell Herrick. She took two steps back. "I'm sorry, I don't need anything."

The man held up his hand. "Wait. I may have something for you. A special balsam mixture you can get nowhere else. I'd never want to disappoint a princess."

His oily voice dripped down her spine and she wished she'd never come. She took another step back.

"What have you brought to pay for it?"

"What is the balsam's value?" She had brought an odd assortment of items from her chamber with which to trade.

He eyed her up and down, as if calculating what she might have to offer him. His eyes stopped at her throat. Gressa's hand automatically clutched the bejeweled cross necklace around her neck. A gift from her father. A high price indeed.

In her rush to get Old Anne to sleep early, Gressa had gone to bed fully clothed, jewels and all, with the covers pulled up to her chin so Old Anne wouldn't question her. Seems that was a mistake.

She set her mouth firm. "I have a comb and brush set. Carved bone. It should earn you a fine trade."

He frowned and held up empty hands. "Alas, I do not think we can do business."

"But my father—the king—will notice it missing. How would I explain?"

"Explaining is not my business. Healing balsams are. And the one you seek is the costliest of all."

How could she trade her father's cross? The one King Rorick gave him after the Battle of Five and Two when the kingdom was divided. And to help a woman she had never met?

Manny was a commoner on the other side of the wall. Why did he draw her heart the way he did? Shouldn't her first allegiance be toward her kingdom? Let the south find their own healing.

No. She couldn't think like that. This was Manny's mother. A woman who deserved every chance at life. Now that Gressa knew her plight, how could she withhold help when it was in her power to give it?

She unclasped the necklace and handed it to the smiling trickster. He made it disappear so quickly that she looked on the ground to see if he had dropped it.

The trickster then reached into his cart and opened up a carved wooden box. Within that box was a locked compartment. He opened it with a key attached to a chain around his wrist, and took out an amber vial decorated with raised leaves.

"A thick liquid enough for two. You might want to save some of the antidote for yourself. Never know how the pestilence gets around. I wouldn't want anything to happen to a princess." He sneered through his beard as he handed her the balsam mixture. "Administer a few drops at a time under the tongue until the patient is well. You may also spread it on any sores."

"Is that my sister?" A deep voice sounded behind her.

Gressa's stomach plummeted as she slipped the bottle into her purse and turned to face her eldest brother.

Herrick stormed out of the castle, arms stretched wide in exasperation. "Must I chain you to your room?"

She'd never heard him so angry and it frightened her to her core.

"I was just leaving," she said. She dashed for the nearest refuge, but Herrick blocked her path.

"What business have you with the trickster?"

She stared down, palms sweating. "I—," she began, searching for something to say.

"Like all young maidens, she was after a beauty potion. Harmless." The trickster crossed his arms and looked evenly at her brother.

Gressa bit her lip. Was he extending a bit of kindness or protecting a new source of income?

Herrick grunted and jerked his head to the side, indicating she could leave.

Gressa ran. Through the castle and up her tower. At the top of the stairs she bent over, breathing heavily. That was close. She was hoping to bring the balsam to the meadow that night, but there was no way she could risk it. Hopefully she wouldn't be too late.

CHAPTER 18

*M*anny pulled himself up another branch, the rough bark nothing against his toughened hands. He hadn't climbed a tree since he was a little boy, and he wasn't sure what put it in his head to do so now. He supposed he might be able to see over the walls, but so far, what he was seeing didn't match his expectations.

His real reason to be in the meadow was that he waited for Gressa, the girl from North Morlaix who may very well be the princess herself for all he knew. How foolish could a tailor's son be?

He was looking for comfort, and the apprentices in the shop were not the ones to give it to him. As the hours ticked by and Mother lived on, but not getting better, the tension in the shop grew.

No one had come for their garments, not even Sir Fletcher's squire. Payday was looming and Manny was unsure how to handle the day. He ought to bring it up with Father, but who can talk of payment when a man's wife lies dying a brutal death? When a boy's mother lies dying?

Manny had a better understanding of why King Simon kept the black death banner hanging from the battlements. The visual reminder kept the pain from dulling, and you wanted to remember the pain.

There she came now across the fields, the sunlight glinting in her hair. She was an angel he didn't deserve. He should stay hidden, stop bothering her, but that wouldn't be honest of him.

"Ho there!" he shouted down before she'd gotten halfway across the field. Even he could hear the uplift in his voice and feel the grin stretch across his lips. He'd better play it cool or this girl would guess how much he liked her.

Gressa squinted up into the leafy branches, searching for the location of his voice.

He remained frozen to not give her any hints of where he was in the dense foliage. The flowers that had adorned the tree when they first met had fallen off, littering the base of the tree, and small berries were beginning to form. As Gressa stepped under the tree, a last petal clinging to a branch fell in the breeze, landing in her hair.

"There you are," she said, matching his gaze.

"I'm climbing to the top to find out if I can see over the walls from here," said Manny. "Seems like the tree is taller than the wall, but I can't see the tree from South Morlaix." He ducked his head out from the greenery to see her better.

"Good morrow," she said. "You are sounding well this morning. Does that mean your mother is better?"

"She sleeps." All the time. Father said she no longer woke to eat or drink.

A look of relief washed over her face and pricked Manny's heart. The girl truly cared about his mother, a commoner.

"And what can you see from there?" Gressa asked, allowing Manny a temporary diversion.

He climbed the last few branches strong enough to hold his weight. "'Tis strange. I see miles and miles of open meadow. Yet I know, from down there, that the meadow is bordered on all sides by the Dividing Wall."

"Strange indeed."

"Can you climb?"

"Me?"

"No, the Panther. Of course, you."

"I've never tried." Gressa gathered her skirts and looked for a foothold on the trunk.

"Grab onto the lowest branch, and swing your legs up."

She looked down at her skirts and he expected her to complain about her costume, but instead, she set her face in determination and swung up as best she could, wedging her legs on the trunk and managing to clamber up onto the first branch. "I did it," she called up.

"Good, now you can stand on that branch and work your way up to me using the branches like a ladder. They are spaced rather well for climbing."

Gressa made her way through the tree. The leaves rustled merrily as she wiggled the branches as she climbed. Eventually she sat on the branch slightly below him. Her arms were scratched and the hair pulled out of her braid, now falling into her face. She looked so full of life.

"Glad you made it," he said.

"You didn't sleep at all last night, did you?"

He shrugged, imagining his eyes were puffy and had dark circles in the thin skin under them, mirroring his father's tired look. He directed her attention out of the tree. "See what I mean?"

Past the green canopy, the sky and the meadow below stretched way out to the sea lining the horizon. Gressa gaped. "You would think we were in a different land."

"Or this land before the castle and town were built." He pointed. "There's the big hill over there and the river that flows into the sea. It's like we can see the land without all the buildings and the people. The way it once was."

"Or will be?" Gressa said softly.

"Come join me," he held out his hand.

She refused. "I'm as far as I want to go right here."

He climbed back down to sit close to her. "Have you thought

about why we have been able to enter this place, but no one else has?" Manny examined his fingertips. "I mean, I don't know why I can, but you—you're the princess."

"Oh! How did you guess who I was? I never told you."

He pointed to her gown. "That, and the items you keep in your shelter. Not common by any means."

She looked away. "If I had the garb of a milkmaid, I would wear it." She picked at the gold embellishments. "The girls in town wear simple brown frocks with waist aprons and blue kerchiefs like the sea. I wish I had the same for everyday wear, but my mother insists."

"Like I was saying, your passage makes more sense than mine, the son of a tailor."

He glanced at her, waiting for her reaction to his position. Would their declarations of status end their friendship? It was one thing to pretend they didn't know, another to show each other who they really were.

"I'm a princess in title only," she said. "No one at the castle treats me with any regard, except maybe the lowest of the servants. Not even my personal maid takes my orders seriously."

Manny raised an eyebrow.

"You don't believe me?"

Her reaction to his being a tailor was puzzling. She didn't shy away from it, nor did she acknowledge it. So, how was he to know what she thought of him?

He shrugged. "I would take your orders."

She studied him, then laughed. "I wouldn't feel so obliged to give you any." She plucked a tiny berry and put it in her pomander.

"What did you do that for?"

"I study plants. I thought my nursemaid might be able to tell what kind of tree this is. Unless you know?"

He shook his head. "I know more about silks and leathers than plants." Besides, there was only one kind of tree he was interested in, and that dream was starting to seem about as likely as kissing this girl staring down at him. "Tell you what, when I get my land you could help me care for my trees." If he was to be refused, he should be refused for something meaningful.

He inched onto a lower limb, and held his hand out to help her climb down. Was he allowed to touch a princess?

Her face paled as she looked at the ground. "I never thought about how I'd get down," she said. Her fingers gripped the branch instead of moving toward him. "You have an interest in trees? So does my father."

He wondered if their interest was in the same trees. "I'll go first and guide you down. Keep looking up and feel for footholds. We'll go down the same way you came up."

"Okay." She didn't move.

"Gressa."

She looked at the hand he was holding out.

"You've got to let go of the branch first."

Meeting his gaze, she reached out her hand to grasp his. Her hand was cool, confirming her nervousness.

"Good, now turn around so you can grip the branch and lower yourself down."

She followed his instructions as he led the way, holding her waist a time or two to keep her from slipping off. Okay, maybe she was never in danger of slipping, as she was being quite careful, but she needed the confidence of knowing he was right there. Near the bottom, he was so distracted with her perfume that he slipped on the last branch and landed with a thud.

"Just showing you what not to do," he said. He stood and brushed himself off. "Let go, I'll steady you."

After glancing over her shoulder, she dropped and landed neatly in his arms. It took everything in him not to turn her around and embrace her. Instead, he leaned in and spoke into her hair, "You're a natural."

She spun with a grin. "That was fun." Then her face sobered. "I have something for you." She dug around in the little bag tied at her waist and pulled out a small amber bottle. "Medicine for your mother. There is enough here to treat two people." She explained how to use it.

He stared at the bottle before reaching for it. "Bless you." He held the bottle high in the air as if in triumph. "The Lord bless you with every good thing."

She laughed, sharing in his hope.

He backed away, eager to get the medicine to his mother. "You know, you North Morlaixers are different than I expected."

Gressa waved goodbye. "And you are not what I expected a South Morlaixer to be. Maybe that's why we were chosen for the meadow. We don't belong to North or South Morlaix."

Manny nodded, still walking backwards. "We're just Morlaixers." He held up the bottle. "Thanks! I'm sorry I can't stay longer, but…"

"Tell me when your mother is better."

Then he was gone, and she was alone again in the meadow. She looked for the wax tablet, wondering if he'd left her another message. This time, the words had been scraped clean and in their place was a drawing of their tree made up of those tiny little footprints. "It's beautiful," she said aloud, hoping to draw out whoever was doing this. She wasn't afraid of them, sensing the drawings were given in peace. When no one answered, Gressa set the tablet in a prominent place in the tent. *Another mystery in the meadow to solve.*

CHAPTER 19

*W*hen Gressa returned to her room, Old Anne had already folded her sheets and slid her bedding under Gressa's tall bed frame.

"Is this to be your normal behavior from now on?" she asked. "Because if it is, you're going to have to tell me what's going on. I can't do my job if you're disappearing in the wee hours of the morning and not telling me where you're off to. I trust you, but it isn't right by me."

Old Anne stopped waving her arms in her frustration and then crossed them, daring Gressa to dodge the question.

"I think that was the last time," Gressa said. She swallowed. "In the morning." She so wanted to tell Old Anne, bring her to the meadow even, but who knew the consequences of that? Besides, there was nothing else she knew to do to help Manny. She could make visits to the meadow when it wasn't so obvious she was missing.

"Good. We'll be eating your meals in here today—"

"But, I said this was the last time," Gressa protested. She'd expected Herrick to confine her to her room again one day, but not Old Anne.

"Got nothing to do with that. The queen is joining us for the day. She's decided it's time for you to be fitted properly for tournament season."

"My mother? All day?" Gressa absently cracked a knuckle. They hadn't spent an entire day together since she was little. What would they talk about?

"Chin up, girl. She's finally paying attention. Use your time wisely." Old Anne patted Gressa's cheek. "Besides, it's the tournament. You've been wanting to go for as long as you could talk."

It was true. In the past, during tournament season, she would open her window wide and listen to the trumpet blasts and the cheering crowds. Delicious smells of roasted meat and yeast breads would waft into her room, torturing her taste buds. Her gentle brother, Siguard always remembered to bring her favorite springerle cookies, and even now, at the thought of the sweet anise treat, her mouth watered.

No matter how much she begged or cajoled or threw a tantrum, she was never allowed to go, not even for an hour, or five minutes. Old Anne said it was because her parents thought it was too risky. There were people from all over who came for the tournament, and who knew what would happen to her if she got separated from the guards amongst the chaos? They preferred to keep her where they knew she was safe.

This year, however, she would be allowed to see all the sights for herself.

Old Anne gestured to a pile of dresses stacked on one of the chairs by the window. "These arrived this morning for you to look at, and there are sketches as well."

"I don't suppose any of them are plain, milkmaid dresses, are they?"

Old Anne gave her an odd look. "Why, whatever for? You can't debut in a milkmaid's dress."

"No, of course not."

"I would think you'd be excited about this opportunity," Old

Anne started to lecture when they were interrupted by a kitchen maid sent up with their food. Normally, Old Anne brought in the food, so the young girl was wide-eyed as she took in her first view of the tower room.

"Over there, now." Old Anne pointed to the table at the window.

The maid ogled the pile of dresses as she went past, then curtsied her way out the door. Gressa held back her laughter. The maid was adorable. Gressa would have liked to ask her to stay and give her opinions on the dresses, but Mother would not be pleased. Nor would Old Anne allow it.

Gressa went through the pile, spreading the gowns out on her bed. They were all expertly stitched, with pleats and flounces in all the usual places. She stood back and frowned at them.

"Here is another," said Ingrid, swirling into the room, wearing one of her own new gowns. The new dress she carried was dark pink, resembling all the other dresses in every way but color. Maybe the dressmaker had run out of ideas.

"They are nice fabrics," Gressa said. "And the colors are true to color."

Ingrid looked exasperated. "Is that all you can say? That the red is red and the brown is brown?"

"What do you think of them, Mother?" Gressa would take her lead. If Mother liked them, Gressa would force herself to as well.

Her mother put her hand to her neck and slightly grimaced. "I asked the tailor for samples of the latest styles, but fancier. You know how the people look to the royal family for a show of fine clothing and trend setting. Given that this is your first tournament, all eyes will be on you. Your wardrobe must be special, especially your gown for the first banquet."

Gressa cringed. She hadn't thought about that part of it. As curious as she was about the greater world, the people in it were probably curious about her, too. She would be free from her tower, but under constant watch by the people and the guards.

Maybe there had been a certain amount of wisdom at her confinement after all.

"Is Father still here?" asked Gressa.

"No, he left this morning for the hinterlands with his barons, looking for rowan saplings. Nothing but a futile treasure hunt, I'm afraid. Those trees are gone for good. We best move on and find another source of riches for the land. Peas perhaps. Everyone loves peas. The peasants could plant them every spring." Ingrid held up the dress she carried. "What do you think of this one?"

Gressa wished Father well in his search for rowan trees, but she did need to talk to him about Herrick. The more she thought about her eldest brother, the worse her imaginings became. She couldn't imagine what he would do with unchecked power.

Ingrid held the new dress to Gressa's shoulders.

"I like these designs well enough," said Gressa. "But remember that dress I wore when I was a young girl? The one with the puffy sleeves and the tiny bunnies stitched around the hem? That's always been my favorite dress. I've never had another its equal."

Ingrid and Old Anne exchanged looks before Old Anne spread the sketches. "What about these?"

Mother looked out the window then back at the dresses, then out the window again, obviously dissatisfied.

"Perhaps we could find that same tailor?" Old Anne said softly. "From South Morlaix?"

South Morlaix? The South Morlaixan tailor had made her favorite dress? Gressa could kiss Old Anne. Gressa didn't have to go to the boy, the boy would come to her. But how would they get him across the Dividing Wall?

The look of shock or fear on Mother's face made Old Anne cringe. "Forgive me, your highness. It was a thoughtless suggestion."

"Jorvik would prefer we use our own tailors, but since this *is* a special occasion...and he isn't here..." Her mother bit her lip. "It would be original, and no one need know." She slapped her hand to her large thigh. "Why not? It is your first tournament. You need a wardrobe that will be talked about for all generations. It must be legendary. I'll have my personal guard take care of it." She lowered her voice. "No one is to tell Jorvik, yes? Perhaps we can have it all taken care of before he returns from visiting his barons."

CHAPTER 20

*M*anny dashed to his house, eager to share the balsam. But when he got there he was dismayed to see the windows and door open. The breeze flowing through the house pushed the curtains so they flapped outside instead of inside.

Hoxham leaned against the outside wall, flipping a copper. When he saw Manny, he pocketed the coin. "Where have you been?" He shoved off against the wall and met him in the street.

"What's happened?" asked Manny.

Hoxham looked away. "'Tis your mother. She passed in the wee hours. They are to take her immediately for burial."

"No!" Manny fingered the vial in his leather pouch. He sprinted up the stairs to find his father. The room was empty, everything left open to air it out.

"Didn't you hear me?" Hoxham had followed him up. "They don't wait for burial in cases like these. You might find them at the chapel. I suppose your father would wait for you."

Manny didn't say anything, but pivoted and brushed past the apprentice. Hoxham wasn't the friend to mourn with. He had about as much compassion as a beetle on a dung hill.

People on the cobbled street parted before him as he stormed his way to the west side of the castle. He found his father with the friar in the small chapel overlooking the sea. Since North Morlaix ended up with the chapel on their side of the wall, the South Morlaixers had erected their own place of worship, a simple building lacking any stained-glass decoration.

"Manny." The tailor smiled weakly. "'Tis over, son. Your mother has entered into her reward."

Manny again fingered the bottle. *Would it have done any good?* It was her time and she wasn't meant to get the balsam. "Yes, Father." He blinked, looking up at the stone roof.

The friar said, "Her suffering is over, but I'm sorry for your loss. You may join me outside when you are ready." He left the room.

After a moment, Manny returned his focus to his father. "What can I do?"

The tailor put his hand on Manny's shoulder. "We had time to plan, your mother and I, these last few days. There is nothing left to do. We'll have a small service at the cemetery. She was quiet in life and wanted to be quiet in death."

Manny walked through the short funeral like he had stepped outside his body. He watched himself walk behind the wooden coffin transported outside the gate on a wagon. He watched as if from above, his mother being lowered by ropes into a freshly dug hole. Then he watched himself sprinkle dirt on the wooden box when it was his turn. He tried to imagine his mother sleeping inside, but he couldn't put her there in his mind. He left her in his memories sitting at the back of the tailor shop, spinning wool and embroidering patterns.

Only a handful of people came, those who knew her best and could take the time off in the middle of a work day. The royal cook arrived late and left early. Some of the women gathered in a knot together, casting pitiful looks at Manny and a few hopeful looks at his Father.

Hoxham even came, although he kept himself apart, more observing than participating. He paced throughout the short ceremony, an irritation in the corner of Manny's eye that reminded him of the Panther across the wall.

Handshakes were given. Awkward condolences made. And then it was over.

Manny forgot about Gressa and the meadow until he was back inside the shop, trying to sleep on the makeshift pallet. His dad was with him as they were airing out the smell of sickness and death that permeated everything in their house above the shop.

The silence was odd. The building creaked and groaned at times, like it was adjusting to only two people living there now.

Manny rolled over to face the wall when he felt the lump in his pocket that was the balsam she had given him. At that moment, it felt like the only kindness in his life.

In the darkness, the tailor spoke out. "It was horrible to see your mother so sick. At the same time, we were able to talk with such openness like we never had before. Truly our last days together, despite the circumstances, were our most intimate."

His father's smile could be heard in his voice.

"She spoke often of you. She wants me to help you fulfill your destiny. Make sure you complete your training so that you will be a knight and move on to something greater. She does not want me to keep you in the shop. I am to make Hoxham my head apprentice and hire another to take your place." The tailor sounded discouraged at this last statement.

"Hoxham?"

"Aye. I've got my work cut out for me on that lad. But maybe an increase in good honest labor will straighten him out. If not, I may send him to the Friar to teach."

Manny laughed at the image of the restless Hoxham in friar's robes.

"I spoke with the constable today. Next week you are to move into the stables to train full time."

Manny opened his mouth to speak but nothing came out. He wanted to protest. He knew his father didn't really want Hoxham to take over the work. Part of him felt like he would be betraying his father if he left his apprenticeship. But his father was giving him an opportunity he never expected. His mother knew his heart and was giving him this last gift to follow his dream.

His father spoke into the silence. "'Twill be fine, son. Your years with me are drawing to an end. You must think of your future."

Manny swallowed. "Thank you, Father."

The next morning, Manny woke with conflicting emotions. He wanted to be full of sorrow, to drag slowly throughout his day, but with all the work piled up there was no time for self-pity for a boy without a mother. Nor could he muster any semblance of self-pity when his parents had just handed him the opportunity to fulfill his dreams.

Father had risen early to make arrangements with several of the spinner women to supply him with the threads he needed for his weaving. Hoxham had already been told of his promotion, and was acting accordingly.

Hoxham noticed the stranger at the door first and jumped up to greet him. Manny was glad his friend was finally showing some initiative. Next week, when Manny fully entered the king's service, Hoxham would actually have to work for a change. The stranger spoke in hushed tones for a few minutes and some coins were exchanged.

"I'll be right with you," said Hoxham to the stranger. After the man had closed the door, Hoxham turned to Manny. "We've got an order from across the sea. Some wealthy woman wants her daughter in one of our fine creations." Hoxham gathered his traveling bag. "Let me check with your father to see if he has any other business while I'm there. Too bad you are moving into those smelly barracks tomorrow."

Manny smiled wryly. A trip to Copello? Sure, he'd like to go. But he'd rather be a knight than a tailor. He would get to travel soon enough. "Be quick about it. I need your lazy hands back here for stitching up these cloaks."

To think that within hours Hoxham would be taking over his stitching while he, Manny the Tailor's son, would finally become a squire. The only path to land ownership he would ever have was to become a knight. And of course, he would be honored to serve and protect his king from the Panther or anyone else who would see him harmed.

But the Panther was Gressa's brother. Of all the girls to meet in a secret meadow, he had to meet the princess of North Morlaix. And now, he was officially being called into service against her family. What would he say to her when they met again?

He regretted that he hadn't returned to the meadow yet to give her back the balsam, but he didn't want to tell her that it wasn't used. Whatever sacrifices she had made to bring it to him were for naught, for surely a princess had no need for a cure of the pestilence.

What tales did she tell to obtain it? Or what subterfuge had she committed? Perhaps he should never return to the meadow. Then he wouldn't have to tell her about his new position. He could leave her thinking he was an ungrateful tradesman and soon she would forget about him. But that was the last thing he wanted to do. He wanted her face to shine upon him in their secret meeting place. He wanted to discover why the wall opened for the two of them. An impenetrable wall. A magical wall.

"Manny! Watch what you're doing, lad." The tailor stomped over and grabbed Manny's hand, stilling the needle. "If that's the way your stitchin's gone, I'll be glad to be rid of you and have Hoxham bumble his way through learning the trade."

Manny looked down at the cloak he had been working on. He had sewn half of a man's cloak to the other half of a woman's skirt.

"Already dreaming of your knighthood, are you?"

Manny began tearing out his stitching, biting his lip and trying not to call attention to his burning ears. His father had only been half right.

"You feeling okay, Father?"

"Quit asking. I'm fine. The doctor must have been wrong. It looked like the pestilence, but it wasn't. No one else came down with it, and glory be we're all safe. Don't go looking for trouble."

CHAPTER 21

On the day of her fitting, Gressa was up early, pacing in the newly minted reception room. Her father's reception room would have been too open, so this particular room had been a storage area until that morning and still smelled of castile soap.

She alternated between worrying her hands and smoothing her skirts, all the while trying to look normal. Normal, meaning not particularly interested in seeing the tailor from South Morlaix whom she'd never met in her entire life and may or may not be Manny or his father.

Ingrid had planned with her guard to send word via the village of Copello across the sea that a wealthy woman was in need of the famed tailor from South Morlaix. Merchants from Copello were permitted into the port of South Morlaix to trade. Once the merchant had made contact, he was to bring the tailor to Copello, where he would be transferred to a boat secretly bound for North Morlaix.

The plan sounded reasonable, though she didn't trust the guard to keep a secret. He was hand-picked for Mother by her eldest brother, thereby making Gressa automatically distrust him. The shuffling in the hallway alerted her to the approaching group.

Her hands began to sweat. She wiped them off on her skirts.

She cleared her throat. She smoothed her hair. Lastly, she pinched her cheeks like she'd seen some of the girls at court do to give themselves a rosy blush. She met Old Anne's quizzical gaze and her cheeks warmed. Guess she needn't have pinched her cheeks after all.

The door opened and in they walked. Just as she expected, her mother, her guard, and....they lifted the secrecy bag from the head of a greasy-haired lad with shifty eyes and foul body odor.

Gressa struggled to compose herself. "Who is this? Surely this can't be the tailor who made my dress when I was six-years old? He couldn't have been but six years old himself."

The lad's eyes narrowed.

Her mother answered, "The tailor's wife has recently died and his mourning is keeping him in the shop. The boy here is lead apprentice, and I am assured is quite discreet." She wrung her hands. "We'll explain to him what we would like, and he can inform the tailor."

Gressa struggled to keep her face from revealing anything but aloof compassion. "Tell the tailor I am sorry for his loss." *And the tailor's son. Poor Manny.* How she would have preferred to hear it from him. But what about the balsam? She clenched her fists. The charlatan of an apothecary would rue the day he traded her cross for nothing but a false promise.

The greasy fellow gave a slight bow in acknowledgment. "Now, about your wardrobe." He lifted a bag at his side.

"Over here," said Old Anne. She cleared a place at the oak table where he could lay out his samples.

"These are commissions we've been working on for the tournament. I mean, our tournament."

Morlaix used to have one tournament, but since the division, north and south held separate events a week apart allowing visiting knights to attend both. It was the only cooperation the two sides exhibited. Anything for a tournament.

The head apprentice pulled out three gowns, wrinkled from the rough way he had crammed them into his bag, but Gressa couldn't deny the skill with which they'd been made. The stitches were even and taut, the fabric of the highest quality, and the styles were elegant. Exactly what she would want to wear to the tournament.

Everyone was watching for her reaction. She nodded and they all relaxed.

"Which do you like the most, miss?" the apprentice asked pointedly. He had to have figured out who she was, and to degrade her title to "miss" rubbed her the wrong way. This meeting wasn't going anywhere near according to expectations.

She held her hand to her temple, feigning a coming headache. "I don't know how you expect me to choose when what I really need is the tailor's ideas."

The fellow stepped forward rather boldly. "I have ideas, miss."

Gressa shuddered. She didn't want to know what his ideas were. She sat on her chair and let her eyes become unfocused. "You must excuse me. I feel a little ill."

The apprentice looked to Ingrid for direction.

"We'll take three gowns. Of course, not exactly like these, but in a similar style of the tailor's own choosing. If he can deliver even better than these, he shall receive double the reward."

Gressa watched the exchange somewhat disinterested. She briefly thought about sending a message through this apprentice, or maybe tuck a note in a gown when no one was looking, but there were too many risks. She'd have to send something that would mean nothing to anyone who finds it, yet meaningful to Manny. No, it was too risky.

"I understand perfectly." The apprentice bowed as he hastened to exit. "You will be pleased," he said.

"Wait right here, for a moment," Ingrid said to her guard. She closed the door quietly.

After the door clicked shut, Gressa let out a deep breath. Her mother patted her arm, the most loving gesture she ever gave. "Don't worry, Gressa. You'll have your spectacular dress. One that will catch a young knight's eye long enough for you to catch his heart. I suppose your father and I must begin looking into a marriage for you." Ingrid blinked as if seeing Gressa for the first time. "We're not used to arranging things for a girl. The boys seem to take care of themselves."

Gressa hung her head. She would rather she would be allowed to take care of her own life.

Ingrid turned to Old Anne. "Please give that apprentice one of Gressa's old gowns to take back with him. They can use it as a pattern to build the new one."

Quickly, Old Anne revealed the dress Gressa had worn the last time she had seen Manny, folded it, and secured it in a plain cloth bag.

Open-mouthed, Gressa stared in wonder at her maid. Not only had she come prepared, but was it another coincidence that Old Anne had chosen that exact dress? Surely Providence could not intervene in such a detail. And would Manny even recall the gown and know the new one was being made for her?

Not meeting Gressa's probing gaze, Old Anne opened the door and handed the bundle to the tailor's apprentice. He put it in his bag and then tossed it over his shoulder, whistling as he walked away with the guard.

Ingrid met Old Anne at the door. "That's enough clothing talk for today. My muscles are aching for my exercises. Old Anne, please go to the kitchen to arrange a mid-afternoon meal. I'll be hungry once I get through my paces. Gressa, are you sure you don't want to learn with me? A girl should be able to defend herself—with more than knife-tossing."

"Not today, Mother." Gressa liked the idea of defending herself, but she had no desire to go down where the men practiced their skills. Old Anne had taught her to allow people to underestimate her. Gressa agreed that was a good strategy. She could practice her skills when alone in the meadow.

Gressa quickly ran up to her room, swiped up her spy glasses, and got on her perch by the window. She checked over the wall to see if she could find the boy she had expected to come to her tower that morning. He was nowhere to be seen. The king's son, however, was strutting through the village with an oversized purple plume in his hat and a passel of servants clearing the way for him through the crowd. He stopped in front of one old man and stood until a servant made the old man bow before him. Then he continued on, out of her view.

Gressa frowned. How would she like him for a king? Nothing but a strutting peacock with an empty heart for the people.

She moved to another window so she could train the spy glasses onto her own side of the Dividing Wall. She searched the crowd for the greasy fellow, wondering how well he was treating her garment now that he was out of the castle. There he was. Being led to the gate by mother's guard, and without the secrecy bag on his head. Oh, no, and here came Herrick. Would Mother's guard give them away?

Gressa almost dropped her spy glasses. Herrick spoke amicably and gave him something. What business would he have with the tailor's assistant? His presence and his coin intruded all too often in unexpected places. A sense of foreboding crept into her thoughts. Old Anne had taught her to trust her instincts. Everything in her was humming a warning.

CHAPTER 22

*M*anny woke early, having barely slept the night. So much had happened lately to set his head to swimming. First the wall opening up for him, then meeting the princess of North Morlaix. His poor, sweet, mother dying. And now he was a squire!

His father was up before him, sitting quietly at the table and staring at the wall.

"Good morning, Father."

He turned, a smile twitching on his face like it was forced there. "Today's your big day. Are you packed?"

Manny nodded and held up his rucksack. He was torn between following his dream and his loyalty to his father and the shop. "Are you sure about Hoxham?"

The tailor shrugged. "If I can't whip him into shape, the friar can have a go at him. Besides, Liam, the Baker's youngest, has asked to be taken on as well. I'll have the Murphy girls take care of all the dyeing and the fancy embroidery. We'll make it work."

The two walked through the early dawn light toward the stables. Neither saying anything. At the gate, the tailor gave him a quick hug. "I know you'll do me proud, son."

Manny watched his father, shoulders slouched, walk with a

slow gait back to the shop. The parting would have come later if it hadn't happened today. It was only poor timing that when Manny's life drastically changed, his father's life had to change so quickly as well.

"Is that you, Manny?" barked a barrel-chested man dressed in work clothes and striding across the yard from the paddock. "You're late. The others are already caring for their horses. This ain't no nursery I'm running here." He dabbed at his bald head with a kerchief. He was already sweating, but it wasn't even warm out yet.

"Yes, sir." Manny picked up his pack and followed the constable to his new bed in the bunk house, then out to the stables.

"Yer to keep your bunk clean. Be on time for work and meals, and most of all, don't be lazy. Can't stand me a lazy squire." As the constable wrapped up his speech, they arrived at the stables where the other squires were tending their horses. All were hiding smirks except for Nigel, the prince. He was scowling, a deep frown marring his pudgy face.

"This is your horse to dress," said the constable, pointing at a magnificent charger. "The boys will show you what to do." And with that he strode off.

A quick look down the line showed Manny that this horse was second in greatness only to the king's horse. He knew what that meant.

"Sir Fletcher's?" he squeaked. And the other squires laughed and passed each other sidelong glances. *Wasn't Nigel his squire?* Manny didn't want to usurp the prince. He glanced his way, but the prince was picking at his fingernails.

A squire named Gus showed Manny what to do. "Feed." He pointed to the feed barrels. "Brush." He tilted his head to the tack wall.

A squire of few words.

Gus dumped a mixture of grain into the horse's trough and stepped back into the line of squires watching with interest.

Nigel broke in. "That's what we do for the sane knights. Your knight, however, requests special measures." He flipped a grooming brush in the air as he spoke. "You must mix the feed thus: three handfuls of chopped alfalfa with salt, molasses, corn and limestone added to the hay in the morning. However, in winter you will use horse bread made of beans and peas instead. After exercises, turn Tannin loose so he can choose his own grass. On heavy working days, give him hay and oats after you rub him down. His water must be kept clean at all times and every third day, bring in water from the clear stream up the mountain. Understand?"

Manny nodded. He understood, but didn't know if he'd remember all that.

"You do know how to groom a horse, don't you?" Nigel looked down his nose.

"With those." Manny pointed to a row of various brushes lined up on a bench, irked that the prince was using such a know-it-all voice. How hard could it be to figure out?

"Fine. But then you have to wet your hands and rub him all over, shine him up with that cloth there. Every morning, every evening. You never know when Sir Fletcher has taken him out or wants to take him out."

"How am I to get all that done in time to be at the great hall to serve?" Manny observed as the other squires wrapped up their work with their horses and they weren't doing near as detailed a job as he was expected to do.

A troubadour was visiting the castle, which meant entertainment today. One of the benefits of being in the king's service and he didn't want to miss it.

Nigel smirked. "From now on you'll have to get up earlier than the rest of us."

Fine. If that's what it took to become a knight, he would do it.

"Happy to pass Sir Fletcher on to you. Enjoy." Nigel tossed the brush into a bucket and strode off to breakfast.

As Manny brushed Tannin's coarse hazel hair, he let a grin

spread across his face. Sir Fletcher was the king's first knight. He would be training under the best—a privileged position indeed. And he was taking over from the king's son, which was even better. He would look like a second-year squire after the lazy prince. Sir Fletcher would likely be grateful for the improvement. His destiny was set. Training under the best, he would be sure to catch up quickly to the other squires.

Manny finished the brushing. He dipped his hands into a bucket of water and rubbed down the middle of the horse. Dirt smeared all over his hands. He added more water and the smearing only got worse. Awk! He used the towel to wipe off the mud. Where had Sir Fletcher been riding? He'd have to take the horse to the water to wash him properly. There was no time for that if he was expected to serve in the hall.

For now, he'd just make the horse look good. A proper washing would have to wait. He ran for the great hall. He would learn today how sharp Sir Fletcher's eye was.

Sir Fletcher was not in the great hall, so under Gus's sparse guidance, Manny learned to serve the trenchers and pour the ale. Had he still been working for his father, Manny would already be getting a cramped neck from bending over his stitching. He smiled at the bustling hall. So what if he had to dart around filling cups? The practice would help him develop keen eyesight. Already, he'd noticed Sir Gordon would clear his throat, look around the room, and then lift his glass when he wanted more. The third time, Manny was at his elbow in anticipation before he lifted his glass, much to the constable's surprise.

The rest of the morning would be spent at the training field. Manny wondered when he'd be introduced to Sir Fletcher when the other squires started elbowing each other, looking over his shoulder.

"Squire!" A great beast of a man marched toward them from the direction of the stables. If Manny had ever seen anyone who resembled Goliath, he was it. Too soon, Sir Fletcher stood over Manny, blocking out the sun. "You my new squire?"

"Yes, Sir Fletcher!" Manny yelled back. The other squires had all stepped away, leaving Manny by himself to face Sir Fletcher.

The knight's nostrils flared. "Did no one tell you that my horse is to be washed down every morning?"

"Yes, sir, but I was not told until—"

"I accept no excuses from my squires. However, being your first day and I have yet to determine your intelligence, I will let you off easy. We wrestle after exercises."

Manny glanced at the other squires standing beside their knights. No one met his gaze.

"Yes, Sir Fletcher."

"Tough break, lad" said Charlemagne, the friendly squire who would make knight in time for next year's tournament. "I hope you bend easily."

The knights laughed. All but Sir Fletcher.

Manny straightened his shoulders. Well, he wanted to learn from the best. Looked as though his education would be swift and somewhat painful.

The morning exercises began with the knights and squires separated into different areas of the small field. The squires practiced acrobatics first, which helped relieve some of the tension Manny was feeling. Then they put the stone, which involved throwing a very heavy rock as far as one could. They were about to bring out the javelins next to see how far each could throw a sharpened stick when all the squires suddenly stopped talking.

"Who thinks they can throw the javelin past that tree?" asked Manny. "Any takers? I'll do your chores this night if you can." Manny noticed the squires' gazes went past him. When the hairs on the back of his neck stood up, he turned around. Sir Fletcher stood behind with a gleam in his eye and a smirk on his face.

"Ready for you, lad."

Manny gulped.

Sir Fletcher laughed at Manny's display of fear.

"I'll make a man out of you yet." He grabbed Manny around

the shoulder and pulled him to the wrestling area. The other knights had already formed a circle in wait.

Manny was not a wrestling novice. Hoxham and the younger apprentices practiced at wrestling. But they were boys and Sir Fletcher was a giant. Manny was nothing but a bedbug to him.

The match began and Manny's survival instinct took over. When the knight barreled down on him, Manny's quick reflexes led him to skirt out of the way and jump on Sir Fletcher's back. Not a very noble or poised position, but safe for the moment. It brought out great laughs from those watching. It looked as though the great knight were giving his squire a pig-a-back ride.

A few shakes from the giant and Manny could feel his hands slipping. He clung tighter until he could hold no more and he was flung out of the wrestling ring. The circle of men was laughing so hard they had tears pouring forth from their eyes. This did not amuse Sir Fletcher. He stalked off toward the castle. It was time for the midday meal.

Manny was unsure of himself. Was he to follow Sir Fletcher? Or had the knight dismissed him?

He looked to the king's son for help. Nigel only shook his head. *What had he gotten himself into?*

CHAPTER 23

he time of planting had long since passed, and harvest and tournament season was mere weeks away. Still Gressa kept returning to an empty meadow. She tried not to be disappointed. After all, she was from North Morlaix and he was from South. She a princess, and he a tailor's apprentice. At best, they could only be friendly, as long as the peace held between their kingdoms. But surely, he had noticed her dress? Wouldn't he wonder why it had ended up in his father's shop?

One day, when she arrived at her shelter, she found a gift from Manny, folded and left on the blue silk pillow. It was a plain, unadorned brown frock with a waist apron and kerchief. The contrast it made against the heavily embroidered silk pillow was as stark as her friendship with the young tailor. But here it was, nonetheless. The note on the wax tablet, written over the tree read "Be free." She didn't stop smiling all the day.

Escaping to her meadow was easier while wearing the dress. She didn't feel like all the town was staring at her. Even though she had stopped looking for Manny—*where could he be?*—she craved her time in the meadow. She hadn't realized that with her expanded freedom her family was also giving her greater responsibilities. She was expected to entertain visitors by playing endless games of backgammon with the ladies who came to court to catch the attention of her brothers.

As dawn broke one mid-summer morning, Gressa dressed in her peasant's tunic and kerchief and slipped down the back stairwell. She was getting better at slipping away unnoticed. Old Anne's hearing was getting worse and her sleeping heavier. And with the tournament getting closer, her brothers, including Herrick, were all busy with training. With all this freedom, Gressa was starting to feel like a regular girl instead of the tower princess.

However, when she reached the opening to the meadow, it was sealed tight. Someone must have been looking her way. While waiting for the opening, she bent down and pretended to tighten her boots. She glanced at the wall. The opening was still closed. She frowned. A girl couldn't stay tightening her boot forever.

She stood, and someone grabbed her elbow and squeezed hard.

"Hello, sister. We meet again at this wall." Herrick's hot breath smelled of the cheese from yesterday's dinner.

Gressa tried to pull her elbow out of his grip. It only made him squeeze tighter.

"I see you wandering near this wall often. And now you are dressed as a peasant. Care to confess what you are up to?"

She chose to remain as unmoving as the Dividing Wall, locking her eyes on the top of the keep. He could squeeze all he wanted but he couldn't make her talk.

Her silence only made her brother angrier. He bent down and whispered in her ear, "Do you think that because you are my sister I will allow you to get away with such insolence? Does our father know that his precious daughter is sneaking around the castle grounds disguised as a peasant?"

Gressa could only hope Herrick would bring her before their father. He was expected home today and though he would be angry, he would only give her a gentle rebuke. Herrick, on the other hand—who knew what he was capable of?

"Shouldn't you be preparing for the tournament?" asked Gressa, trying to change the subject.

"Perhaps I was setting a trap so that I could catch me a song-bird." Herrick turned Gressa around so she was facing the wall. "Open it. Now."

"The wall? I cannot."

"Cannot or will not?"

"Cannot. 'Tis the Dividing Wall, brother, not a door." Gressa held her breath, hoping that feigning ignorance would help her escape. She had grown careless. But because the wall never opened when someone was watching, he had never actually seen her enter. He would have no proof that she could enter the wall.

"You and I both know there is magic in this wall." He stroked the rock. "You will teach me its secrets, sister." His voice was cool and commanding.

Gressa's legs began to tremble. A memory flashed of a day when she was but seven years old and witnessed Herrick's return from a hunt. The other huntsmen had brought their spoils to the cook for tending. But Herrick chose to butcher and prepare his hart in the middle of the town square. From her tower, she saw the massive amount of blood spilled onto the dirt. That was the first time Gressa understood that her eldest brother was different from all the others. He wore his bloody shirt all that day, Old Anne said, even during mealtime when their father commanded him to go change. Herrick had stood up to the king, stared him down for a full minute before throwing down his eating knife and taking his leave.

"I don't know its secrets," she whispered, her throat as dry as the thread she embroidered with. She told the truth. She had no idea how the magic worked. "But father will know how you've treated me when he gets back."

Herrick laughed. "Our father is of no consequence. His reign will end soon, and I'm not going to let you ruin what I've been working for my whole life. I know how to deal with you once and for all."

Her blood chilled. *What could he possibly mean?*

He yanked her into the castle and back up to her tower. His force was so strong that he ripped Manny's careful stitches, tearing her sleeve from the bodice. He shoved her into her bedroom and made such a commotion that even Old Anne awoke. With wide blinking eyes the old woman took in the scene, looking from Gressa to Herrick, to Gressa's lumpy bed and back to Gressa.

"She is not to leave her chambers," said Herrick. He spun around and slammed the door. A key was shoved into the keyhole and the lock turned.

Gressa didn't even know her room could be locked, or that Herrick had the key. Suddenly, her brother seemed at great advantage to her. She stood trembling, staring at the locked door.

Old Anne got out of bed and led Gressa over to the table. She was silent, for which Gressa was grateful.

"How long do you think my brother can keep me locked in my room?"

"Until he gets what he wants."

Gressa lay her head on the table.

"And what is it that young Herrick wants?" Old Anne began to stroke Gressa's head.

"Magic."

∽

GRESSA RATTLED THE DOOR. She pulled on it with all her strength. Then she kicked it in all her anger. "He can't do this to me. Wait until our parents find out."

Old Anne sat in the window box in the tower, her gaze into the distance. She was silent.

"Since when has my door had a lock, anyway?"

"Since your birth."

Gressa turned, startled. She had been asking herself questions aloud for the past hour and Old Anne had yet to answer any of them until now.

"I never noticed."

"Hmm. I believe it was a precautionary measure."

"What for?" Gressa settled herself in the window box opposite Old Anne.

Old Anne was silent.

"You can't tell me that and then not give the full story."

"I suppose you should know. When you were but a babe, your mother and father took you for a stroll in the inner courtyard. To show you off to the people and to give you some fresh air. However, on that walk, you heard another babe cry. On the other side of the Dividing Wall. There had never been another baby on that side of the wall before. At least, not in the king's court. You reached your hand out as if to comfort the other baby. Then you began to cry. As soon as the other babe heard you cry, he stopped. Then you stopped crying and clapped with happiness. It was as if you became friends."

Gressa waited for Old Anne to explain how that incident would result in a lock on her door. Old Anne said nothing else.

"And, this made them put a lock on my door because?"

Old Anne smiled a curious smile. "Because, dear, they feared that you and the neighboring king's son were destined for one another."

Gressa stared at Old Anne, trying to determine if she was serious. "Bwaahhh—hhaa." Gressa exploded with laughter.

"Your brother has told many a tale about wayward princesses bringing down kingdoms, or determined suitors stealing such princesses away. As such, your parents fear several things: that you will run away from home to be with the southern prince, that he would use you to destroy the north, that your love would destroy everything."

Gressa couldn't believe what she was hearing. "That lazy, louse of a boy? I'd be surprised if anyone could fall in love with him. 'Tis a most foul creature over there."

Anne continued with her queer smile. "And how would you know what the prince next door is like?"

Gressa blushed. "There are rumors." *And I have my spy lens.*

"You know, his mother died the very day he was born. When the king unfurled the boy's banner of arms, the crowd cheered so loudly we could hear them over the wall. The cheers were followed by an eerie silence. Then confused murmurings. Then the women began to wail. The king had let out the black banner of death. They say Good King Simon has not been the same since. Perhaps the same is true of the boy. Maybe he has never felt the love of a woman."

Gressa lowered her head. Maybe she was too quick to judge. Or maybe not. She frowned. She wished she knew another girl to talk to. Her sheltered tower had left her knowing little about life. She had to rely on Old Anne for the truth.

A rattle of keys brought Gressa back to attention. The door opened and in walked her mother. Gressa flew to her. "Mother! Are you here to release me?"

Ingrid flicked her gaze to Old Anne. "No, daughter. But I am here to explain things to you."

Gressa flung herself onto her bed, face down. "What?"

"Your father and brothers are concerned that your behavior might bring harm to the kingdom."

Gressa sat up. "My behavior? What behavior? I sit in here and embroider. Occasionally I go into the garden to grow herbs." She stood and paced the room "I do my lessons and practice my lute. A more perfect daughter you could not have."

Ingrid frowned. "Herrick has caught you sneaking out of the castle in disguise. A peasant? A peasant! What have you been doing, Gressa?" Ingrid spread her hands out to indicate Gressa was still dressed in her disguise.

"Nothing. I only get tired of everyone watching me all the time. I wanted to feel what it is like to be a townsperson."

"It feels cold and poor and hungry."

"Did you say Father has returned? May I speak with him?"

"Your father is with his advisers." Ingrid turned to the nurse-maid. "Old Anne, you must be more vigilant. Do not let her out of your sight. Jorvik will be interviewing potential suitors in time for the tournament season." She looked back at Gressa. "Your rest-lessness will go away once you have a husband and your own children to care for." Ingrid let the sentence fall into the room and echo against the walls. She left and locked the door behind her.

Gressa stood in the center of the room, gaping at the closed door. They really were going to marry her off so soon? She wanted to escape her tower but not as a wife to some baron, for surely, they would not be including any boys from South Morlaix. Nor any tailors.

"Why doesn't she help me?" Gressa whispered. "She should be on my side."

"This is her way of helping. She knows you're unhappy, but there is only so much she's able to do. Just because you cannot see what she is doing, doesn't mean 'tis nothing."

Maybe. But that didn't mean Gressa had to accept her fate. She had to get a message to Manny. He could help her figure out the magic in the wall. Or maybe he could take her into South Morlaix. She could find some place that needed a girl helper. She could be a nursemaid like Old Anne.

CHAPTER 24

*E*arly morning rising soon became the norm. Though Manny looked longingly at his warm bed as he tiptoed past all his fellow squires, he needed to be the first to the stables in order to get started on his long routine. Given the extra time he was spending in the stables, Manny was learning quickly and catching up to the other squires who'd been there long before him.

He'd learned his grooming mistakes lay in his brushing technique. The curry combe was used to bring the dirt up from under the hair. Then he used a horse-hair brush to flick the dirt off. He followed with a straw broom, and then the wet hands and the polishing cloth. He developed a nice rhythm and Tannin seemed to enjoy it. These quiet mornings with the horse were turning out to be enjoyable, a relaxing time that gave him time to think.

If only he didn't have to work beside Nigel. Though Manny had a few dealings with the prince in the past, he hadn't realized how truly awful the heir to the throne was. The other boys wouldn't talk about it, but through long looks and anguished faces, they all realized that South Morlaix was in trouble should anything happen to King Simon.

This morning, Manny was right on schedule and almost finished with his horse by the time Nigel strolled in, yawning. He scooped his usual small bit of food for his horse and brushed a few strokes before putting away his brush.

Manny couldn't take it anymore. Prince or not, Nigel was endangering the life of a knight. "You'll starve that horse if you don't give him his proper share. You'll make him weak." He was about to launch into grooming techniques when Sir Fletcher burst into the stable and stood between the two.

"Squire, pack your things. The king is sending me out to the manor houses of the land. Seems the Panther has been busy these last few months rounding up support for himself on our side of the kingdom. King Simon fears there may be a revolt in the works."

Nigel raised his head. "And what are you to do?" His voice edged condescension.

Manny looked at him sharply. Nigel may be the prince, but this was Sir Fletcher. No one spoke like that to Sir Fletcher.

"I'm to smooth things over so that you, piddly Nigel, don't find your head removed from your body and tossed into the moat."

Nigel baulked.

But Sir Fletcher was not finished. "I did my best to train you to defend yourself and your castle, but you have more interest in spearing your next meal than any foe. You pray we find allies who are willing to defend the target you wear on your back."

Nigel looked stunned, as if he had never considered the possibility that, as the king's only heir, he would be at risk of anything, save being spoiled by his nursemaid. His lower lip trembled, and he took his leave to the great hall.

"Squire. Say goodbye to whomever you need to. I know not when we shall return. By the tournament at the latest. We leave upon the hour." Sir Fletcher hastened to the barracks.

Manny could think of only two people he needed to tell. Father and Gressa. With his new schedule, he'd only been able to slip away from his duties once, when he delivered the peasant's outfit for her. She hadn't asked him for it, but he had heard the longing in her voice to be able to slip through the crowd, and it was a simple task for him to do.

The other squires teased him for spending his time sewing women's garments when they were playing dice, but all he needed to do was imagine her smile when she found it and that was all he needed.

He had stayed away from the stables as long as he dared, but she had not come that day. He had wanted to tell her of his change in fortune. It did not seem the thing to put into a note.

Father first.

Manny found him working on a fine green silk gown. Laid out on the edge of the table was the dress he was making the pattern from—it looked like Gressa's. Couldn't be. She was just on his mind was all. He cleared his throat to get Father's attention.

The tailor nodded grimly when Manny told him the news. "Things are happening quickly for you, boy. God be with you."

Manny gathered what few belongings he thought he would need, and tossed them in a bag. The rest would be at the barracks. After a hearty hug from his father, he ran to the Dividing Wall.

Glancing around to see if anyone was watching, he slowed to a saunter. With his back to the opening, he slipped in.

What were the odds that Gressa would be in the meadow? They'd have just enough time to climb the tree before he'd have to rush off. Would she be proud of him when she learned he was now a squire? But she was not in the tent or in the tree or throwing pebbles into the brook.

The meadow seemed even more quiet than usual. Like she hadn't been there herself in a long time. One side of the tent had fallen down and Manny quickly fixed it. The dress was gone, and the wax tablet read, "It's perfect." He grinned, imagining her surprise at the gift.

The mysterious drawing this time was of a person with long legs and spiky hair. *Himself?* He patted down his hair. Who else was using this meadow, and what were they trying to say? Words would be a whole lot easier.

He put her unused balsam beside the tablet. Ideally, he would have told her in person, but she would know what had happened when she saw the full bottle. He couldn't think of what to write on the tablet that would convey all that needed to be said, so he took to pacing along the North Wall for as long has he could afford.

It didn't open for him, though he didn't expect it to. Besides, what would he do if he suddenly found himself in North Morlaix anyway? With one last hopeful glance behind him, Manny left the space between the Dividing Walls.

As he was sprinting through the open courtyard in South Morlaix, Manny heard Hoxham call out.

"Ho, Manny!" Hoxham caught up with him. He was looking as disheveled as ever. "Where'd you come from? Could have sworn you stepped right out of the Dividing Wall." Hoxham peered over Manny's shoulder, looking intently at the wall. He swatted the space between them. "Och, these bugs! Won't leave a person alone."

Shifting his weight to block Hoxham's penetrating gaze, Manny joked, "You best be careful; too much work is affecting your eyesight. I was here the whole time."

Hoxham shrugged, still trying to see around Manny. "Your father tells me you are leaving with Sir Fletcher. On what task do you, a novice, warrant?"

"Kingdom business, Hoxham, kingdom business." Manny slung his bag over his shoulder, trying to portray an air of importance, and continued walking away from the wall.

"Funny, tailor's son. Really, what will you be doing? Will you be gone long?"

Manny sobered. "I don't know how long we'll be gone, nor do I know exactly what we'll be doing. Sir Fletcher has the orders and I'm along to serve him."

"Anything to do with talk of an uprising?" Hoxham picked at a piece of string on his arm.

"How did you hear of that?"

Hoxham shrugged. "I'm surprised you haven't. Always got your head stuck in your future, and you miss what is happening around you. Maybe you should leave me your precious cross for safe keeping."

Manny shook his head. Hoxham had always liked Manny's necklace. He usually kept it hidden under his jerkin like his mother asked him too, but one day while he was rough-housing at the beach, it had fallen out and Hoxham had seen it.

"I'm about to get very involved in the affairs of the king now. Kind of exciting. I've never left these walls before. I'll get to see what's out there in this world." *And maybe pick out my piece of land.*

"So, you're leaving the village." Hoxham crossed his arms. "Where are you spending the night?"

"I just told you I don't know anything. Why do you care so much about where I'm going and what I'm doing?"

"With you gone from the shop, I have to do a whole lot more work. I was hoping you'd be bored of your new work and return."

Manny laughed. Of course, Hoxham would be thinking of himself. "Hard work is good for you."

"For you, yes. Me, not so much." Hoxham opened his arms wide. "There's got to be an easier way to make a living."

Manny put out his hand to shake with Hoxham. "Take care, old friend."

Manny sprinted the rest of the way to the barracks. He felt Hoxham's gaze, so he turned to look. The apprentice stood in the middle of the square, hands on hips, watching him. Manny had little time to think about his friend, so he gave a curt wave and entered the barracks to collect the rest of his things.

Sir Fletcher was waiting in the stables. His horse was ready and another was tethered for Manny.

Manny immediately apologized. Readying the horses was his job. "I was only saying goodbye."

"'Tis fine, lad. I am not so lazy a knight that I cannot ready my own horse."

The horse Manny would be riding was grander than any he had expected. He briefly wondered how long a trip this would be and how his backside would handle being on a horse for extended periods of time. He knew how to ride, but only in small intervals.

Sir Fletcher led the way through the inner curtain, the outer bailey and the outer curtain. At the gatehouse, he stopped to speak with the gatekeeper. They continued on over the draw-bridge. Their horses made a satisfying clip-clop, clip-clop on the wood. Now that they were on their way, Manny took a deep breath as if he could taste excitement mixed in with the scent of pine and dirt. He didn't realize how much he was longing for adventure until he was faced with one.

*a*n entire week in her bedroom and Gressa was ready to claw her way out. Old Anne was good company for the first two days, but now they were both tired of endless games of backgammon and their fingers red-raw from working the embroidery needle. Gressa needed to escape. She needed to go to the meadow. On day five of captivity she had broken her secret and brought out the spy lenses. She simply had to see if Manny was going into the wall without her. If Old Anne was shocked at the hidden spy lenses, she hid it well.

"May I have a turn?" Old Anne asked after Gressa had spent the morning spying out the window.

Gressa handed them over. "May as well. Nothing interesting going on out there, either."

Old Anne smiled. "We'll see about that." She chose another window and leaned into the corner, training the glasses on the grounds of North Morlaix. "Hmm," she said.

Gressa looked over Old Anne's head, trying to see what she was seeing. "What is it? I can't see anything."

Old Anne stood and handed the glasses to Gressa. "By the gate. Tell me what you see."

Gressa focused the spy lenses on a group of travelers that had just crossed the moat. Rich men, from the look of their clothes. They stood holding the reigns of their horses, with Herrick in the midst of them, gesturing toward the castle. He was likely inviting them to join him for dinner.

No, he was gesturing to the tower. Her tower. Even from such a distance, his attention unnerved her. She stepped back in case he could see her, trapped like one of the rats the cook oft caught in the kitchen.

"W-ho are they?" she asked. Her voice trembled.

"Me thinks a suitor."

"A suitor?"

"For you."

Gressa's mouth went dry.

Moments later Ingrid entered the room. She had a bright smile on her face. "Daughter, good news. Tonight is a very special feast."

Gressa cast a frightened glance at Old Anne, who had deftly tucked the spy glasses away. "Special feast? 'Tis not a holiday or a Saint's day."

Ingrid clasped her hands together. "We have special guests dining with us tonight. From the old country."

"Oh, Viking relatives? Grandfather, perhaps?" Gressa asked hopefully. Willing for there to be another explanation for the guests. "We haven't seen him in ages."

"No, daughter. Not someone from your past. Mayhaps someone for your future."

Ingrid went over to Gressa's gowns. She pulled out a rose-colored one. "Wear this tonight. It's your prettiest." Gressa looked out the window. *Where are you Manny?*

At dinner Gressa found herself seated at the front table beside a very old, very vile lord. He grinned at her with crooked, black teeth. When he spoke, the stuffed peacock he was eating lolled on his tongue. Wherever did Herrick dig up this suitor? He was punishing her, that much was for certain.

She leaned into the table to see past her father to where her brothers sat. Herrick was staring directly at her with his hard, black eyes. He flashed a flicker of a smile before wiping it away with a napkin. Her brother was concerned with keeping up appearances.

Viking Ulf, on the other hand, was not. A trickle of grease from the roast duck leaked out his fat lips and dribbled into his beard where it joined bits of food from previous meals. Gressa's stomach churned.

She knew that tonight her brother would pay her a visit. He would give her an ultimatum: tell him about the Dividing Wall or be married off to Ulf for a life lived in sacrifice to the secret.

Quickly, she reviewed her options. Marriage was definitely out. So was bringing Herrick into the Dividing Wall. There was no telling what he would do, how he could manipulate the magic. Whatever he did, it would only benefit him. Not her father. Not the people in his kingdom. And certainly not the people in Manny's kingdom.

Her people. Even though she had been sheltered from much of the common life, she did watch over the people daily. She knew that the washerwoman liked to get her washing done early so she could visit with the baker's wife. The gatekeeper with the green hat was funny because he made everyone laugh. The falconer appeared to have his own magic the way he could command the hawks and other birds to fly on his command. She couldn't let the Panther get to them. Right now, her father the king stood in his way, but Jorvik wouldn't be king forever.

Viking Ulf sneezed. All the food he had in his mouth splayed out before him.

Gressa couldn't keep the disgust out of her face. She looked over at Herrick. This time his grin could not be contained. He looked like he had already learned her secret. She could cry, but she wouldn't give him that satisfaction. She would rather run away.

Later that night, Gressa paced back and forth in her room. She was locked up again after the dinner. She was given a night's reprieve until breakfast when she would have to sup again with that dreadful man. She had not even Old Anne to pass the time with. She was all alone in her room to imagine her dismal future. Herrick was letting her fret alone so that when he did make the offer she would jump at the chance of getting rid of the insipid Viking.

Fret she did not. Instead she plotted. There had to be a way to escape. She couldn't do so from the tower. The castle was as difficult to break out of as it was to break into.

So, it was decided then. With or without Manny's help, she had to go through the Dividing Wall. Any other place her brother would be able to track her down. He had eyes and ears everywhere, and she had no one. No one who wasn't under his control or influence. No one except Manny.

Only, she hadn't seen Manny in weeks. It was as if he had vanished. As if Herrick knew about him, too, and had taken care of her last way of escape.

She would stay wary. Be ready to go at a moment's notice. Tonight, she would begin storing away food. Viking Ulf was too busy with his own food to notice what she did. As long as Herrick thought he was winning, maybe he would not keep such a keen eye on her.

The key turned in the lock. So soon? Of course, that was the real reason why Old Anne was sent on a task, so she would be alone to be manipulated.

Her brother stood in the doorway, hands clasped casually behind his back. Traces of victory playing about his lips.

"Sister, did you enjoy your dinner today?" He managed to rein in the smirk on his face.

"Stuffed peacock is my favorite dish, brother. I thought it was delightful." She could play the game, too.

His lip curled into a snarl. "And how was your dining companion? Did you find him to your liking?"

"He seemed to enjoy the food very much."

"What about your company? Did he enjoy that?"

She shrugged. "We didn't talk much."

In two steps Herrick was standing before her, the key to her room held close to her face. "Make sure you talk at the next meal. You may as well get to know him better since he is working out your betrothal with Father as we speak."

Finally, the words were spoken and hanging in the air. She waited for Herrick to stake his claim.

He paced, slowly and assuredly around her room. "Now, sister, I wouldn't want to see you married to someone whose company you couldn't tolerate. Perhaps I could put in a word for you. Convince father that Ulf is not a worthy match for you."

Still, she waited.

"You have something I want. I have something you want. A simple exchange." He drew in his hands between them. "Tell me the secrets of the Dividing Wall. I know you go in there. Show me the way. That is all."

"I don't know what you are talking about."

His lips clamped shut. He spun on his heel, slammed the door, and locked it.

Gressa collapsed on her bed. The sooner she escaped, the better.

CHAPTER 26

*M*anny was exhausted. For serving only one man, there certainly was a lot to do. Apparently, Sir Fletcher's methods of training a squire consisted of making the squire do absolutely everything. From preparing the fire and campsite when they were between manor houses, to washing their clothes in any streams that came by and also catching fish. Seems the only thing Sir Fletcher was willing to do on his own was hunt for game. He said he needed to keep his killing eye sharp.

Presently, Sir Fletcher came out of the woods, holding a fowl upside down by the legs. He thrust the bird into Manny's hands. "Clean it up."

Manny looked back at the fire he had just barely gotten started. They'd had a wet day, and he was lucky to find any dry kindling at all. "Could you at least keep the fire going while I clean your bird?" Then he remembered to add "Sir Fletcher."

Sir Fletcher smirked. "Of course. Squire."

Face warm, Manny took the bird away from their camp. He plucked the feathers, releasing his irritation. This was likely part of his training, to be tested beyond his limits, and he had started to let his temper get the best of him with Sir Fletcher. He must do better.

When Manny returned with the bird on a spit ready to roast, Sir Fletcher was in a talkative mood.

"I'm finding our visits curious," he said.

"How so?" Manny set the bird above the flames. He'd been fortunate to find two strong sticks with a Y to use for his spit, and he'd packed them on his horse from camp to camp. These past few weeks they had traipsed up and down the south side of the kingdom, talking with all the wealthy landowners and some of the peasants, too. They'd been welcomed into manors and peasant cottages alike and been shown acres of fieldwork. Beside many a hearth fire they'd been entertained with folk stories and music. Last night, in fact, the family they stayed with were accomplished singers, singing in harmony right down to the youngest, a precocious five-year old girl with a drippy nose.

"The people are too content. There is no talk of unrest. The split kingdom remains at peace. The further we go away from the castle, the more at peace the people appear to be. They seem to be happy to be away from any day-to-day nit-pickiness of the kings."

Manny listened as he rotated the spit using the positioning sticks like Sir Fletcher had taught him. It was quite clever, actually. The way Manny first set up the spit, the heavy weight of the animal always made it hang upside down over the flame, but Sir Fletcher's method controlled the spit's rotation.

When Sir Fletcher grew quiet, Manny glanced up. Was the knight asking for advice or merely talking aloud? Sir Fletcher stared into the flames, and Manny sat back, waiting.

He hoped they would continue with their travels, since he hadn't found his land yet. What he had found was a greater appreciation for South Morlaix and its people. The land was fertile, growing any manner of grains in a patchwork of fields. The people were adept farmers, producing gardens filled with tomatoes, cucumbers, peas. And they were a happy people, enjoying one another's company, coming together to feast and entertain Sir Fletcher and himself. The only site to mar the land was the ugly wall. Always, there was the wall. A constant reminder of what had been and what had been lost.

"So, unless the people are good at hiding their upcoming revolt, where have these rumors come from?" Sir Fletcher stood and paced around the fire. "I find no evidence that the Panther has been stirring up the people on our side. Maybe the people in North Morlaix, but that is not new news. We hear them shouting at our wall after training. Taunting us." He stopped pacing. "Our people seem as content as ever with Simon as their king. They show not the slightest desire to launch a revolt, nor to risk having that twit Nigel become king."

"No sir." Drippings from the bird sizzled as they hit the flames, and the aroma of cooking fowl made Manny's mouth water. He missed the regular meals he received at the castle. Not that he wanted to get soft, like Nigel. No, he'd rather feast off nuts and berries than turn out like Nigel.

Sir Fletcher sat back on his haunches, poking a stick into the embers. "We're missing something, squire. Where there is smoke, there is fire. We've seen the smoke, but I can't find the fire."

Manny thought for a moment. "Rain can put out a fire so that by the time you get there, there is no flame. What if they were discontent, but have gotten over it?"

"Possible, but we should still find evidence of the fire being there. Charred wood. Something. But everyone seems genuinely surprised to see me. Genuinely surprised that I am testing their allegiance."

Smoke from the actual fire in front of them swirled and then blew directly into Manny's face. He coughed. "Wind can blow smoke in a different direction."

Sir Fletcher looked up at him. "Different direction?"

"Like a smoke screen. Maybe the Panther was trying to get you away from the castle." Manny removed the spit from the fire and slid the cooked meat onto a bed of fresh leaves he had prepared.

All this talk of the Panther and the kingdom brought Manny's thoughts to Gressa. He didn't like not being able to say goodbye to her. He snorted. Distracted by a girl. He never thought he'd see the day he'd start acting like Hoxham.

"You might have something there, Squire." Sir Fletcher took the cooked bird and divided it between their plates. His plate received the most. "New plan. Tomorrow we return to South Morlaix Castle."

CHAPTER 27

At the first blush of day, Manny and Sir Fletcher set out to return to the kingdom. The horses sensed their return and seemed happy to be going back, too. When the sun was at its peak, they reached the Ranger's Forest.

Here, the trees grew so thick they blocked out the strong noonday sun so that it appeared as if it were evening time. Fleetfoot snorted and danced a little sidestep. Manny patted him soothingly. "It's okay, boy. Nothing to get spooked about. You probably heard a rabbit." Though the trees lined up like a palisade, Manny tried searching through the branches for a larger animal such as a cougar that might be stalking them. Unusual behavior, but not unheard of.

Sir Fletcher rode on ahead, his horse riding strong and true.

Manny's horse continued having a hard time staying to the path. He kept trying to veer off and turn around.

"Sir Fletcher!" Manny called out. He didn't want the knight to think he didn't know how to handle a horse, but he also didn't want to get left behind. Sir Fletcher either didn't hear him, or he kept going.

"Come on, Fleetfoot." Manny dug his heels into the horse. The beast refused to move.

Then Manny heard a scuffle ahead. War cries. "He-yaw!" Manny said to his horse. He kicked him hard. The horse finally obeyed. They arrived on a scene that sent Manny's heart into his throat. Ambush.

Sir Fletcher was off his horse in hand-to-hand combat with three burly men. Manny pulled out his small sword, wishing he was further along in his training. He pulled his horse to a stop. The men hadn't noticed him yet, as the noise from their own fighting had covered his horse's approaching hoof steps. He paused to assess the situation.

The three men appeared to be taking turns attacking Sir Fletcher. The skilled knight was easily able to deflect the blows of one man at a time. If they all attacked him at once, it would put him under.

Manny was skilled for a squire, but these were all fighting men. He had to be clever if he were to be of any assistance.

Forming a plan, Manny charged forward, thwacking a man's head as he rode past.

"Aaaargh," yelled the hairy man. He took off after Manny, but Manny was too quick on his horse. The man retreated to the forest and came out with his own war horse. A giant of a beast.

Manny's plan was working. At least as much as he had thought it through. He was hoping that, by picking off one attacker, Sir Fletcher would be able to overcome the other two, then come to Manny's rescue if he should need it.

What Manny didn't expect was what happened next. The hairy man that was following him called back to the others. "Get the boy. Here he is."

The boy? Him? Why would they want him? The fear that gripped his heart made him push on even faster. Poor Fleetfoot must have felt as scared as he did because the beast ran faster than Manny thought a horse was capable of running, foam and sweat pouring off.

The hairy man's horse was bearing down. Manny veered off

the path and into the thick of the forest. "Sorry, boy, but you're smaller than their horses. Maybe we can shake them in here."

Manny's heart pounded against his rib cage. In the forest, they could no longer run and the going was slow. If the man carried a bow and arrow, Manny could be done for. Thankfully, Fleetfoot was also surefooted and easily picked his way through the underbrush. Several times Manny had to duck or risk being scraped off his horse's back.

The man cursed as he tried to follow. His horse was too big and he had to double back to the roadway. Now Manny had a new problem. What to do about finding Sir Fletcher? A squire couldn't abandon his knight any more than a knight would abandon his squire.

Manny and Fleetfoot picked their way back to where Sir Fletcher had let off his horse. Maybe they could find Tannin and still meet up with Sir Fletcher. He tread carefully in case others waited nearby.

When he got near the roadway, Manny tethered Fleetfoot in a dense place in the forest, and then stealthily crept forward. The fir trees kept him well hidden and the thick underbrush smothered the sound of his footsteps. He walked half a mile in each direction, finding nothing. Two birds in separate trees twittered at each other. All else was eerily silent in the forest.

Manny decided to return to Fleetfoot and take his chances on the road. He had to find Sir Fletcher before those men could regroup and come up with a new plan.

A snap of a twig was Manny's only warning. Before he could defend himself, a hand was clasped over his mouth and a strong arm pinned him down.

"Don't make a sound," came the whisper.

Adrenaline shot through Manny and he twisted free, turning to see that his captor was Sir Fletcher, holding his forefinger to his lips. Blood was beginning to crust on Sir Fletcher's knuckles and a cut over his eye looked painful.

"What happened?" Manny mouthed silently.

Sir Fletcher pointed to the road. The three men passed by, one in the center on horseback with the other two walking along, poking into the edges of the forest. When they were out of sight, Sir Fletcher untied Fleetfoot and held him while Manny swung up onto the saddle.

"They will double back shortly. Meanwhile we'll have to make our way through the forest and return to the castle as quick as we can. Tannin was spooked," said Sir Fletcher as he mounted Fleetfoot behind Manny and took the reins.

Manny felt as he did when he was first learning to ride a horse. He hoped they still wouldn't be riding like this when they made it back to the castle.

"They were after both of us, Squire. Perhaps you even more than me. What have you done?"

Manny shook his head. "Nothing." Except enter the Dividing Wall. Could someone know about that?

Sir Fletcher grunted. "Who else knew of our trip?"

"You told me to say my goodbyes," said Manny defensively.

"To whom?"

"My father." *And the Princess of North Morlaix.* "My father's apprentice. No one else."

Manny sensed Sir Fletcher's disapproval in the shift of his muscles. "What are you not telling me?"

"Nothing. I don't know why they would want me." He was as bewildered as Sir Fletcher. "I'm nobody."

CHAPTER 28

*G*ressa woke in the dim light, groggy after having cried herself to sleep in the middle of the afternoon. She pushed herself to a seated position. "Old Anne, is that you?" A figure was bustling around her room, flitting from one side to the other. "Is it time for dinner already?" She stretched and yawned. "I'm not hungry. I won't go down."

"I will tell your family." Old Anne helped Gressa to her feet. "But now, you haven't much time. Put on this outfit." She held out a strange frock. A peasant's outfit that was green, not brown, like those popular in North Morlaix, and with an apron overlay that was entirely too large and a polka dot kerchief that Old Anne was tying around Gressa's hair.

"What? Why? It's not very pretty." Gressa tried to duck away from the kerchief.

Old Anne smiled. "It is what they wear in South Morlaix."

"South Morlaix?" Gressa thumped back onto her bed.

"You do not intend to stay here, do you? There are secret places you can go…if you can find them." Old Anne placed the peasant outfit on the bed.

Gressa looked at Old Anne curiously. "What secret places?"

Old Anne glanced out the window. "Where your brother, the

Panther wants to go."

"How do you—? Have you seen—? What do you mean?" sputtered Gressa.

"Dress quickly. It might take you more time than you have to find the door."

Gressa didn't hide the shock from her face. "I know where the door is. But what do I do when I get there? There's no food. I can't live there by myself forever, and the other side doesn't open up for me."

Old Anne shook her head. "Not that door. There is another."

"Another?" Gressa pulled the peasant dress over her head. Old Anne helped her with the ties. "Where is it?"

"I don't know. You have to find it. We think it is somewhere in the castle. If it exists."

"We? Who is we?"

"Never you mind. Focus on getting out of here. I fear your brother will do something worse than marry you off to an old Viking. He means to break you, tonight, however he can."

Old Anne shoved her out the bedroom door and locked it behind them.

Gressa looked at the lock. "How did you get a key?"

Old Anne just smiled and guided Gressa down the circular stair, which led to the back part of the castle where the divided hallway was.

Gressa's heart pounded so hard that it felt like it was in her throat. She was scared she would get caught escaping. She was scared she would find the other door and have to face whatever lay on the other side in South Morlaix.

"Won't I be hanged if they find me in their castle?"

"Don't let them catch you."

Old Anne led Gressa to the little-used hallway. "I must leave you here so no one gets suspicious. I cannot tell you how to find the door. I don't know how. But since you were able to find one, we hope that you can find another."

Gressa was desperate to hold on to Old Anne. "Can't you

come with me?"

"No, child. My business is on this side."

Gressa looked at her curiously. Her business was taking care of the king's daughter. Shouldn't she carry that through the Dividing Wall?

Old Anne pulled a small wrapped package out from her pocket. "Almost forgot. Here is some bread and cheese to see you through. Be quick on your feet when you get there. Hide first, then figure out where you are. The tournaments are starting soon, but whatever you do, do not attend their tournament. You would surely be caught. Look for the village healing woman; she will help you."

Gressa's lips began to tremble. "How will I find her if I must stay hidden? And I haven't said goodbye to my mother. She will be frantic. Or to Siguard. Surely I can speak with my brother at the chapel."

"There is more unity than you know of. Look for this symbol." Old Anne pointed to the leaf on her necklace. "Those who wear the rowan leaf do not want a divided kingdom. They will help you."

Gressa fingered the necklace. She had seen this emblem elsewhere in North Morlaix. She thought it only a pretty decoration. A remembrance of the old rowan groves. Surely the daughter of the king should know more about what goes on in her kingdom than she did. What must her people think of her? No wonder they talked about her.

Old Anne hugged her tight. "You are young, but now is the time for you to grow up. You have been sheltered far too long. God be with you." Old Anne turned and trod whisper-quiet down the corridor and around the corner.

Gressa noticed for the first time how dark this part of the castle was. The Dividing Wall had closed off most of the windows, making the passage dark and the air stale. How was she to find a hidden door? The door to the meadow she found by noticing a shadow. Here, everything was shadow.

Perhaps the magic in the Dividing Wall knew she needed the meadow and so it opened up to her. By necessity. She needed a new opening now by even greater necessity. "Well, Dividing Wall? Here I am, but I don't know where your opening is." Gressa felt foolish talking to a wall. She ran her hand down the length of the wall in the passage. High, low. It didn't matter. The rock wall was solid. She began to understand a little bit of Herrick's frustration and why he paced back and forth in front of the Dividing Wall, examining it as a potter examines a pot for cracks.

A tiny light caught her eye. Was it a trick of the dark? Her eyes strained to see something, anything. There it was again, floating around her head like a firefly. How odd. There were no fireflies in Morlaix. She reached out to catch it, but it flew out of reach and then was gone.

The bang of a door echoed in the corridor above her. "Where is she?" railed Herrick's voice.

Oh no. He'd come for her. Frantically Gressa probed, prodded, pushed, and pummeled the wall.

"Guards!" exclaimed her brother.

The men ran in all directions, their footsteps echoing through the corridor. She found the darkest corner and pressed her body into it, hoping they wouldn't notice her. But then she saw torch-light reflecting off the corner, dancing against the stone bricks. They were bringing lights; there would be no shadows when they came. They would find her.

The footsteps grew louder and the light brighter. They would be upon her in seconds. She would have to think of an excuse as to how she got out of a locked door. She couldn't implicate Old Anne. The nursemaid would be confined to the dungeons for certain.

Gressa pressed even harder into the wall. She felt the stone give way, then she fell over backwards through the Dividing Wall. Her breath caught in her throat. She was saved. Then she remembered Old Anne's warning. Hide.

CHAPTER 29

*G*ressa scrambled to her feet and took quick stock of her surroundings. The dim room contained a crib, a rocking horse, a rag doll and some other playthings, a braided rug, and pretty rose draperies covering a window. *A Nursery*. But not just any nursery, one decorated for a girl.

She darted for the curtains, afraid that her sudden thumping into the obviously abandoned room would cause someone to come running to check it out. She did her best to cover her feet with the fabric, then held her breath and waited.

Had the king and queen of South Morlaix once had hopes for a daughter? The room had been decorated with such care, never used, and then kept preserved for years as a testament to hope unrealized. That poor king and queen. Her own family was so large, but in South Morlaix they only had the one son and such a son as he.

Once Gressa's heart stopped pounding, she ventured a peek around the curtains. No one had come, so she was safe for now. She let out a deep breath. She'd made it!

She'd made it out of North Morlaix on her own. Well, with a little help from Old Anne.

Gressa examined the spot where the door was, not surprised

to see it was a solid wall again. It was possible Herrick was there on the other side, listening for her. But something in her gut told her that door wouldn't operate like the one in the meadow. Other forces were at work here. Someone was looking out for her wellbeing.

How did Old Anne know about the doors? Perhaps the healing woman would know. Until she could find the healing woman and ask, she would make this room her sanctuary.

She returned to the curtain to see the view the princess would have had if she'd existed. Past the open space in front of the castle, the rows of encroaching town life began. The marketplace with shops below and homes above were constructed the same way as those on her side of the wall.

Her gaze locked onto a sign with a picture of a needle and spool of thread. *The tailor's shop.*

Gressa tried to see through the window to the inside of the shop, but she was too far away. Her heart wanted to run over there for safety, but she locked her knees to keep her legs from following her heart.

Could she risk visiting him there? Or perhaps she should wait, and when he walked out, will him to look up to the abandoned nursery and see her standing there. What a fright it might give him to see a ghostly figure staring down from the empty room. She grinned and backed away so she'd be harder to notice. If she was wont for mischief, she could give many a fright staring out this window.

Won't he be surprised when he finds her on his side of the wall? They could see each other every day instead of hoping to meet up in the meadow.

Old Anne said to look for someone with the leaf symbol. What if someone liked the look of the leaf and was wearing it for decoration?

Gressa imagined how the conversation would go: "Hi, I'm the princess from North Morlaix, can you hide me?"

She shook her head. No, it would take cunning on her part to navigate this side of the wall. Who knew what they would do to her if they found her? And worse, what would it mean for the peace treaty?

The smell of roasted pig drifted in, reminding Gressa of the time. The servants would all be busy until after the meal. She took out her little stash of food and broke off a small piece of bread and a small piece of cheese. She would save the rest, eating bits at a time since she didn't know when she would have access to food again.

No. What am I doing? She was reverting to her former self, trapped in a room. If she was going to get her freedom, she'd need to move. In a burst of bravery, she ventured out into the hallway. Now, to get out of the castle and into the village. Find some kind woman wearing the leaf and beg a job and lodgings from her and then find the healing woman.

The castle was probably the mirror image to hers, so as long as she remembered to go left for her normal rights, she should be out in no time. Gressa rounded a corner that should take her to a stairwell when she collided smack into a servant.

"Och! What are you doin' skulkin around 'ere?" said the short, stout woman. Her hair was thinning on top, and she was wearing jewelry that looked like it belonged to a queen. The woman, seeing Gressa staring at her jewels, quickly pulled them off and pocketed them. "If yer the new girl then I suspect yer as dimwitted as the last. I need a servant wot can attend to me needs. I needs the help for dressing in the morning, fixing my hair and runnin' this here nursery."

Gressa's mouth hung open. There were so many odd things this woman had said that she didn't know what to rest her mind on first. Here was this unusual woman wearing the queen's jewels, thinking she, Gressa, was a servant, and there was a nursery in need of running? Why, there were no babies.

"Well, don't stand thar gaping at me. Fetch me some dinner." She pressed her palm to her forehead. "I wos not up to eatin' with the rest of them tonight."

Not knowing what else to do and afraid the woman would sound the alarm if Gressa didn't bring back any food, she followed the smells to the great hall. Strangely, she felt right at home in the castle. If only she had not been so scared of getting caught, she would have enjoyed exploring this half of Morlaix Castle.

In no time at all she found herself hovering at the entrance to the great hall. Should she go in, grab a trencher and sneak away with it? She could go to the kitchen, but that would only increase her chances of getting caught. At least here in the great hall, everyone was busy with their food and they were used to strange faces when visitors came calling. Scanning the tables for an empty place, she spotted a loaded tray on a side table. In and out. She could be fast.

CHAPTER 30

*W*hen they neared the gatehouse, Manny hopped down and walked the rest of the way to preserve his dignity.

Up ahead, the Gatekeeper greeted Sir Fletcher with a hearty handshake and a glistening in his eye. "I thought ye was dead. Tannin came back three days ago. He had a nasty gash on his rump. We sent out a search party. They found....well, not you, obviously, but evidence of, of blood and, and other things." The gatekeeper turned a shade of green.

"We did run into a little trouble, just not the kind we were expecting." Sir Fletcher's voice was weighty, as if he were trying to convey more information to the gatekeeper without actually saying it. Manny stepped in closer. They didn't see a search party. Granted, they remained in hiding all along the way, but they should have crossed paths.

"Everything all right out there now?" The gatekeeper tapped a leaf pin that he wore on his lapel.

Sir Fletcher nodded. "Yes. Kingdom life as usual."

"Then what of the horse?" The gatekeeper said horse in a sing-song way, like it was code.

Sir Fletcher's gaze flickered to Manny, then back to the gatekeeper. "We'll talk later, my old friend. I can smell the roast pig being served in the great hall from here."

"Of course. Of course. The king will be glad to see ye. He's been sore upset, he has." They clasped hands.

Manny frowned. Clearly, the gatekeeper and Sir Fletcher had more to say to one another and it appeared to be talk about him. Did Sir Fletcher really think the attack had something to do with Manny? It had to be a case of mistaken identity. Maybe the attackers had thought he was Nigel, and they were commissioned to kidnap or even assassinate the prince. Manny hadn't thought that taking Nigel's place beside Sir Fletcher would carry that risk, but it made perfect sense. Maybe that was why Manny was given to Sir Fletcher. He was a decoy. Well, that galled. A decoy for that sop of a prince?

A new black banner of death hung from the castle keep beside the old, tattered one from the queen's death.

"I'm flattered," Sir Fletcher said. "It's nice to know you'll be missed when you're dead. Just wished they'd looked harder for us before mourning our untimely demise."

Inside the great hall, Sir Fletcher's coat of arms was lowered and black draperies garnished the room. When Manny and Sir Fletcher entered, the king immediately noticed them. He stood, like a great heaviness had just fallen off him. How touching a king would care so deeply about his subjects.

A hush descended the Hall as one by one people noticed the king, and rose with him. Murmurs sounded as the people saw Sir Fletcher, thought dead, but now alive. The king met them halfway to the dais. He shook hands with Sir Fletcher and clapped him on the back.

"We thought we had lost you," he said. His voice was thick with emotion as he looked at Manny.

Then he shook Manny's hand and clapped him mightily on the back. Manny had to step forward to keep from losing his balance, so great was the welcome.

"Dine with me at my table tonight."

Manny went to sit with the other squires, but the king called him back. "You too, Manny. You deserve to sit at the king's table." He turned to Sir Fletcher. "Tell me all that has transpired these days."

Surprised, and honored, Manny ignored the sour look Nigel was giving him and settled beside Sir Fletcher.

As Sir Fletcher told his tale, Manny thought it interesting that he did not mention to the king what he hinted to the gatekeeper about. Were Sir Fletcher and the gatekeeper involved in some treasonous activity? Was that the reason for the attack in the forest?

"We were all sorry to hear of your death," whispered Charlemagne as he poured ale at the table closest to him. "Well, most of us." He winked.

"When you can, could you run and tell my father that I am alive?" He would prefer to go himself, but one did not leave the king's table until the king did.

Charlemagne nodded. "Happy to. And by the way, I challenge you to an arm wrestle at the gate. I'm the top squire, now. You're the only one I ain't beat but I intend to change that."

"Ha!" Manny flexed his arm and grinned.

The king and Sir Fletcher were still bent together over hushed whispers. As the next course was served, Manny thought back over their trip. Sir Fletcher was the ever gallant and chivalrous knight. He carried out his duties faithfully. Nothing about him indicated he was a traitor other than the one conversation that Manny could be reading into. He couldn't be a traitor. So, what was missing? Why did it feel like Sir Fletcher was holding something back from King Simon?

"Eat," said Sir Fletcher, nudging Manny. "It's not every day you eat with a king. Don't insult him by refusing his food."

In response, Manny took a big bite from a buttered roll. There would be time to mull over recent events later. Now was the time to celebrate. He took in the wealth of food laid out at the king's table. Eel, peacock, herbed breads and sweet breads, hog and stuffing.

Absorbed as he was with his food, he wouldn't have noticed her if she hadn't dropped a tray. But she did.

A clattering to his far left caught his attention, and there she was staring at him.

"Gressa," he whispered. As soon as he mouthed the words, the girl with eyes like a cat broke her gaze and hastily picked up the food she had dropped.

Sir Fletcher stiffened. He leaned casually toward Manny. "Gressa? The king of North Morlaix's daughter?" he whispered harshly. "What business have you with her that you would speak her name now?"

Manny cleared his throat and looked away. Nothing got past Sir Fletcher. "I-I said ressa-er recipe. This is the best food I've never eaten in my life." He ate a large helping of potatoes and leeks in order to end the conversation.

Then he furtively watched Gressa clean up her spill. Everyone else ignored her or made faces like she was a nuisance. What was she doing here? He half-rose from his chair when she fled out the door with the tray, but sat back down when he realized Sir Fletcher was still watching him, suspicion in his eyes.

CHAPTER 31

*G*ressa felt the gaze of everyone in the room. Head down. Clean up the greasy pork and the fowl and stuffing. Wait for them to get bored. She hadn't meant to drop the tray, but when she saw Manny sitting at the head table, she didn't know what happened. Her limbs went weak and her hands let go in shock.

She thought he was the tailor's son, but he was seated in a place of prominence. Was he not whom he seemed to be in the meadow? Imagine if she had tried to visit him in the shop, she would have made a fool of herself. Could he be a king's spy to try to get into North Morlaix? If the tailor's clothing had been a mere ruse, she fell for it. Fell hard.

Was he still watching?

She couldn't look, but since the usual sounds of eating and talking had resumed, she could assume she wasn't the center of attention any more. Not that she could assume anything on this side of the wall. She thought she knew what she might be heading into, but now she wasn't so sure. Maybe she should try to go back and throw herself on her mother's mercy. Make Mother promise that Herrick would have nothing to do with finding her a husband. Agree to a marriage that would take her far away, but not to someone who would treat her badly. A simple marriage of convenience with a kind man. That she could agree to.

She'd foolishly let herself get her hopes up, but the Tower Princess should have known her life was not her own to direct. She was a pawn for both the North and the South. Why did anyone care so much what she did?

She grabbed another trencher and filled the tray. Before leaving the room, she risked a glance up at the head table again. Manny had gone back to his meal, talking intently to the knight beside him.

He'd seen her, she knew. Wasn't he surprised to see her there? Or did he not care? He didn't even come to her rescue to help clean up the spill.

She thought she knew who he was. Granted, they'd never spoken anything intimate to each other, never actually shared any future dreams, merely a curiosity at why the meadow opened up for them and them alone. Sentimental foolishness. Of course, she would fall for the first boy she met on her own. A foolish girl was all she was. Naive and easily persuaded. She hardened her heart as she looked for the odd woman whose tray of food she was carrying.

An ill-tuned harp accompanied by b-flat voice was spilling out of a room past the girl's nursery. It was the most elaborate nursemaid's room Gressa had ever seen. It shamed her how shabbily they treated Old Anne, having her share Gressa's room in the tower. Nor had they even considered giving her a room of her own. And not once had Old Anne complained or asked for more.

"About time," said the woman, her jewels back on. "Thought I'd die of hunger in here, like that wilting princess across the wall." She ran her hand along the strings. When Gressa stood in shock, the woman made a face. "Are you daft? Bring it 'ere." She shook her head. "They always give me the daft ones."

Gressa rushed in and set the tray on a mahogany tea table. She folded her hands awaiting further instructions.

The woman took a bite and nodded. "That chef. I'd marry him

if he weren't already taken." She eyed Gressa. "Quiet one, aren't ye? I dare say I like the quiet ones best. You'll do. Be sure to be back here with breakfast in the morn. Not too early, mind you. Wait until the food is on its way back, then ask the cook for my portion. He'll know what you want."

Relieved, Gressa backed out, curtsied at the door, then took measured steps back to the nursery. She doubted the nursemaid would check on where the lower help slept, so if the wall wouldn't open, she could probably find a corner in the nursery to curl up, maybe tucked behind the rocking horse.

So, her backup plan of meeting Manny was not a good plan at all. She would follow Old Anne's advice and seek out the healing woman. Gressa had a lot of head knowledge of medicinal herbs, thanks to Axell and the books he'd given her. If the woman would have her, maybe Gressa could make her way.

Then, once she'd established herself, maybe she could return home via Copello. She didn't have any papers to get through the port, but given that she was the princess, they should let her in. She touched the wall separating her from her tower room. It wasn't for forever. She'd see Old Anne again. Mother. Axell and Siguard. Even Varin, Jutland, and the others. Not that they would even notice she was gone.

She wished there were a way to find out what happened to Old Anne. What became of royal nursemaids when there were no royal children to care for? On this side of the wall, they were treated like queens, apparently. Given jewels and a fancy room and a servant of their own. Old Anne would likely be sent back to the village to find a wealthy merchant. Surely, she would be treated kindly. It would be a status symbol to have the royal family's nursemaid raising your littles, wouldn't it? Gressa chose to paint a happy picture of Old Anne playing pat-a-cake once again with babies, but in reality, she had a feeling Old Anne sacrificed her safety and happiness for Gressa's.

It all happened so fast. If she'd had time to think about it, she would have refused Old Anne and attempted to live in the meadow instead. What had she done? She had to find a way to make it up to her friend. The only true friend she had.

CHAPTER 32

inally, they were dismissed from the king's table. When King Simon stood to go, the rest of the table stood as well, and then the entire room. The king exited first, through the doorway leading to his private rooms. After the king left, everyone else moved toward the large doors at the back.

Manny lulled behind, planning to slip away down the corridor where Gressa had disappeared. What was she doing here? She must have figured out a way to cross over the meadow. Perhaps she was stuck here and needed his help. How long had she been here? Stealing food from the great hall must mean she was desperate to eat.

Seizing the moment when Sir Fletcher was surrounded by the other knights, eager for the tale of what happened, Manny followed the hallway Gressa had disappeared down.

The further away from the great hall, the quieter the passageways became. Manny skulked down the dark corridors into the heart of the castle, being careful to walk with silent footsteps. The passageways seemed oddly familiar, like a memory or a dream. He instinctively wound his way up one of the turrets and into a room prepared like a nursery. There was a crib adorned in rich dark colors, toy knights with snapped off arms and play horses with scuffed paint. Nigel's nursery.

Manny tilted his head, listening. He'd wandered into the prince's wing. Nigel would not be happy to find him intruding in his rooms. Hearing nothing, he set out for the hallway when a toy knight with a white cross emblem caught his attention. The toy was third in line up on a shelf with a row of other knights, and looked like the victim of a great battle. He was missing his right arm and his left leg, and his armor was chipped.

Looking at the toys, again, Manny saw a fleeting shadow of his past. He'd played with these toys before. Perhaps he and Nigel played together when they were younger. He couldn't imagine he and Nigel ever being playmates—even when they were children.

Hastening to another and yet another room, Manny kept up his search, positive he had seen her. No other girl, no matter her garb, looked like Gressa. If she was on this side of the wall, she was in trouble. But if she was in trouble, why did she run from him?

He looked into a few more rooms until he came across a girl's nursery. He frowned. South Morlaix had never had a princess. But upon closer inspection he realized all the toys were in pristine condition. Never played with.

He was about to turn and leave when the curtains moved. Under the curtains were a pair of dainty shoes more befitting a princess than a peasant.

"Gressa," he whispered. "It's me."

He reached behind the curtain, and grabbed her arm. When she lifted her face to him, she looked frightened, her eyes darting around as if looking for escape.

"What are you doing on this side of the wall?" he asked gently, trying to ease her fear. "I thought it was forbidden?"

When Gressa saw it was him, she didn't relax like he expected her to.

"It's okay. I won't let anything happen to you," he said.

"Who are you, really?" she asked. "I saw you up on the dais. I thought you were the tailor's son?"

"I was given a promotion," he said. "I've been working toward it all my life."

She let out a long, long, breath, like she had been holding it ever since she had crossed the wall. "I'm glad for you. It was a surprise, is all. I'm sorry about your mother. I saw you'd returned the balsam."

"Thank you. I never had the chance to use it. She died in the night."

A look passed her face, like she was chiding herself.

"It was too late," he said. "Even if I had rushed it over hours before. There was nothing we could have done."

"I wish—" she started, then stopped. "Why do you have all those scratches on your face?"

He touched his cheek. "A race through the forest. The branches must have got me. Doesn't hurt. Why are you here?"

"Herrick found out that I could go through the Dividing Wall. He was holding me captive until I told him—" Gressa clamped her mouth shut. Her eyes widened like a scared rabbit caught in a snare.

Manny turned around to see Sir Fletcher standing in the hallway, arms blocking the door and a grim expression etched on his face.

"Is that who I think it is?" drawled Sir Fletcher.

Manny stood protectively in front of Gressa. "That depends. Who do you think it is?"

Sir Fletcher's eyes narrowed, and he was silent long enough to make Manny squirm under his study. Eventually, he said, "Someone who could get us all killed."

"I don't think it's as serious as that." Manny swallowed as Gressa touched his shoulder.

"The princess?" Sir Fletcher said. "How could it be any more serious?" He looked over his shoulder, then motioned for the pair to follow. From around his neck he pulled out a necklace with a leaf on it. The same one that the gatekeeper wore. "Come with me. We can't stay here."

Manny reached for Gressa's hand to let her know she could trust him, if not Sir Fletcher. Was Sir Fletcher a traitor or a friend? Not knowing what that symbol meant, Manny would stay alert and be quick to reach for the dagger in his boot. Perhaps Sir Fletcher was leading them into a trap—sending Gressa straight into the arms of her brother. Right now, they had no choice but to follow.

Sneaking through the castle turned out to be surprisingly easy. They came across only one servant and he kept his head down after one gruff look from Sir Fletcher. Next, they were walking out the castle grounds and toward the gate. Twilight had come so the streets were near empty of women and children.

"Keep your head down, princess. Don't let anyone see your eyes," said Sir Fletcher. He was the only one of the trio who spoke. As they walked he'd stop suddenly, or have them duck behind a building. Manny kept a firm grasp on Gressa's hand, though he didn't need to. She was holding on so tight their flesh might fuse together. Fear emanated from her fingertips.

When they walked past the gatekeeper, Sir Fletcher simply waved and kept walking. Manny analyzed their movements to see if Sir Fletcher was sending a secret message and giving Gressa up to the South Morlaix authorities. However, he could sense nothing amiss. Sir Fletcher, by all indication, was looking out for them.

Which led Manny to wonder. Why? Why protect the enemy? Gressa was from North Morlaix. Bells should have been ringing and the cry sounded for a breach in the wall. But all was silent and the king's own knight was ushering them to safety.

The closer they got to the wall, the more skittery Gressa's movements became. The slightest noise made her jump, and she tried to peer into the darkness to discover the source of each sound. Her fingers dug into Manny's, making him want to protect her all the more. But he didn't know where Sir Fletcher was taking them and Manny had no place to bring her. She couldn't stay in the barracks, and he had no idea how his father would react, never mind that shifty Hoxham.

As the sun completed its course for the day, and the moon rose in its place, Sir Fletcher led them to a house near the Dividing Wall. The houses here were built close together, small, and with adjoining chicken coops. Simple wattle and daub construction with oversized thatched roofs made the cottages look plain, but cozy.

Sir Fletcher knocked quietly. *Tap. Tap. Tap. Tippity-tap.*

The door cracked open an inch, and an old woman peered out. When she saw Sir Fletcher, she cried and opened the door wide to embrace him. Placing her hands on either side of his face, she smiled as wide as a mother seeing her boy alive from the dead.

"You are yet living!" she said. "Living, but thin."

Then, noticing he was not alone, she backed out of the doorway and invited them all inside. "Come, come. Let me fix you something to eat and you can tell me how my son who they told me was dead is not dead." She did a little dance, removed the black mourning shawl from her head and then tossed it in the corner.

Pease porridge was cooking on the hearth stove and there was bread on the table. Manny didn't think he was hungry after dining with the king, but the smell of food stirred his stomach again. He held a chair out for Gressa and sat beside her, still holding her trembling hand.

Sir Fletcher lifted a heavy bolt across the door, closed the shutters on all the windows and bolted them. Then he turned on Manny and Gressa. "All right, you two. Tell me the whole story and don't leave anything out."

CHAPTER 33

*G*ressa stared at the knight towering above her. His demeanor was calm now that they were secured in the cottage, but his lips twitched, out of irritation, or amusement, she could not tell. But for the first time since she had fallen into South Morlaix, she began to relax, her shoulders releasing their tension. Strangely, she felt as comfortable here as she did in her chambers at home. She wasn't very good at this sneaking around. And even though she didn't know this knight's name, or his role in their kingdom, she knew she could trust him. He had shown her Old Anne's sign. Maybe he could help her get settled in the village and start a new life. And in time, she would find a way to let Old Anne know she was all right, and her mother, too.

The knight continued to look between them, waiting for an explanation.

Gressa opened and closed her mouth a few times before she could get any words out. She coughed, not used to the smoky air in a peasant's cottage. "I suppose I should start since I'm the one who shouldn't be here."

The old woman served steaming cups of tea and biscuits. She held a cup out to Gressa, but getting a good look at her, dropped the cup, which smashed on the hard-packed earth.

"Oh, I'm sorry, miss. Pardon, your highness. I didn't burn you, did I?" She quickly wiped up the spill with her skirt and picked up the broken pieces. "I never realized 'twas you. Welcome, welcome." She retreated to the other side of the room but kept her gaze focused on Gressa, a look of bewilderment on her kind face.

"How do you all know who I am? I'm wearing a disguise from your kingdom." Gressa held out her arms to indicate her South Morlaixan attire.

The old woman laughed. "You don't know?"

The knight's expression turned grim.

"Know what?"

"Your eyes. Everyone knows you have green eyes."

Manny wrinkled his brow. "They do?"

"No one else in either kingdom has green eyes." The old woman's voice was cracked, but awe-filled.

"I had no idea." Gressa thought of her mother, father, her brothers. All brown or blue. She examined Manny's and Sir Fletcher's eyes. Both brown. Then she stared back at the woman. Her eyes looked somewhat familiar.

The knight pulled up a chair at the table and made introductions. "Be pleased to meet my mother, Abigail. I am Sir Fletcher, first knight to King Simon of South Morlaix."

First knight? Gressa's heart fluttered. He was an important man. As close to the king as Herrick was to her father.

"Continue, Princess Gressa," said Sir Fletcher.

She fought her mind for a place to start. Should she tell them about the Dividing Wall and how she met Manny? Would they think she was daft in the head, or would they force her to lead the way back into North Morlaix? She looked at Manny for help. He nodded.

"Tell them everything," he said. "Well, as much as we understand."

Nodding, Gressa began. "My brother, the Panther, is famous for pacing back and forth at the Dividing Wall. I thought he was obsessed with battle strategy and how he was going to conquer the South when my father passed on. But that isn't it, not completely, anyway. His obsession is the wall itself. He's been looking for a way through the wall. A magical way."

Sir Fletcher and the old woman exchanged glances. "Has he found this way?" he asked.

Gressa was taken aback. "You think there is a magical way, too?"

The old woman stepped closer, and the rush light's flame flickered orange on her face. "Legends and rumors from the day the kingdom was divided say that the woodling king never meant for the kingdom to be divided forever. That he was clever enough to best the two knights who thought they had bested him."

"You mean, the woodling king from our nursery songs? *Beware the woodling king. He hides and spies amongst the rowan trees. Try as you may, look upon a rowan limb, but try as you might, you'll never see him.*"

"The verra ones, child."

Although Gressa could accept a magical wall, she was having trouble wrapping her mind around the fabled woodlings who live amongst the roots of the rowan trees. She had seen no sign of any creature other than birds in the meadow.

"And has he found the way?" asked Sir Fletcher again, urgency in his voice.

"No. But I did. And so has Manny."

The old woman dropped another cup. It, too, shattered into smaller pieces on the hard dirt floor. She scurried around the room, grabbing a broom and sweeping up. She avoided Sir Fletcher's scowl.

Gressa looked at Manny, and he grinned at her. She took courage in his support.

She began her tale: "A few months ago the wall opened up to me and Manny within days of each other. We weren't looking for it and we can't always get in."

Abigail interrupted. "The legend is true then?"

"We saw no woodling," said Manny. "There is a tree and a brook through which flows a most refreshing water."

Sir Fletcher crossed his arms. "Nothing but wives' tales and superstitions. Perhaps the entrance is simply difficult to find. The ivy has taken over much of the wall. I don't believe in a door that opens and closes of its own will."

Gressa shook her head. "If there were a permanent opening, my brother would have found it long ago. But when I go through the wall, the space is like another place entirely. As if there were no castle at all. Right, Manny? He climbed high up in the tree and the castle disappears."

Sir Fletcher scoffed and began pacing the room. His movement brought back Gressa's anxiety. "I didn't know it, but Herrick had been watching me. He guessed that I was getting into the wall and he wanted me to tell him how."

"And did you?" Sir Fletcher asked.

Again, Gressa shook her head. "I would never. But Herrick has a way of getting things out of people. Old Anne thought it best if I escape. She helped me find another doorway, inside the castle. It led into the nursery."

"Old Anne?" said Abigail. "Is she well?"

Sir Fletcher interrupted, "Later. You can ask your questions later. The princess will stay here for the night." He turned back to Gressa. "Did anyone else see you since you've been in South Morlaix?"

Gressa nodded. "A nursemaid. She was a wide as she was tall and she was wearing fancy jewelry, which she quickly hid. She thought I was there to serve her and she ordered me to get her food, which was why I was in the great hall. I didn't expect to see Manny sitting at the king's table, so I dropped my tray." She looked hesitantly at Manny to see if he would explain why he was at the head table. When he didn't answer, she continued. "And then you found me."

"You've described Prince Nigel's nursemaid," said Sir Fletcher. "I'll simply tell her that you were an unacceptable servant and we will get her another. It happens often enough as she is difficult to please."

There was a knock at the door. Everyone but Sir Fletcher jumped. He motioned for Gressa and Manny to stand behind the cloth divider while he went with the old woman to the door.

Manny stood in front of Gressa, blocking her from view of anyone who may come around the corner. Her nose came up to his shoulder.

The front door groaned as the bolt was withdrawn. Seconds later, there was a volley of low voices. Gressa rested her cheek on Manny's strong back. She was suddenly weary and ready to find a safe corner to rest tonight.

"Manny? Let's go," called Sir Fletcher from the doorway.

Manny turned to Gressa. "I'll be back at first light."

She gave him a small smile to let him know how grateful she was. Then he was gone, the door clicking shut behind him.

The old woman pulled back the cloth and motioned for her to have her tea. "Fletcher has business to attend to. He would like you to stay with me while he figures out what to do next."

"I hope I'm not bringing you trouble." Gressa settled herself back at the table, holding her own teacup lest Abigail drop another of her precious cups. "I didn't think things through when Old Anne gave me a way of escape."

"If Old Anne was advising you, it was the right decision." She rubbed her neck. "I didn't expect something to happen so soon." The woman's voice sounded worried.

Gressa tilted her head. "You speak as if you know Old Anne well."

"I do. She's my sister."

"Your sister?" That's why Abigail's eyes looked familiar. Gressa had been looking into those same eyes since she was a baby. But Old Anne had never talked of her family. In all those years, they'd been separated by the wall. Why hadn't she said anything? Maybe because it was Gressa's father who was responsible.

"You young people forget that the kingdoms used to be united." Abigail bustled about the house, arranging a bed for Gressa. She flicked a bed sheet in the air, making it crack with an authoritative snap overtop of a straw mattress on the floor.

"When the kingdom was divided, it wasn't only the buildings — 'twas the families, too, who were separated. The woodling king divided the castle himself, but our stonemasons helped build the wall down the rest of the kingdom. Until it was done, we could go back and forth, knowing there was a time coming when we'd have to decide on which side to live. At first, we thought we'd be allowed to enter freely, to trade and to visit with family and friends. Decisions were made rather lightly, because we didn't realize." She began punching up a pillow with great force, as if channeling her frustrations into its feathers.

"For once the wall was complete and the new gate houses went up, we were no longer allowed into North Morlaix, nor were they allowed into South Morlaix. The rivalry between the two kings was so bitter they wouldn't allow it. They began as prideful and stubborn and have grown to be prideful and bitter. The whole kingdom suffers for it. I haven't seen my sister in forty-seven years." Abigail reached her hand out, like she was reaching for her sister, grasping at an empty space.

Secluded in the castle, Gressa had no idea what the villagers had been suffering. Old Anne had taught her about the time of the dividing, but she had given the facts, not the stories. It was the stories that told the truth.

"I'm sorry," Gressa whispered, ashamed of her family.

Abigail tossed the beaten pillow onto the pallet. She laughed. "What for, child? 'Tis not you who caused the dividing."

"But my father…." And my brother Herrick. If given his way, he will make things worse. He would have us all under his selfish hand.

"Tut, tut. There's nothing to be done tonight. Finish up your tea and tell me about Old Anne. What is my sister up to these days?"

CHAPTER 34

*M*anny followed Sir Fletcher into the dark night. A few paces ahead slinked the shadowy figure they were following. Manny kept glancing back at the quiet cottage, as if the closed door could tell him anything that was going on inside.

"She'll be fine," spoke Sir Fletcher. "No one knows she is in South Morlaix, though her brother might soon guess. Old Anne can hold him off from the truth for only so long."

Then what? Would he demand Gressa's return? King Simon would quickly comply. He had no interest in the daughter of his rival. And then Gressa would be in a worse position than when she left. He couldn't let that happen. He would run away with her before he would let any harm come to her. Thanks to his recent trip, he knew the lay of the land. There were any number of places to hide.

"Who's that?" asked Manny, jerking his chin to the dark form ahead of them.

The knight was silent, the banging of pots and shouts of children being shooed to bed filling the space. Finally, he said, "You saw me speak with him earlier today."

They continued following the man until they neared the castle and the figure disappeared into the shadows. Sir Fletcher continued to the castle.

"But aren't we following him?"

"No."

Manny sighed.

The castle lights had all been put out but for a few lonely candles here and there to shed light for the working servants. Sir Fletcher led the way to the kitchen, where he spoke in hushed tones with the cook, a short, well-fed man.

The cook called forth a young serving girl, a tiny slip of a thing. "Please tell nursemaid Gretchen that the last girl was incompetent and you will be serving her starting now."

The young girl's face went slack and she stood paralyzed at the news.

The cook waved his hand. "Are ye daft? Off with ye now and be pleasant."

Sir Fletcher nodded his thanks and backed out of the kitchen.

Double-timing again to keep up with the knight as he powered back through the castle and into the night air, Manny grabbed his arm.

Sir Fletcher spun around, anger lining his mouth.

Quickly dropping his hand, Manny asked, politely, "What are we to do now?"

"Sleep." Confirming Sir Fletcher's pronouncement, the curfew bell rang.

"Sleep? But what about Gressa? And the Panther? Shouldn't we be getting her as far away from here as we can?"

Sir Fletcher bent low and hissed into Manny's ear. "You have no idea what you two have done, do you? A silly little princess and a tailor's boy. You best follow every instruction I give you and don't demand any special explanations. There are many who have worked too long and too hard for you and that girl to mangle our plans."

Manny's eyes flashed. "What do you expect us to do? I don't know what plans you've got going on, but if you care to enlighten me, I may care more than I do right now." Without meaning to, he let his voice get louder. His hands were now clenched as he fought back the adrenaline pulsing through his body.

Sir Fletcher stared him down and said, "Lower. Your. Voice." A muscle twitched in his jaw, amplifying his point.

Manny backed down. "Are you going to tell us what is going on?" He whispered. He said "us" because he wanted Sir Fletcher to know whose side he was on. Gressa wasn't a North Morlaixer to him. And she wasn't a bartering piece, if that's what they were considering using her for.

The knight clenched his jaw. He took quick stock of the court-yard before seizing Manny by the upper arm and pushing him into the shadows. Once hidden, he whispered, "The kingdom should never have been divided. There are villagers—on both sides—working toward reunification. But, we also know that there is a spy on this side of the wall working for the Panther."

"Who?"

"Until recently, we thought it was you."

"Me?" Manny took a step back from Sir Fletcher. "Why would you think that?"

"We planted several rumors around the village to determine where the information was getting out, and we traced the source to be your father's tailor shop. We cleared your parents when your mother became ill and your father was quarantined while the false information continued to spread."

"How could you even think my father was a spy? He was a favorite with the king."

Sir Fletcher rolled his eyes. "Are you so naïve? At times like these we look at everyone. We rule out suspects one by one. You were a difficult source to track when you would disappear for hours on end and no one could find you. Suspicious behavior, wouldn't you say?"

Manny nodded. Yes, he could see why they would suspect him. And he did spend an inordinate amount of time hovering near the Dividing Wall. "Do you still think I'm a spy?"

Sir Fletcher snorted. "You're nothing but a lovesick boy."

Lovesick? Lovesick! Protective, yes, but who wouldn't be with the princess? Her brother was a monster and he'd set his sights on her. She needed his help. She was like a puppy being swept away in a flooded river. That was all. A cute puppy. One with flowing red-gold hair and unusual green eyes as captivating as any glittering gem.

"Ach! Even now, your eyes cloud over with romantic thoughts," said Sir Fletcher.

Manny blinked. *Lovesick?* Him?

"You better snap out of it, son of a tailor, squire to myself. She's a princess from North Morlaix. We should be hoisting her back over that wall this very moment. But I, too, cannot bear to think what would become of her if we did. I'm hoping Abigail will have a plan for us tomorrow. Until then, can we finally return to the barracks?" He crossed his arms in wait.

"Yes," Manny relented. "And what of our trip into the countryside? Were you testing my loyalty?"

"Our trip served multiple purposes. Testing you was one. While we were gone, information of our mission was spread to our informant in North Morlaix." Sir Fletcher walked toward the barracks.

"Wait! You have a spy in North Morlaix? And who is the spy on this side of the wall?"

Sir Fletcher cracked a crooked smile. "Of course, we have a spy. And their spy over here? I'll not tell you yet. You have to prove to me you can hold your tongue. I don't want you tipping our hand. Now that we know who it is, we can use him."

THAT NIGHT MANNY tried to get some sleep. The loud snores of the squire in the bunk next to him were not helping. He rolled away from the sound and thought of his friend Hoxham. They had met the day he came looking for an apprenticeship with the tailor. A scrawny, malnourished runt of a boy with an eye for mischief and funny jokes. He had come on a particularly busy day, when Manny wasn't yet old enough to be of much help in the shop. His father hired him on the spot, his soft heart willing to take a chance on a castle rat, an orphan boy who begged and stole to get by.

Since Hoxham had no one else, the tailor treated the apprentice with more familiarity than he ought. The apprentice and Manny grew up as close as brothers. Hoxham didn't get along well with the other boys, so Manny often found himself defending his friend. Prince Nigel was particularly tough on Hoxham, finding in the poor boy a character weaker than himself.

Time and again at the risk of widening the rift between himself and Nigel, Manny defended Hoxham to the prince, thus cutting off any hope of becoming a knight in South Morlaix once Nigel took over.

Which is why Hoxham's betrayal stung even more—for Hoxham was the spy. Manny was sure of it. He was the only person Manny told about leaving the castle with Sir Fletcher. But how to find out for sure?

Father had never liked the boy's shifty ways. It wasn't that Hoxham was necessarily lazy, though he was, but he would disappear at odd times and for long periods of time. And all that extra coin Hoxham pocketed. Manny had always suspected his friend had some side business going, but he never imagined it was treason.

Worse, why did Hoxham try to have him killed in the ambush in the forest? And now that Manny knew, how was he going to act like he didn't?

Then his thoughts turned to sweet Gressa. She must remain hidden at all times from Hoxham, for if he ever saw her, all would be lost.

CHAPTER 35

*E*arly in the morning Gressa's lessons began with Abigail. She repeated the names and uses of the herbs lined up on the scarred wood table: nettles, calendula, burdock, chamomile, and others. These lessons helped keep her mind off why Manny and Sir Fletcher had not been back to check on her in days.

Yesterday, Gressa had helped Abigail mix some of these herbs into a poultice for a neighbor suffering from a pain in her arm. And the day before that it had been a cough syrup with honey, elderberries, cloves and schisandra berries. Gressa was hoping for another neighbor to come down with an illness just so she could see what Abigail would mix up next.

"I'm so glad Old Anne told me to find you. Although, she didn't say *you* in particular, she said the healing woman. It would have been nice if she'd told me you were her sister."

"From what I remember of Anne, that doesn't surprise me. When we were little, she let me do most of the explaining for the two of us. Probably because I was the one who talked her into doing whatever mischief needed explaining in the first place." She laughed at the memory.

"I can't imagine Old Anne doing anything to get herself in

troub—" Gressa went quiet. Even now Old Anne might be taking the blame for Gressa's disappearance.

Abigail reached over and squeezed Gressa's hand. "Don't fret about my sister. She never did anything she didn't want to do. I'm sure she's the same way now."

Gressa gave a slight smile. That may be true, but Herrick could be harsh and Old Anne was a servant. He wouldn't have to hold back his cruelty.

"If you'd have told me last week that I'd be sitting here with the princess—" Abigail started laughing so hard she nearly fell off the chair.

Gressa laughed with her. For being sisters, Old Anne and Abigail couldn't be more different. Old Anne, so serious and reserved, more capable than people gave her credit, while Abigail was all tea cakes and fun. Although, as Gressa had seen, she was also surprisingly capable.

"What do you think is going to happen to me?" asked Gressa.

Abigail's smile dimmed, then brightened right up again. "I dunno. Let's take this one day at a time, shall we?"

"Is Sir Fletcher going to tell the king?"

"He may."

"I hope he doesn't."

The two were interrupted by a knock at the door. *Tap. Tap. Tap. Tippity-tap.*

"It's Fletcher." Abigail rose to answer the door.

But it was Manny who awaited on the other side. He slid in quickly and closed the door, bolting it behind him. He nodded to Abigail and grinned at Gressa.

"Forgive me for not coming sooner. Sir Fletcher didn't think it wise." He flopped into the closest chair. He tilted his head and studied her. "I'm still surprised to see you on this side of the wall," he said.

"Me too. Yet I feel right at home. Abigail has been most gracious. Did you know her sister is my nursemaid?"

Manny glanced at Abigail. "I'm not surprised."

Gressa grew serious. "Is Sir Fletcher going to tell the king about me?"

There was so much at stake. Not just her life, but the peace treaty. But where else could she go? If it were true that she was the only one in the kingdom with green eyes, she would be found out everywhere she went. Herrick would hunt her down like one of his rabbits. He would enjoy the game immensely. And who knew what he would do with her once she was trapped?

If Abigail would let her, she'd stay as long as she needed to in this tiny cottage. Even though it was smaller than her rooms at home, she didn't feel any despair. Today, surrounded by fragrant herbs, and the constant chatter of Abigail, Gressa could breathe as free as when she was in the meadow.

"We don't know what affect your crossing the wall will have on the treaty. Sir Fletcher thinks that if the king doesn't know, then he can't be guilty of any wrong doing."

Gressa relaxed. She tilted her head. "So, then. What's next?"

"I don't know what you should do, other than stay out of sight. Sir Fletcher has me helping him prepare for the tournament. Everything has to continue as normal so as not to arouse suspicion." Manny's face grew hard. "You never know who is watching."

"Still haven't found the spy?" Abigail stepped forward. "I told them it wasn't you. It's not in your blood."

Gressa had briefly questioned Manny's intentions when she saw him up on the dais with the king. He was full of contradictions, so no wonder others had questioned him, too.

"When Sir Fletcher and I were touring the villages, we were attacked on the way home. I appeared to be just as much a target as Sir Fletcher. Maybe more so, and we suspect the Panther was behind it."

"But why? What would my brother want with a tailor's son? Unless…"

Manny reached for Gressa's hand. "What do you know?"

She shook her head. "Likely nothing. My mother sent for your father to make my tournament gowns—"

"I knew that was your dress I saw on Father's workbench." Manny snapped his fingers. "Your mother sent for our shop to make it? It must have been after I'd already transferred to the bunkhouse."

Gressa's face warmed. She couldn't admit she was hoping Manny would have come in his place. "I saw my brother talking to the head apprentice at the gate. Maybe he was sending us all a message by trying to hurt the tailor's son?"

"Maybe," Manny said, but that didn't feel right either. It would have been Hoxham talking with the prince. Confirmation enough for Manny that his friend was the spy. It still didn't explain why they'd want to hurt him.

"My brother can be petty. If something is not of his doing, it isn't well done in his opinion."

Manny shuffled closer to the door. "I best get back. I don't know when I'll be able to see you again. Maybe tonight. Maybe tomorrow. Or not. I'm at the mercy of Sir Fletcher's whims." His gaze flickered to Abigail.

She laughed. "He's my son. I know how focused he can get."

Gressa walked him to the door, grateful that Abigail returned to her herbs to give them some privacy.

"Thank you for helping me. I know I've put you at great risk."

"What is a knight without a damsel in distress?" Manny tried to sound casual, but Gressa could see a deep intensity in his eyes. He was still worried, but he didn't want to alarm her.

He opened the door a crack and the morning light streamed in. He quickly looked about before he ventured a foot into the lane. "I'll be back as soon as I can."

"Manny?" Gressa stopped him. "You'll let me know if Sir Fletcher changes his mind, won't you?"

"Immediately." He met her eyes. "Then we'll run away together."

CHAPTER 36

*M*anny began to run back to the barracks when he saw something familiar out of the corner of his eye —Hoxham's ragged hat disappearing around the corner of a hut.

He stopped in his tracks. "Hoxham!" Manny changed directions to chase after his friend, or, former friend. By the time Manny rounded the same corner, Hoxham was gone. What had he seen? If Manny had led him straight to Gressa's hiding place, he'd never forgive himself.

Manny spent a few minutes exploring the side houses and small yards before giving up his search. He was already late for exercises and would have to confess to Sir Fletcher why. He kicked a stone, sending it flailing into a loose pile of hay.

"Ouff," said the hay pile as it moved.

Manny dove into the pile and pulled out Hoxham. He was holding one eye, tears streaming down his ruddy cheeks.

"Now what did you go and do that for?" said Hoxham angrily. "You near poked my eye out. I've got enough of me own troubles without being made half-blind."

"Let me see it." Manny tried to peel Hoxham's hand away.

"No! It hurts too much. Leave me be. Ain't you supposed to be with the knights?"

Hoxham's reminder stirred up Manny's ire. But then he remembered he couldn't confront Hoxham about the spy business. Sir Fletcher wanted to use him to spread false information back to the Panther.

Manny pretended to be concerned about Hoxham's injury. "Give off your hand!" Manny managed to unveil the eye. Already it was puffed up, almost all the way closed, and the skin turning any number of colors. Manny flinched at the sight.

"Aye, it's bad?" asked Hoxham. "My one good feature was me eyes. The girls can't resist 'em." He buried his face in his hands.

"I'm sure it will heal just fine. You'll have a black eye for a week or two is all." Manny plunked down on the hay. "What are you doing way out here?"

"I'm on a delivery for your father."

Manny raised an eyebrow. "Oh, is this hay pile in need of a jerkin or two?"

Hoxham fussed with his eye. "I felt like I was being chased so's I hid. Didna know it was you." His voice sounded as one who was caught poaching on the king's lands. He turned away and picked at the hay.

Manny sighed. Hoxham must have his reasons for betrayal. Hopefully something more than just filthy lucre. "I best get back to the stables."

"H-how was your trip?" Hoxham asked.

Manny brushed off the hay clinging to his clothes. The fine dusty bits floated in the morning sun. "Eventful."

"How so?"

"We were attacked is all. Didn't you hear?"

"Of course, I heard. The whole village thought Sir Fletcher was dead when his horse came back with blood all over it. Though, I suspected you would eventually find your way home. Who'd want you dead?" Hoxham stood with his hands on hips and legs apart in his usual arrogant stance.

"Same thing I was wondering. You have any ideas?" Manny

cocked his head, squinting to shield his eyes from the morning glare.

Hoxham looked genuinely shocked. "A tailor's son? Only reason to see you befall trouble would be if you sewed a man's britches too tight, eh?" He grew thoughtful. "They did na hurt you too bad?"

Manny shook his head, not sure why he was reassuring a traitor. He walked away, backwards. "Tell my father I'll try to see him later." He turned around and continued a pace before glancing over his shoulder. When Hoxham wasn't looking, Manny darted behind a cart and then doubled back the way he had come. Even though Sir Fletcher would likely want him to stay away from Hoxham, who better to learn his spy game?

Hoxham sat sulking in the hay for several minutes before picking up his hat and making his own way through the village. He walked this way and that, with no apparent purpose other than following his own whims. No wonder Hoxham always took so long on an errand. He never took the straight route. Just when Manny thought Hoxham was leading him to some place special, they ended up at the tailor's shop.

Disappointed, Manny chided himself for wasting time. Sir Fletcher would not be happy. Maybe Hoxham wasn't the spy after all. The errands he ran all over the village might make him look suspicious, but how would he get information over the wall anyway? Hoxham was decidedly un-athletic. To throw even a message tied to a rock would take great strength and skill. Let alone stealth. Wouldn't people become suspicious to see him hurling objects at the wall?

But what was this? Hoxham had slunk around the back of the shop. He continued past, on to the small field behind the aviary.

Manny maintained his position. Hoxham glanced left and right before raising a leather-gloved hand. With his other hand, he swung a ball on a string. A hawk circling high above dove for Hoxham's hand. Hoxham fed the bird, affixed something to its talons, then released it immediately. The bird shot up high before diving again on the other side of the wall.

So that's how they did it. Messenger birds. Manny hurried to tell Sir Fletcher.

He found Sir Fletcher in the weapons room, laying out his equipment for the day. Doing Manny's job.

"I just saw Hoxham send a message. He does it by hawk."

Sir Fletcher nodded slowly. "We suspected. The birds are the only ones free to go over the wall. Plus, we have noticed an abundance of circling hawks of late." He tossed a training baton at Manny. "And how did you happen to witness this when you were supposed to be here preparing my equipment?"

"You know what I did." Manny didn't try to cover up his actions.

"You put the girl in jeopardy every time you visit her. By now the Panther knows she is missing. He has searched all the boats and closest ports on the mainland. He is already suspicious about the wall. Don't you think Hoxham will be paying closer attention to anything amiss here in South Morlaix?"

The blood drained from Manny's face as he realized Sir Fletcher's rebuke. Gressa. He led Hoxham straight to her. If anything happened to her! He dropped the baton and took off in a run.

Sir Fletcher reached out his long leg and tripped Manny. "Not so fast, hot-head."

Manny lay on the ground and spat dirt out of his mouth. He squinted up at Sir Fletcher. "I have to warn her."

Sir Fletcher placed a well-worn leather boot on Manny's shoulder. "Not without a plan of what to do with her. There are only so many places we may hide the lass. Let's not be rash and leave her open for exposure. A knight protects. A knight thinks. A knight plans." Sir Fletcher pointed to his equipment and signaled for Manny to perform his duties as a squire. "We have some time before the Panther can act. And besides, my mother is wise in her own right. She won't be easily fooled to give up the girl."

All through practice, Manny kept his watch on the skies over the wall. He was waiting for the Panther's response sent by another hawk. He couldn't send his own knights to breach the wall. Would he send them by ship?

Manny looked toward the sea. All calm. Knights walked the castle walls, vigilant at their posts. THWACK! Manny's head was struck by a baton, and it knocked him to the grass.

"You seem a little distracted today, tailor-boy."

Manny groaned. He had spent too much of practice lying on the earth. He blinked and focused on a pair of royal boots. *Nigel.* "Nice hit. Didn't know you had it in you." A sucker punch. The only way Nigel could get a hit in on anyone.

"You've been away from the castle for a time with that wretched knight. Maybe I've been practicing while you were gone." He held his hand out for Manny and helped him to his feet.

Indeed, Nigel did carry himself with increased meekness, a far cry from the strutting, peacock-like swagger he usually held. And he had slimmed down some as well. Maybe the prince finally realized that his life truly was in danger. A threat from the Panther would make any man's knees quake. Sir Fletcher said you should hold every enemy in high regard. Passion went a long way in a battle.

"You do seem different."

Nigel bowed slightly, showing a touch of modesty. "If you'll excuse me," he said, stepping away at the sight of Sir Fletcher's approach.

"I've decided we need to move her to one of the outlying villages. I've got a brother living on my estate. She can stay under his guard until we find something more permanent." Sir Fletcher handed his equipment to Manny and started for the garrison.

Manny juggled all the practice equipment and scrambled to keep up. "Isn't your estate past the forest and near the far sea?"

"It is."

She would be a full week's journey away. How could he protect her?

"Is that a problem, squire?"

"I don't like how far that is, should something happen."

"It's not a perfect plan, but my brother is capable."

"What if she hid within the Dividing Wall? Since only I can access it. She would be safest there."

"A temporary solution, and a good one for today while we make other arrangements."

They had reached the garrison and Sir Fletcher stood, hands on hips, surveying the grounds. "Go get her some food, and I'll bring her to the wall. Can you enter through any length of the wall or does it need to be a specific door?"

"I've only managed to enter at one point. Gressa found another—one inside the castle itself."

"Go now," urged Sir Fletcher, his eyes to the sky where a circling hawk swept high overhead before diving into South Morlaix. "I believe Hoxham has his orders."

CHAPTER 37

"When is the last time you and Old Anne saw each other?" Gressa sniffed the lotion she was mixing. It needed more lavender to cover up the smell of the main ingredient, some herb she had a hard time pronouncing. It worked well for the aches and pains of the elderly, Abigail said.

"We were children. She'd gone with a friend to watch the potter who lived on the north side. That was the day the wall separated us and we never saw her again. My mother died never laying eyes on her first born again."

"I'm sorry," Gressa said. Her family had caused such pain.

"Wasn't your fault. You weren't even a twinkling in your father's eye." Abigail handed Gressa a sprig of the lavender. "Copello refused to get involved in our politics, so they didn't allow any Morlaixans to step onto their ports in those days, Northern or Southern. It was their way of staying neutral, but really, they didn't want an influx of disgruntled folks pouring into their town and starting fights. Can't say I blame them, now, but back then it almost drew them into the conflict."

"But some go to Copello now. One of my brothers is there."

"Yes. Over time, regulations have been relaxed and people

have calmed down. On this side. I don't think the north allows as much freedom as we have on this side."

Gressa frowned. She didn't know enough to comment. But if her circumstances ever changed, she'd look into it. She would do what she could to make things better for her people.

"Sorry, princess, but I've got to go out to check on Mrs. Tallow. She'll send someone to fetch me if I don't pop in for tea. She's a creature of habit and expects us all to be as well. My, her tongue does wag."

Gressa opened the cupboard and removed the blankets stored there before crawling into the hidden compartment at the back. Abigail insisted Gressa tuck in the cubbyhole whenever she went out as a precaution. "The princess won't be found on my watch," she said.

"I'll do my best to make it quick, but not too quick. She'll get suspicious." Abigail locked the panel into place. She was still talking, but her voice was muffled. Gressa assumed she was asking if she could still breathe, because that was the question she always asked.

"Yes!"

Blankets were thumped back in and the door closed.

Gressa shifted to a more comfortable position. She hated this part, sitting in the dark not knowing how long Abigail would be gone. It was really hard to keep track of time. Sometimes she could hear street noises, in particular the two little boys who lived next door. She strained her ears to listen, but heard nothing. They must be out for a walk. The mother tended to run their energy outside.

Another sound came filtered through her hiding place. Abigail had just left; did she forget something? *Scrape.* Something hidden behind the furniture? *Thump.* That she had lost and couldn't find?

Gressa froze. Someone was searching Abigail's house. It sounded like they'd found the root cellar. The door made a big thump when it dropped on the packed earth. Good thing Abigail wouldn't let her hide in there. Root cellars must be common in these houses, so of course anyone looking for her would know to look for one.

The cups in the cupboard rattled when the door was opened. Gressa pressed back into the corner, then changed her mind. They would just grab her. She needed to be ready to run. If she stayed inside, they'd have her. If she could get into the street, she had a chance to get away.

Slowly, she moved to a crouch, balancing on the balls of her feet. Sweat dripped down the small of her back. She couldn't take it anymore. It would be better to catch them by surprise, than have them catch her. She made ready to burst through the cupboard when the sounds changed.

There was a scuffle, more thumps, a crash.

Gressa listened, listened. Her heart pounding loud in her ears. Nothing. What was going on out there? A giggle next door sounded entirely too normal after what had just taken place. If only she could ask one of those little boys to come over and report back what was going on.

The false panel was ripped open, revealing Sir Fletcher's concerned face.

"You all right?"

Gressa couldn't find her voice. She nodded.

He held a hand out and helped her untangle herself from her hiding place. The table had been upended, and broken pottery and herbs lined the floor.

"Where is—"

"I've taken care of them, but we need to move you, now." Sir Fletcher rifled through his mother's clothing chest until he found a dark cloak with a hood. He held it out to her. "Try it on."

She did. Too big. It felt like she was playing dress-up. "This might make me stand out more than fit in," she said, still shaking. She didn't want anyone looking at her. That was a close call.

"No matter. I don't care that people know I'm hiding someone. I don't want them knowing who you are."

"But won't they just follow us?"

"Not where you're going. You know how to get through the wall?"

She shook her head. "I can't go back now."

"To the meadow? Manny is getting supplies for you now."

"What is this?" Abigail stood in the door, light streaming around her. She quickly closed the door. "Fletcher?" Her gaze took in the ransacked room.

"Thank you, Mother. I'll come for dinner on Sunday night."

Gressa raised an eyebrow. That was how he explained her once-tidy house? "I've been found out. Your son saved me in the nick of time and now he's secreting me away to a new location."

Abigail grabbed her hands. "You are trembling dear. Do you need some tea before you go?"

Sir Fletcher let out an exasperated breath, and Abigail patted Gressa's hand. "Best you leave now. This isn't goodbye. We'll see each other again."

CHAPTER 38

*T*hunder clapped in the distance, warning of an impending storm. Manny paced along the Dividing Wall, carrying a sack filled with hard cheese, dried meat, and bread. *They should have been here by now.* He could imagine all sorts of ill will befalling them if he gave in to his fears.

He scanned the faces of anyone who had Gressa's form, suspecting Sir Fletcher would try to disguise her somehow. The crowds were beginning to swell as folks made their way in for the upcoming tournament. He even kept an eye on an old man with a wheelbarrow in case Sir Fletcher was especially clever. But when the old man parked his 'barrow near the east garden, Manny couldn't take it any longer. He left the wall to go get Gressa himself.

It was a shock when Sir Fletcher gripped his arm. "Going somewhere?" he said. Sir Fletcher pushed him back toward the wall.

"There you are," Manny said. He looked around, but no Gressa. "Where is she?"

"If you didn't notice her, that's a good thing. We thought it best to travel separately. She walked in front so I could keep an eye on her, while my mother walked slightly behind as a decoy."

Abigail nodded slightly as she turned and retreated.

Manny scanned the people by the wall, but he still didn't see Gressa.

"She's waiting for you in the shadow of the castle."

Sure enough, a dainty, cloaked figure hovered uncertainly by the wall.

"When I see you in place, I'll give you the best diversion I can. You sure that's all I have to do?"

"Yes." Manny's mouth had gone dry. He was the son of a tailor. What was he doing trying to rescue a princess? "The wall does the rest." He spoke with more confidence than he had. *We hope.*

They'd never gone through together, so who was to say it would work? The wall seemed to be on their side, if that were possible, and that's what they were counting on. If not for his sake, for hers. She was the tower princess, escaped from her tower. Manny refused to be the one who sent her back to it.

Gressa peeked out at him from her oversized hood, and he silently took hold of her elbow and brought her to the correct location at the wall. He forced his legs to keep a steady pace instead of break into a run.

His gaze darted at every movement, every shadow. Gressa remained silent, hidden in the cloak as a soft rain began to fall. No one would look suspiciously at her hooded head in this weather.

When they were in position, Manny nodded to Sir Fletcher, now across the courtyard. The knight grabbed the nearest lad.

"Thief!" he yelled. Sir Fletcher pounced on a bewildered boy and spun him around, swiping his leg out from under him. "Lie here while I check your clothing."

All eyes riveted to Sir Fletcher, particularly the merchants', wondering whose shop had fallen victim of theft.

But the wall wouldn't open.

Sir Fletcher made a grand show of checking the boy for stolen goods.

Still, the wall would not open.

"Look away," Manny said to Gressa. "I'll go in first and pull you with me." He searched the wall for an opening until he heard Gressa cry out.

"Let me go!"

He spun around to see her in the grip of Nigel's nursemaid.

"Let me see your eyes," cried the nursemaid as she threw Gressa's hood off her head. "It is you!" she crowed. All attention was still on Sir Fletcher, but for this woman.

She stuck her thick finger in Gressa's face. "You were the thief wandering in the castle. I saw you steal the Queen Margaret's jewels!"

"I did not!"

"Here's the thief!" The woman cried out to the crowd, drawing attention their way.

Manny pulled Gressa's hood back over her head and tried to pull her away from the nursemaid. The woman would have none of it. Her grip tightened on Gressa's arm until the princess cried out.

By this time, people were beginning to tire of Sir Fletcher's charade and turned their attention to the new disturbance. The Dividing Wall would never open now.

Sir Fletcher let the scared, yet innocent boy go and joined the trio at the wall.

"What is going on here?"

The nursemaid pointed a finger at Gressa. "That's the princess from the North. I knew it t'were. Stole the queen's jewels and now the Panther will attack us because of 'er. He said he would. Her and that boy, they should never have been near the wall."

"She knows something," Sir Fletcher said. He grabbed the nursemaid by her thick arms and dragged her into the nearest doorway, the kitchen. Once inside, he yelled for everyone to leave them. His booming voice echoed in the space, and the kitchen workers scattered, instantly dropping their pans and ladles and root vegetables.

Manny and Gressa pressed themselves flat against the wall as the servants poured out. So, this was the quick obedience Sir Fletcher sought from him.

"Help! Someone! The knight's gone mad! He thinks to kill me!" The nursemaid's cries went unheeded as Sir Fletcher flung her into the potato bin.

"You will tell me everything."

Her face turned red with her efforts to escape. "Do ye know who I am?"

"A waste of flesh." Sir Fletcher spat at her feet.

She caught up her legs and tucked her feet safely under her skirts.

Manny's eyes grew wide. He made a note to be quicker with his answers and obedience to the knight.

The nursemaid sealed her mouth into a tight line and crossed her arms. She stared vacantly past Sir Fletcher's shoulder.

The knight clenched and unclenched his hands, his gaze not leaving the uncooperative woman.

Manny stepped forward, hoping to come up with a way to help. When the nursemaid caught sight of him, her eyes turned to hatred as she stared him down. Manny blinked. He'd never had anyone look at him with such venom. It made his blood run cold. Who was he, but a tailor's son? Why would she look on him thus?

Sir Fletcher caught the exchange and now also looked at Manny.

"Who is this lad to you?" he asked the nursemaid.

She tore her glance away from Manny. "He is less than nothing."

Sir Fletcher smirked. "Then you won't mind if this less-than-nothing boy fetches the constable to have you thrown into the dungeon, eh?"

Manny spun on his heel to leave the room.

"Stop!" cried the nursemaid, her voice quaking.

"It does no' matter anyway. Yer too late. The Panther knows. He knows all about tha' girl." She pointed a quivering finger at

Gressa. "It breaks the treaty, it does. He'll be seeking vengeance soon." At this, she began to laugh, a choking, sputtering laugh.

Gressa shrunk back against the wall.

"Why laugh so, cretin? If he breaches the wall, he'll kill you simply for being in the employ of the king," said Sir Fletcher.

The woman laughed harder, like a lunatic under a full moon.

What did she know that they didn't?

Hoxham entered the kitchen and made a move as if to speak when his eyes fell across Sir Fletcher with his thick muscles and sour expression.

Sir Fletcher raised an eyebrow.

Hoxham closed his mouth and took a step back. He looked to the nursemaid for support, but she was too busy struggling to rise up amongst the tumbling spuds to be reliable. Instead, he fixed his gaze on Manny and Gressa. His eyes narrowed. "That's the princess," he said. "She's wot you've been hiding."

Manny stepped in front of Gressa. "What do you want, Hoxham?" He spoke carefully, trying to decide whether to lean on Hoxham because of their friendship, or to speak in a commanding way, as a future knight and protector.

Gressa whispered in Manny's ear, "He's the one I saw talking with my brother in North Morlaix."

"This has nothing to do with you, Manny," said Hoxham. "Even Sir Fletcher needs to step down." Hoxham risked a look at the fuming knight, and involuntarily took another step back. "We either forfeit the girl or the kingdom."

Gressa stepped forward. "He lies. There has been no attack. I haven't done anything to the people here in South Morlaix. The peace treaty still stands."

This silenced Hoxham. For a minute. He crossed his arms. "It's a matter for the king. You have no say, princess." Hoxham spat out the word princess in disgust.

Manny lunged for his former friend, who first looked surprised, then amused.

Sir Fletcher grabbed Manny, pinning his arms. He hissed in Manny's ear, "Don't make it worse. We take it to King Simon."

The nursemaid, with all the attention off her, was now on her feet, flicking dirt from her voluminous skirt. "King Simon! King Simon!" she shrieked. She led them to the great hall, laughing the entire way and muttering to herself.

CHAPTER 39

They found King Simon in his library, a circular room lined with bookshelves from floor to ceiling. Four thickly padded chairs were placed in the center around a table loaded with bread and cheese. Gressa marveled at the proliferation of books in South Morlaix. Her father had no patience for reading; he would rather be outside on a fox hunt or conducting boat races. If it weren't for Old Anne, perhaps no one in the royal household would have been taught to read. She insisted that not only Gressa learn, but the boys as well.

King Simon stood, book in hand, and looked confusedly at the odd gathering inside the doorway. He rubbed the back of his neck, a tired old gesture that reminded Gressa of her father as of late. The two famous knights-turned-kings were both aged. In her mind, King Simon had remained the stubborn young knight of which the minstrels sang. Seeing him for the first time, she wondered what her life, no, everyone's lives would have been like had the knights remained friends instead of becoming enemies.

The skinny lad burst forth first, perhaps trying to get his accusations out before he grew too fainthearted, or to put his spin on it before Sir Fletcher could have his say. Gressa shivered, the long reach of her brother felt even here. She leaned closer to Manny.

"Your people have kidnapped the princess of North Morlaix." Hoxham pointed an accusing finger at Sir Fletcher and Manny.

The nursemaid squeezed her way past the group and stood before King Simon. "Look. Look at the girl. She's the one that did the cryin', remember? You've gots to get rid of her." She spoke forcefully, as if she were the one in control, not King Simon. She said no more, but implied much with her eyes.

Gressa watched with interest. What crying had she done? She'd been too much in a whirl since landing in South Morlaix to let her emotions catch up with her. Of course, she oft cried in her tower when no one was around to hear and after Old Anne had gone to sleep. What did this woman know of her tears? She was a crazy thing, that's what. Gressa kept her gaze on the woman. The crazy ones needed watching. Manny could take care of the weasel-boy.

Gressa almost missed it, keeping her focus on the nursemaid, but out of the corner of her eye she saw King Simon, clench his chest with his hand when he looked at her. Or was it when he looked at Manny? She turned her attention to the king.

"What is the explanation?" King Simon addressed Sir Fletcher.

"If it please the king, may I introduce Princess Gressa of North Morlaix."

Gressa, out of good training and habit, curtsied as if she were being presented at court, not as if she were facing a possible trip to the dungeon, or worse, a forced return to North Morlaix.

"North Morlaix?" was the king's immediate response, followed by several stunned minutes during which he alternated looking at Manny and looking at the housemaid, before finally resting his eyes on Gressa.

Gressa rubbed the skin near her thumbnail while simultaneously biting her lip. Two nervous habits from childhood that made her aware of how vulnerable she felt in this moment.

What would her father do if he caught someone from South Morlaix in *his* castle? Folks said he had softened since her birth, so maybe he would be lenient. She didn't have to wonder how her brother would react.

"You look like your father's sister. She had eyes the color of yours." He returned his attention to Sir Fletcher, seemingly not noticing the surprise in Gressa's face. It was strange to hear someone accursed to her family talk so familiarly about them.

"We must send her back. Take the skiff and go by sea."

Gressa's insides collapsed with the news. She mustn't go back. She mustn't.

"Your majesty!" Gressa splayed herself face down before the king. "If it please you, do not send me back. They don't know where I have fled, so they should do you no harm. But if I go back…" She dared not think what would happen.

Her pleas were met with silence and Gressa's thoughts of Good King Simon soured. He was as impassive as her father. For knights who wanted to rule so badly, neither seemed to care for the rule once they had it.

"Sire, I will take responsibility for her."

It was Manny. From her prostrate position Gressa noted his boot as he stepped beside her. Her heart expanded threefold for him.

"Alas, you cannot," said the king. "You are but a squire and have no means to care for even yourself." He bent down and gently lifted Gressa's chin from the stone floor. He helped her to her feet. "Do not think me unfeeling. I have heard tales about the Panther and I fear for what consequences you may face for running away. However, we have a treaty. We are not to interfere in each other's kingdoms. Harboring a runaway princess is interfering, I dare-say."

He turned away. "I would expect your father to do the same for me."

Gressa felt as if her soul had detached and was floating somewhere behind her body. She had never been this scared in her life. Her physical body still breathed, though she didn't know how it could.

Sir Fletcher whispered to the king. That traitorous skinny boy who should be going to his own dungeon cell stood smirking. Why wasn't he going to the dungeon? And the strange nursemaid was stealing a candelabra, tucking it amongst the folds of her voluminous skirt. The world had gone mad.

Manny reached for Gressa's hand, and her soul allowed the touch. He grounded her. What would happen once she was aboard the vessel and on her way back home? What would keep her from floating away then?

CHAPTER 40

At the seaside, with the salt wind whipping her unbound hair, Gressa stood on the rocks and stared out at the endless rolling blue-black waves. Sir Fletcher stood ten paces away, speaking with the captain of the vessel she was to board and ride home to her imprisonment. The nursemaid had remained behind, giggling and likely stealing her way around the castle. But, much to Gressa's irritation, Hoxham floated in the background, watching near the sea wall.

"Why won't you look at me?" Manny squeezed her hand.

Gressa couldn't talk.

"Make a run for it as soon as the boat lands on your side. Get to the meadow. I'll meet you there. We can still outsmart them."

She shook her head once. It was impossible. Her brother would have patrols scanning the waters, waiting for her. She would be in shackles before her toe ever touched ground. She licked her lips, tasting the sea. Perhaps this would be the last time she would ever have freedom such as this again. She should try to remember it. Every detail. The way the wind continually blew, causing her skin to prickle in goose flesh. The distant call of the sea birds. The endless view, not blocked by walls or prison bars.

She felt a gentle tug on her arm.

"Please," Manny whispered. "Let's run now."

Gressa glanced around. Sir Fletcher was distracted. The captain equally so. But Hoxham, his gaze had not left her since the king had issued his verdict. Why did they let that weasel go free?

"He's lazy. He'll sound an alarm, but he won't come after us." Manny guessed her thoughts.

"Everyone will be watching us run through the square. The door won't open."

"What about the door in the castle?"

Gressa's eyes opened wide. "But that leads directly into North Morlaix. Not the meadow. There's no safety there." She shuddered to think what would happen to Manny under her brother's hand. At least she was a blood relative and her mother and father still lived. The Panther's retribution toward her would be limited.

"No one will be expecting us, so that will give us time." He wrapped his arms around her and gently placed his chin on top of her head. "I can't bear to think what might happen to you."

For a moment, she allowed herself to lean into him and feel his strength, to relish in his warmth. To pretend things were different, and that she could give in to this blossoming love.

But he was a tailor's son. A knight in training on the other side of the wall. She had to make him see that he had to give up the idea of the meadow. It would not be their salvation, not when there were so many other people to think about.

He lowered his head until their cheeks were touching, but she pushed herself away before he could kiss her.

"Old Anne is there," she said.

Manny chuckled ruefully. "And what good is an old woman against the Panther?"

So often Gressa had thought the woman out of touch, naïve. But the whole time, Old Anne was there to protect the young princess and work toward a united kingdom. Sly Old Anne.

"I am his only sister. He will likely marry me off as soon as possible." She watched the waves crash against the shore carrying flotsam from far away. "Perhaps once I am queen in another land,

I can return to save Morlaix. My brother's machinations will only serve to destroy him."

Manny stiffened. "Do not marry." His voice was quiet. Hurt.

Gressa turned and finally looked at him. "Why not?" An image of the slobbering Viking with bits of food in his beard, leaning toward her for a kiss, made her throat close up. But surely, she could find happiness amongst her gardens and serving her people. A happy marriage wasn't everything.

Sir Fletcher returned before Manny could answer. "I'm sorry, milady." He steered her by her elbow toward the dock. He discreetly handed her a small leather pouch. "From my mother. She said to give it to you if you were caught and forced to return."

Gressa slipped the pouch amongst the folds of her skirt and tied it to her belt. She doubted that, being the princess, she would be searched. It would be enough that she was returned in disgrace.

The captain brought over a small skiff and tied it to the dock. "He is none too happy to be docking in North Morlaix," said Sir Fletcher. "He's afraid of capture. I had to threaten him with our own dungeon. As it is, he will only bring over this little rowboat. The waves may jostle a bit, milady."

Gressa nodded. She didn't like the looks of the small vessel, already sitting low in the water with the highest waves crashing over it. She would arrive home cold, disgraced, and dripping wet. The Panther wouldn't have it any other way.

The captain stood at the ready, thoroughly agitated. He wiped his brow with a grimy handkerchief, which he then tucked into his shirt, only to pull it out seconds later and wipe his brow again. His nervousness did nothing for her confidence in him.

Sir Fletcher held his palm out, directing her to the boat. "You best go."

Gressa smiled at Manny. Not a forced smile, but a warm smile as she wanted her best friend to remember her. For, she realized at that moment, he was her best friend. She'd never had one before in her secluded life, and her jaunt with him would provide her with many warm memories, no matter where she ended up.

"Remember me well," she said.

He smiled back as if he, too, were trying to fix this moment in his mind. "Always."

CHAPTER 41

*A*s soon as Gressa was out of earshot, Manny turned his anger on Sir Fletcher.

"What have you done!"

Sir Fletcher continued staring out to sea. "There was nothing we could have changed. The king was correct in his decision. He has a responsibility to protect South Morlaix, not the princess of the North. As soon as he learned she was here, he had to send her away."

Manny hated to admit their reasoning held true. He only wished he had more time to come up with a better plan. He lifted his arm in one last wave as the skiff went around the corner. He couldn't tell if Gressa was looking at him or not, but if she was, he wanted her to see his last wave.

"I must report back to the king. Please tend to my horse. We'll meet up again at the evening meal."

Manny trailed behind Sir Fletcher, and noticing an absence, said, "Where is Hoxham? Surely we have enough evidence to bring him before the king for treason."

Sir Fletcher nodded. "We do, but we're not finished with him yet. He knows he must be more careful now, but I don't think he is bright enough to be scared. He's been a spy for a long time and he considers himself invincible."

"I need to warn my father."

"Fine. But be discreet."

❧

HOXHAM WAS in the middle of the tailor shop when Manny arrived, wet from the pounding rain that had begun to fall.

"Oh, if it isn't North Morlaix's future prince?" Hoxham scoffed, bowing low.

Manny flicked some rain water at Hoxham's face. "Back off. You had no right to expose her."

"What were you doing with the princess, anyway? How you two crossed paths, that I'd like to know. Did she need another fitting? If your father sent you instead of me…"

Manny's father entered from the back room. "What's this? A busy squire has come to pay his father a visit?" The tailor hugged Manny. "What's new in the king's world?"

"The princess of North Morlaix was here seeking asylum." He looked at Hoxham, trying to read his reactions. "But the king wouldn't allow it and so sent her back by skiff."

The tailor's eyes widened. "You don't say? Wonder how she got here? 'Tis a strange one that princess. I've heard stories."

Manny forgot about Hoxham. "What stories?"

His father shrugged. "Oh, haven't been new ones in a while. Just the old stories the women used to tell. Can I get you a drink?" he asked, noticeably trying to change the subject.

"I'm fine. What stories?" he repeated.

"She was born near about the time the prince here was. People said the two babes would cry at the wall for each other. Women heard eerie wails at the wall day and night. Say the two were destined to be together." He shrugged. "Hopeful thinking, those women. Come up with any old romantic story, they will."

Gressa and Nigel? Destined? Manny shook his head. He didn't see it. Kind, sweet Gressa. Pig-headed, lazy Nigel.

Hoxham laughed. "Well, as usual, the prince missed his chance. That one is slower than a slug in a race against a snail."

Manny couldn't help grin. Hoxham was always good for a laugh. Too bad their entire friendship amounted to nothing but betrayal.

The tailor chuckled along with them. "If you have a minute, come look at my latest creation. Hoxham secured a high-paying customer. I think I've outdone myself."

In the back room, the tailor had laid out the richest fabrics they had, in bright colors that were expensive to obtain. "Oh, that your mother would have liked to touch these, eh?"

Manny nodded. His mother, though always dressed in the common garb of a tailor's wife, did enjoy the fanciful creations made for the manor houses and royalty. She spoke often of the days before Queen Margaret died, and all the finery the queen ordered. The king had held nothing back from his beloved queen.

While his father went into detail, showing the new techniques on the sleeves he was experimenting with, Manny couldn't help but think how pretty these dresses would look on Gressa.

Soon, Hoxham grew bored and withdrew into the front room. *Finally.*

"The real reason I'm here," Manny said in hushed tones, before pausing to check on Hoxham. Likely the boy was hovering near the curtains eavesdropping. Ah, a customer had come in. Manny returned to his conversation with his father, satisfied that Hoxham was sufficiently busy.

"Hoxham is a spy for the Panther. Take care in your speech when you are around him."

The tailor scoffed. "I knew something was wrong with that one. But what care do I need to take? Afraid the girth of the king will get back to the other side?"

Manny hung his head. "No, you're right, I suppose. Thought

you should know was all." He smiled ruefully. "I always stuck up for him. But you were right all along. How did you know?"

"Your mother's intuition. I'm quite daft about these things myself, but your mother *felt* things about people. There are a few folks about this place I'm extra careful around. You never can tell about people. Even your own kin."

CHAPTER 42

$\mathcal{T}$he skiff was rickety. The waves relentless. The wind bitter. And Gressa's stomach, already tied up in knots, was queasy.

"How much farther?" she gasped out. She hung over the water-bloated wooden side, closing her eyes to the splashes of sea water as she retched again over the edge. She was down to stomach acids and little else.

"Not much," said the captain, his voice gruff. His disposition had improved little since casting off. Dark clouds had gathered on the horizon and the waves had begun to swell. He stopped rowing. "Here's good. Out you go."

Gressa raised her head. The coastline of North Morlaix floated in front of her. A shallow beach area wide enough only for the guarded docking area, and the cliff rising to their half of the castle. Ten men stood ready to greet her, but the dock was still a good deal away. "Aren't you going to row closer?"

"No."

Gressa eyed the distance with her seasick eyes. "But the waves. And I'm freezing. I'll never make it."

"Not my problem. I was told to bring ye back to your side. This is your side."

"But..."

"Look, miss. I'll not be captured meself. If'n they want ye back, they'll send someone to fetch ye once ye take the plunge."

Gressa rested her cheek on the skiff. How would the people of Morlaix muster enough courage to fight the Panther if they had so little compassion for each other? They would all have to band together if they were to best him.

"Thank you for your kindness," she said and meant it. She felt sorry for the old captain. He had tried to row as gently as he could, and he did bring her closer than he obviously felt comfortable with.

He cleared his throat in return and dropped his chin to his chest, though his gaze didn't leave the coastline.

All right then. She gathered her skirts about her, calculating how long it would take for the water to soak through and drag her down to the bottom. One of her brothers had better be quick.

She stood, making the boat rock even more, the water sloshing over her feet. She slung one leg over. Two legs, and lowered herself slowly into the water. She caught her breath. Ice. So cold. She couldn't bring herself to let go of the edge of the skiff.

The captain cleared his throat again. "I'd rather not wait for them to capture me," he said.

Gressa looked over her shoulder. A boat was on its way for her. A real boat with four oarsmen rowing fast. She need only tread water until they reached her, surely, she could do that. She let go.

The old sea captain rowed away with renewed strength while she bobbed in the waves, fighting her heavy skirts from drowning her.

CHAPTER 43

*G*ressa's brother Siguard sat in the chair opposite her, staring into the fire. Second eldest, he was second in line for the throne, and the first of the brothers to let it be known the throne didn't interest him.

The lines on his face were softer than Herrick's. His eyes, the gentler eyes of a man won out to living a life of peace and prayer. He had shocked the family when he announced he was entering the monastery. Gressa had always thought her parents hoped he would change his mind and King Jorvik could name Siguard as successor instead of Herrick. Though that would likely spell his instant death, and maybe that's why her parents let him go so easily.

Why didn't he speak? Was he sent to get a confession out of her? Gressa pulled her arms in tighter around her body as she shivered again. Her brother Axell, the one who had given her the pomander before leaving for Copello, had plucked her out of the stormy sea just when she thought she could hold her head above water no longer.

She had prayed her final prayer and was about to commit her soul to God when, like a guardian angel, Axell reached over the edge of the small Viking vessel and rescued her. He had returned a knight, and, if Siguard was correct, soon to be a husband as well.

"Do you need another blanket? More stew?" Siguard asked. He moved comfortably about the small abbey, despite the armed men guarding the door and each window.

She shook her head. No, just answers, gentle brother. Like where was Old Anne? And even more to the point, where was Herrick?

"Our father was heartbroken when you left."

"Father? I'm surprised he even knew I was gone."

"I don't always understand him, either. They say he was a different man when he was young. Before."

"Before?"

"Before he became king. Before the *way* in which he became king."

"Can't you talk to him? Make him see that Herrick is getting out of control. Now that Axell is home, if the two of you went together, you can make him see reason."

"Father is acting with reason. He's giving Herrick more power so he can learn to rule while Father is still here to help." Siguard pulled an illuminated book off his shelf and absentmindedly flipped through it. "Herrick has set up a meeting with South Morlaix. Peaceful talks, he says."

Startled, Gressa sat up straight, her shivering ended. "Not with their prince, truly Herrick wants to kill him, and that will be easily done."

Siguard closed the book with a snap and returned to his chair at the fire. He methodically poked at the charred log, sending streams of sparks up the chimney. "Yes, he does. But Father won't allow it. He is going too, to make sure Herrick behaves."

Gressa sat back, deflated. "The two kings are going to meet? But that hasn't happened since the wall went up."

Siguard looked thoughtful. "No, it hasn't. Was this your original intent? Run away to bring about lasting peace?"

If only her actions had been that measured. She shook her

head. "Herrick was going to wed me to that horrible Ulf." She buried herself deeper into the coarse blanket.

"Hmm. There seemed more to it than that," Siguard muttered.

Gressa cocked her head.

"Can you think of any reason why the Panther would want a meeting with the South?"

"You called him the Panther." Siguard was always so careful with his word choices.

He held her gaze. "He is acting more like the Panther and less like my brother. I have concerns. And you've been over there. How did you manage that?"

"I don't like your tone. Are you trying to get answers for Herrick?" Aside from Axell, Siguard was the brother she trusted most. However, he'd been out of the household since she was a child, so maybe she didn't even know him as much as she thought.

Siguard picked up the book once again. He flipped through several pages and when he spoke, his voice had softened. "I am not working for Herrick. I work for God." He closed the book without reading anything. "I sense something different in Herrick's demeanor. He seems.... happy."

"And that worries you?"

"Since when has our brother ever been happy?"

When he knows he's about to win.

"Look, Gressa. We all know that South Morlaix is weak. The only reason Herrick hasn't attacked them is because of Father, who, for some reason, perhaps loyalty to his old friend, is protecting South Morlaix."

"Father? Protecting South Morlaix? Since when?"

Siguard continued, "So why is Herrick jovial of late? Even after you left. He was angry, no doubt, but he didn't stay that way for long."

"What changed?"

"I don't know. I thought it might have been you. That you

were somehow part of his plan. Did you pass on any information? Bring anything with you?"

She shook her head. She only wore the peasant clothes Old Anne had given her, and she was still wearing them when she went down into the sea water. She thought of Hoxham and his smug look as she boarded the skiff.

"He has a spy. A boy over there who sends messages by way of the birds."

Siguard shook his head. "Something new. Something different happened. Axell arrived shortly after the trickster left the castle— you know how much Axell dislikes that man—and Herrick welcomed our brother home with a clap on the back, no less."

No, she didn't know Axell's feelings about the trickster. His feelings for Herrick, on the other hand, were well known by everyone in the kingdom.

"That is unusual." But there was something that bothered her more than her brother's cheerfulness.

"Why did the trickster come back? He's been around a lot lately." She hoped he'd never come back. Something about him made her skin crawl.

"I don't know. He didn't perform, so I'm not sure what his business was."

She was glad she'd been in the other kingdom when he came. She didn't need him to slip up and ask in front of her family if his balsam worked. She may have failed at her escape, but she would do everything in her power to keep Manny out of Herrick's sights.

"What are you thinking?" Siguard asked.

"About the last time the trickster was here." In her mind, she relived the night she'd purchased the balsam: sneaking out in the dark of night, him mistaking her for Herrick coming for a remade potion.

"It couldn't be," she whispered. Her veins turned to ice. *I was distracted and should have thought more about it. If I missed it, it'll be all my fault.*

"What?"

Gressa glanced at the guards, and Siguard took her cue, asking them to step outside. As he did, his robe shifted and a gold leaf attached to his belt glinted in the firelight.

He's one of them? Then he could be trusted.

"Manny's mother fell ill with the pestilence, but she was the only one. It acted more like a poison than a plague. The trickster sold me a balsam, but when I went to him, his back was turned and he thought I was Herrick. It sounded like he'd sold him a tincture that didn't work. What if he made a poison that would look like the pestilence? What if it was supposed to spread in the south, but it only affected one person?"

Siguard rose and looked out the small window. "That is a serious claim."

"I think Herrick is trying to kill King Simon, maybe even the prince." She stood. "I have to warn them. Tell these men to stand down so I can leave. And I can't be followed." The best thing she could do was get to the meadow.

"Herrick left strict orders for these men. They'll not just let us pass."

"Has the convoy left for South Morlaix, yet?"

He nodded. "I believe so. They planned to sail as soon as the storm passed." He looked out the window. The skies were still dark, but the rain had stopped.

"Maybe there is time yet. Will the knights permit us to go to the dock, if they stand guard?"

"I don't know."

Gressa yanked open the door and a burst of cold air blew back her hair. Immediately, two knights crossed their lances, barring her way.

"I need to speak with Herrick. I have information he wants. I'm ready to give it to him." The men didn't move. "It's about the Dividing Wall." Would Herrick's men know anything about what Herrick wanted from her?

One knight nodded to the other. He set out running while the other blocked her way.

"But I need to see him now. If you make me wait, I won't give him the information. I must tell him before he leaves North Morlaix."

CHAPTER 44

"They're coming here? But why?" Manny was beside himself with worry ever since Gressa had floated away on that rickety boat, a look of severe resignation on her face. Now he faced the sea once more, watching a small Viking long boat bob its way toward the dock. "We should be armed and ready."

Sir Fletcher shook his head. "No, it is not an attack. At least, not one with weapons. Tactical, maybe. We'll have to stay alert. No part of this meeting makes sense. But King Simon is tired. He has never recovered from Queen Margaret's death. His decisions are not always the best." His jaw twitched.

King Simon waited in the great hall. The North Morlaixers would be welcomed with a private banquet and audience with the King. Only a handful of the king's most trusted knights stood guard.

"How many are like you?" Manny asked. He was referring to the leaf pendant he wore around his neck and the matching one the guard at the gate wore on his collar.

"Now is not the time."

The long boat was lashed to the dock. King Jorvik climbed out first. He was an imposing figure. Wide, thick chest, heavily bearded face and with sunbaked leathery skin. Beside him hopped out a knight, possibly another one of his sons. Next came the Panther. There was no mistaking which one he was. Athletic and observant, he had been surveying the land before exiting the vessel. His gaze swept over all the armaments, the position of the guards, and with the movements of his mouth, he looked to be counting to himself the number of boats docked at South Morlaix. Sir Fletcher was stiff, expressionless, but watchful. He and the Panther had already met eyes and summed each other up.

If King Jorvik was disappointed King Simon was not there to greet him, he didn't show it. He smiled heartily as if he were here on parade, or greeting his future subjects. Well, he would have to try harder than that to win over the people of South Morlaix who loved their own king, apart from the business with the Dividing Wall, and did not trust these North Morlaixers any more than they could spit into the strong sea wind and not get wet.

Sir Fletcher led King Jorvik alone into the library where King Simon sat waiting by the fire. Manny would have liked to witness the meeting of old friends, now sworn enemies. Would they shake hands? Smile? Fight?

They remained secluded for over an hour, Sir Fletcher guarding the door and the Panther sitting with his boots on the king's table in the great hall, which had been decked out with fruit and cheese and rolls. He stared down each knight one at a time, like he had measured them and found them wanting. At Nigel, he laughed, causing the young prince to break out in a sweat.

When he came to Manny, he stared longer than most. Manny held his gaze, channeling all his anger and possessive feelings about Gressa toward her tormentor. The Panther's expression turned quizzical. He waved Manny over to him.

Manny looked at Sir Fletcher. Sir Fletcher shrugged and nodded at the same time.

In order to appear strong and confident, Manny stood tall and walked purposefully over to the Panther. His resolve weakened and he burst out, "What is your business here?"

The Panther chuckled. He tossed a baked roll from hand to hand. "Who are you to the pretender king of South Morlaix?"

Manny was taken aback. What kind of question was this?

He hardened his face to look more knightly. "I am a squire. One day I will defend my king in battle."

"And who is your family that you take on position of squire?"

Manny's stomach tightened. Something about this line of questioning bothered him. He thought back to his trip with Sir Fletcher into the hinterlands when they were ambushed. "My father is the greatest tailor in the land."

The Panther's mouth twitched. "So, I hear." He sat up, his leather boots hitting the floor with a deep thud. "But what I can't figure out is why the king cares enough about a whelp such as yourself, enough to sponsor your career. And my sister? You have caused her a great deal of pain."

Manny lunged forward to strike at his taunter. The Panther, showing more quickness than Manny expected, stood and had Manny's head pressed against the table and a knife at his throat before Sir Fletcher could react.

"Know thy enemy," hissed the Panther, glancing up at Sir Fletcher, who was advancing with drawn sword. With one last shove, the Panther released Manny.

As Manny got to his feet, the two kings swept into the room. King Jorvik nodded to the Panther, and they said their goodbyes before King Simon directed Sir Fletcher and Manny to escort their guests to the docks.

Sir Fletcher silently led the way until the three North Morlaixers were back on their ship and paddling to deeper waters. He and Manny stood as unmoving sentries, watching the long boat dip and rise on the waves.

As they watched, another figure rose in the boat. Manny squinted. A rough, lopsided hat. "Hoxham." He turned to Sir Fletcher. "He's gotten away!"

"He only thinks he has. If the Panther didn't invite him, life won't go well for him."

After the boat had gone around the bend, Sir Fletcher said, "What was that between you and the Panther?"

Manny shrugged. "I don't know. He suspects me of something. Or some connection to the king."

"Do you have a connection?"

"Not a one. Other than we have always tailored the royal clothing."

Sir Fletcher stared at Manny. Then, without another word, led the way back to the castle. The king was going to make an announcement.

CHAPTER 45

"*I*t's too late, sister." Herrick brushed past Gressa, wiping the rain off his leather-clad shoulders.

"What do you mean? What have you done?" She followed him from her shelter underneath a dripping roof in the marketplace, the closest to the port any of her brothers would let her wait. She'd finally been released from Siguard's rooms after they had returned from the south, and it worried her. She'd twisted her apron in knots as she'd waited, wondering why she had been let go. Herrick would never give her her freedom unless he didn't need her anymore. And if he didn't need her anymore...

"Me? Nothing. It's father who's done it." He walked on in the direction of the aviary with nary a glance behind her.

Gressa's stomach churned. Siguard was right. Herrick had done something. He was smiling when he looked at her. *Smiling*.

"'S'cuse, princess?" said a voice from inside the window of the shop where Gressa was huddled.

"Yes?" Gressa turned to find the potter woman watching her.

The potter woman curtsied. "Are you all right, princess?"

Gressa sighed and forced a smile. "Yes, mistress. How is your hand?"

"Good as new." She held it up for Gressa's inspection. "And so will our kingdom be one day. Chin up." She backed out of the window and boarded it up to the rain.

Oh, the dear people of Morlaix. What has Herrick done to them now?

She ran to the keep to see her father. But when Gressa arrived, only her mother was to be found, talking earnestly with the cook. As soon as she saw Gressa, she beamed at her daughter, dismissing the cook with a wave.

"Gressa, darling, we have good news!" Ingrid clasped Gressa's hands. "Your father has secured your future. There is to be a united tournament with South Morlaix, and afterwards, you are to be wed."

Gressa skimmed right over the shocking news of a united tournament to the news that affected her directly. "Wed? To whom?"

She pictured the leering Viking. That would make Herrick glad, indeed, to see her suffer so.

"To the prince of South Morlaix. I believe his name is Nigel or some such." She waved her hand like his name was inconsequential. "He's not like us. Not the least bit a Viking. Not very bold, or..." Ingrid blushed. "With your strong will and Viking blood, you will be ruling as queen, no doubt, with a king on your arm for decoration." She bustled around the room folding linens. "I don't know why we hadn't thought of it sooner. Your father and I used to be..." She paused again, leaving her thought unfinished. "Gressa? Are you ill?"

Gressa had stopped listening at the name Nigel and had slowly sunk to the floor. She was neither happy nor sad. Indifferent, much like the prince was. Her thoughts quickly turned to Manny. He had implored her not to marry. Not to marry the Viking and move away? What would he think of her marrying Nigel and living in his kingdom?

But to have a hand in unifying the kingdom, or at least bringing peace, how could she refuse?

"What does Herrick say of this?" she asked her mother.

Ingrid's hands paused for a second. "It was his idea."

Gressa blanched. This made no sense. No sense whatsoever. *Herrick has spent my whole life making sure I didn't marry the prince next door.*

Mother turned away and continued fussing with the linens. The words tumbled out of her in excitement. "A united tournament. Never thought I'd see the day. I didn't live here back then, but they were famous. The whole world will come to see the tournament. Everyone will want to watch to see if we get along." She huffed. "Of course, we'll get along. I was worried your brother might not come around, but he's maturing quite nicely to suggest such a thing. And your father, I think underneath, he's missed his best friend and rival. It's not as much fun to gloat when you've got no one to gloat in front of."

Mother had never spoken in such a torrent of words before.

"Mother, look at me." Gressa pulled onto her mother's arm until she turned and met eyes with her. "Why does this arrangement seem so off?"

She shook her head and patted Gressa's hands. "Never mind me. I never was one to get so emotional. Must be getting old. And you're my only girl." She dabbed at the corner of her eye. "I want you to be close."

"Do *you* want me to wed Nigel?" After all these years of keeping her and the southern prince apart, they were making it happen.

Ingrid stopped her twittering. She nodded. "I think it's best. You saw the other choice Herrick had for you. A man only concerned with satisfying his appetites. You would only be a possession to him, not a companion."

"I would be a companion to Nigel?"

"I don't know. At least there's a possibility."

Gressa chewed her lip. Her strong mother only pretended to be strong. She could be as physical as the boys, but when it came to courage, she was lacking. A mother should fight for her daughter, not hand her over to an uncertain future she does not want.

"It is the best you will get," Mother said.

Gressa searched her mind for any reason why anyone had agreed to this. "Will it reunite the kingdom? And if so, where does that leave Herrick?"

Ingrid began her fussing again. "Not exactly unite, but maybe we could open up the wall for trade." She waved her hand as if it was of no consequence either way. "I don't know the details. You'll have to ask your father when he returns. He's gone north."

"Again? Without seeing me first? I thought he was worried about me."

Ingrid patted Gressa's arm. "He was, dear. But you're safe now."

Flustered, Gressa asked, "When will he be home?"

"In time for your wedding."

CHAPTER 46

*S*ir Fletcher found Manny out behind the stables, chopping wood with a vengeance.

"Does building blisters on your fingers make you feel better?" asked Sir Fletcher.

Manny scowled and swung the ax again, deep into an uncut log. Chips flew and landed in the rapidly growing pile surrounding the chopping stump and his feet.

"Yes. Makes. Me. Feel. Wonderful," he replied between breaths. He'd been at the chopping for nigh an hour, but being winded and with sore hands were the least of his troubles.

"You know this isn't your job. You wouldn't want Charlie the Cutter to get boxed for slacking off, would you?

Clink. Clink. Clink. Thump.

At last, Manny sat down on the log pile. No, he didn't want to interfere with Charlie's job, he only needed something physical to do. Something to keep him from scaling the wall barehanded in an ill-conceived attempt to rescue Gressa.

He pulled out his handkerchief to wipe the sweat dripping into his eyes. "What do you make of the news?" he asked. But before Sir Fletcher could answer, Manny stood and paced in a circle. "The Panther would never allow it unless he had another plan. And if he has another plan, what can it be? And will Gressa be safe?"

"What about Nigel?" Sir Fletcher crossed his arms and looked down at Manny.

"What? Oh, bah. His future has already been decided as long as the Panther is alive."

"As a future knight, you might want to change your opinion. After all, your future is linked closely to the prince's."

"I know it. Especially if he marries Gressa. I fear for both their lives from the moment they are wed. The Panther won't let their union stand. He can't."

"I don't know what to make of it either. The king isn't talking to me. He's shut himself up in his chambers and won't let anyone in. It's not like him at all."

"So, what do we do?"

"Wait for the Panther to make his move."

Manny kicked at the wood chinks. Seems like that's what the entirety of South Morlaix had been doing for all of his life. They trained and waited. The more they waited, the more tentative and weak they became.

But it was the southern prince who made the first move. He came to Manny in the middle of the night.

"Psst." Nigel called through the window of the bunkhouse near Manny's bed. "Manny, you awake?"

He was, staring at the dark ceiling, trying to decipher the Panther's motives and figure out what the grand scheme was.

"Come with me," whispered Nigel in his loud, not a whisper voice.

Manny slipped past his sleeping bunk-mates, who'd all gone down fast and heavy. Outside, the half-moon barely lit the court-yard. Nigel, probably assuming Manny would obey him, was already halfway to the castle. Manny shook his head and followed.

It was strange to march right into the castle knowing everyone else was asleep. His steps were loud against the stone walls even though he was trying to be quiet.

Where was Nigel taking him and why? Manny wished he'd taken the time to dress and add a weapon or two to his person. Sir Fletcher's voice rang in his ear. *A knight is prepared.* Well, not always. And he wasn't a knight yet, anyway.

Nigel led the way to his personal rooms in the castle and indicated Manny should take one of the plush chairs near the empty fireplace. Manny couldn't help a pang of jealousy as he settled into the comfortable chair. It was like sitting in a cloud. He imagined this room in the winter with that fire blazing. The prince probably never slept a cold night in his life.

"Tell me about her," Nigel said.

Manny squirmed. He knew Nigel was asking about Gressa, but how could he answer such a question? He didn't want Nigel to know anything personal about her. He wanted Nigel to refuse to marry her. He could lie and tell him she was a contentious, whiny girl who was only interested in arguing with everyone.

"What do you want to know?" He hedged. "She's the tower princess."

"What is she like? Is she pretty? Does she have a nice voice?"

Manny's mouth went dry. Did they really have to talk about this? Besides, "pretty" wasn't exactly the right word for Gressa. He didn't have the words to describe her. She was like a sunrise casting her glow over the world. She was the ocean meeting the shore. He examined his fingernails. The kind of girl who made a squire think of poetry instead of archery practice. She was exactly who she should be and she should be left alone.

"Awk, I shouldn't have asked you." Nigel placed one hand above the fireplace and leaned in, as if staring into an imaginary fire. "It's just you're the only one who's talked to her. Is she nice at least? I mean, it won't be terrible to be married to her, would it?" He turned and looked earnestly at Manny.

He was worried that *she* would be a poor mate?

"No. No, it won't be terrible to be married to her." His voice probably betrayed his true feelings for her, but Nigel didn't seem to notice. *For you, at least. You could do no better. It'll be terrible for me. I'll have to leave South Morlaix for good. I couldn't bear it. I can't bear this conversation.*

"It's just. I've always wondered. Her being on the other side of the wall. The closest princess to our kingdom. It seems like destiny, don't you think?"

Manny dug his fingernails into his arms. It never bothered him before that Nigel had a crush on the unseen princess.

"But with the tourney and everything, there's been a lot of lords and ladies and their daughters arriving, and I've been thinking."

What's this? Manny rested his hands on the leather arm rests. "Yes?"

"There are many more kingdoms outside of ours. We're isolated on this island, but there are other alliances that could help us with our Panther problem."

"You're worried the marriage won't bring peace to our two kingdoms?"

Nigel held Manny's gaze, and for the first time, Manny saw a glimmer of understanding in the prince's eyes. Perhaps Nigel did know how precarious his life was. All this time, his behavior could have been an act to hide how scared he really was. How would Manny have grown up if he had known all the ruckus over the wall was centered on killing him?

"What does it matter, anyway? I don't get a choice."

"But if you had a choice?"

Nigel shook his head. "You think I've got it all, being the prince and living in this castle, don't you? Never mind." He straightened and looked around. "It's not a bad life. I'm sure we'll make it work. As long as she does what I say, we won't have any problems."

Manny balled his fists. Maybe he was giving Nigel too much credit.

CHAPTER 47

Gressa sat on the floor of her bedroom with Old Anne at her side. Her dowry chest, a cedar box bound by thick leather belts, was open in front of her, and the two of them were rifling through it to see what she had and what she still needed. The trousseau was complete and overflowing, as the years of confinement had given her and Old Anne plenty of time for sewing her linens.

"Let me see your hands again," said Gressa.

Old Anne continued folding bed sheets. "T'will do you no good to dwell on the past."

Gressa frowned. "I'm so sorry Herrick locked you in the dungeon. He only did it to get back at me."

"I knew the dungeon would be my fate if I helped you escape. I may not agree with much your brother does, but on this account, he was within his rights."

Gressa reached for the vial of balsam to rub into Old Anne's chaffed skin. The marks where the shackles held her were red and blistering, and Gressa took great care to be tender as she applied the balsam. "Is that why Abigail knew to send this healing salve with me?"

"My sister is a wise one."

"I cannot place the smell. It's got a hint of peppermint, but underneath there is something else. Do you know what it is?"

Old Anne smiled. "The tiniest bit of rowan oil. My sister has always been careful with her rations. She honors me with this gift."

"Rowan oil, truly?" Gressa smelled again. "It's familiar. Though I've never smelled rowan oil, I know this scent." Somehow it reminded her of Manny. Did he smell like rowan oil?

Manny. What must he think of her engagement? She needed to explain to him why she agreed. It wasn't because she didn't care for him. But how could he understand that? He hadn't grown up knowing he would one day be part of a kingdom alliance. Not a girl, but a princess. The role took precedence over the heart. They could have never been together, but she would always treasure the memory. Now she had to grow into her role and serve the kingdom as best she could.

Gressa returned a stack of bedclothes to the chest, nestling them next to the clay crocks from the woman she'd met at the marketplace so many months ago now. "Do you think we will live in the castle, or do you think we will move away to a manor house somewhere in the kingdom?"

"I think it best if you can stay within the castle keep." Old Anne added Gressa's jewelry box and the wimple she would wear to cover her hair once she was married. Then she added more figures on her parchment.

"How many are like you in North Morlaix?" Gressa stopped her packing and tilted her head to examine her nursemaid.

"What do you mean?"

"You know," said Gressa, not wanting to say it out loud. "Remember, the walls have ears?"

Old Anne looked about the room. "Yes. Simply take comfort knowing you are not alone. No matter where you live, you'll be protected as best we can."

Gressa leaned in close to Old Anne, so close she could smell traces of the dungeon filth still clinging to her hair. "What do you think is coming? What is Herrick planning?"

"No one knows. None of us expected this." Old Anne waved at the stack of items waiting to go into the chest, the beginnings of wedding preparations. "Did you know the knights—from both sides—have been ordered to tear down a portion of the Dividing Wall near the old tournament grounds? There is to be a joint tournament this year."

Gressa gasped. "I knew about the tournament, but to tear down the wall? How can that be? The peace treaty forbids it."

"The joint tournament is an act of peace. Everyone who has read the treaty agrees that an event such as this is allowed. They will simply rebuild it when the tournament is over." Her eyes shone. "If the wall will allow itself to be torn down, we will all have seven days to see our loved ones."

"You'll see Abigail again. Would you want to stay with her in South Morlaix? Will that be allowed?"

"After the seven days, I suppose we'll all have to be back on our proper sides, or be forced back like you were. We'll take every allowance made."

"But if I'm moving there, wouldn't you come with me?"

She frowned and thought a minute. "You'll be married. I don't think we could make a case for you needing a nursemaid."

"When I have children of my own, wouldn't my parents want a North Morlaixan nursemaid to watch over them and teach them our ways?"

Old Anne's eyes softened. "We could hope. I'll be good for rocking babies. But you'll need a younger nursemaid who can keep up with little feet. Does this mean you're warming up toward the union?"

"I've no choice, do I? I have to hope that Nigel isn't as bad as I think he is."

"We are both full of hopes today, are we not?"

Gressa didn't answer. None of this made any sense. Was Herrick faking peace in order to take over? And what about the trickster? If not a poison to kill King Simon, what did Herrick get from him? And why rebuild the wall again if there is true peace— why not allow free passage between the kingdoms? Gressa rubbed the back of her neck. Her head hurt thinking of all the possibilities. She needed to get Manny's opinions. She needed to know what they were saying in South Morlaix.

hey started tearing down the wall early in the morning, before the moon had left the sky. Torches were set up on both sides, creating an eerie flickering glow on the stone. The North Morlaixers had already begun. The loud scraping and chipping of stone and mortar split the air while muffled voices filled the cracks from the other side. Manny pressed his ear up against the wall but couldn't make out any distinct voices. He didn't like what was happening today. It didn't feel right.

"Report!" commanded Sir Fletcher to one of the wall guards standing in a turret atop the wall. The turrets were evenly spaced along the wall, with every second one belonging to South Morlaix, the others, to North Morlaix.

"The wall is crumbling easily. I've witnessed the North taking stabs at the wall a'fore. They couldna' even leave a mark." He looked over the wall again to assess their progress then turned back to Sir Fletcher. "You best get started or they'll do all the work. Don't know what's changed." The guard spit over the edge, on the North Morlaix side.

Sir Fletcher nodded to his men, and they swung their clubs at the six-foot-thick, eighteen-foot-high wall. The demolition could have gone faster if the men hadn't also carried their weapons.

Sir Fletcher had every man alert: ready to fight if this was all a trick, a way to breach the wall voluntarily. South Morlaix's wall-man had confirmed that the men on the other side also had their weapons ready. Since they would know the south's wall-man could see their weapons, an ambush was unlikely. Could it be that the men in the North were just as suspicious as those in the South?

The work was difficult, and Manny welcomed the strain on his shoulders, the sweat beading his forehead. There was no lack of volunteers, as this was the most exciting event since the wall went up and everyone wanted a part in it. They took turns striking the wall and removing rock. The local justice stood watch over the pieces of wall to make sure all the pieces were accounted for. When the tournament was over, they'd need to repair the wall, and Sir Fletcher had no patience to chase down token pieces carted off in pockets and under hats.

Later that morning, as the sun poured its light on the wall, villagers began to line up and watch. They were curious, nervous, and anxious. They stood well back of the knights, giving themselves plenty of room to run if the North Morlaixers should attack.

At last it happened.

A pick ax from the other side protruded through the wall, its silver tip glinting in the sun and sending dried mud and small stones trickling down the wall. Everyone was silent. The knights stopped their work and stared at this foreign object sticking through their wall, its shaft being held by an enemy knight on the other side.

The North Morlaixers were also silent, recognizing what had just happened.

The townspeople stood agape.

Manny lowered his ax and waved at the swarm of gnats in front of his face. Truly, the wall was coming down. He looked around to see if there were any repercussions. No trumpet shout from an invading army. No heavy storm rolling in from the sea.

Simply, the scraping of the ax returning to its side of the wall. And then a hole. A small shaft of light shining through.

Manny couldn't help himself. He rushed forward and looked into the gap. Another eyeball stared back at him. They both jerked back in surprise. Then there was a loud cheer rising up on both sides of the wall. An ease of tension.

The townspeople craned their necks to get a better look. Everyone wanted to be the next to catch a glimpse of the other side. Slowly, inch by inch, then faster, block by block, the opening grew larger. Enemy hands now worked side by side. Eyes stared into eyes.

When at last there was a hole large enough for a single man to walk through, Sir Fletcher stood in the way and stared at the man across from him. It was the Panther. He was smiling.

Sir Fletcher gripped his dagger. A vein on his neck stood out as he clenched his jaw. "Here is your hole," he said.

"Excellent," answered the Panther. He boldly stepped through it and surveyed South Morlaix. His eyes roamed over the villagers and came back to land on Manny. "Care to see my side, Sir Fletcher?" he asked, his eyes not leaving Manny.

Sweat dripped down the back of Manny's neck and trailed between his shoulder blades. He struggled to maintain eye contact with the Panther. He would not be the first to look away.

With a smirk, the Panther turned and led Sir Fletcher through the small tunnel in the wall. Sir Fletcher came back moments later and signaled for the hole to be made wider. "It must be large enough for the horses."

Work on both sides resumed until they'd carved out an archway large enough to accommodate two chargers with mounted knights riding side by side. The knights tried to keep the townspeople from entering, but the pressure and excitement was too much. Finally, the knights stood back and allowed citizens of north and south to step across into each other's kingdoms. They passed each other through the tunnel, suspicious eyes, which quickly darted to take in their respective forbidden lands.

Manny remained on his own side. His curiosity with the north didn't hold as much sway without the hope of Gressa in it.

He still struggled to make sense of it all. For the first time since the kingdom was divided, the tournament would be held in the Morlaix tournament grounds. On the North's side. Just what did King Simon give up for this honor?

CHAPTER 49

*G*ressa paced in her tower room, her brows knit together in consternation. She didn't know what to make of what she had seen. Using her spy glasses, she had looked through the crumbled portion of her wall and seen the people of South Morlaix constructing a new wall within their castle grounds. The new wall was a mere two feet back from the current wall. Now, why would they be doing such an odd thing?

Her brother Axell had told her not five minutes ago that the wall near the tournament grounds had been hollowed out into a tunnel to allow the people of the South to attend the festivities. Why tear down one part of a wall and at the same time build a new one further along the same wall?

Herrick was at the root of it, of course. He had never been so happy in his life as he had been these last few days, taking all the praise for the joint tournament. If he had been any other of her brothers, she would want to share in their joy.

Axell, for example, was obviously happy in love. His head was so high in the clouds for his young maiden that he didn't listen to Gressa with his usual attentiveness.

"Have you ever noticed how clouds form shapes?" he asked her one day when he joined her in her garden. She wanted to show him how well she'd taken care of the plants he'd sent her, but all he wanted to do was lay on the grass and talk about his love. "Look, that one is like the building in Copello where we met."

Of all the times for Axell to fall in love. He assumed everyone was as happy as he was, so Herrick's odd behavior wasn't setting off alarms for him. It was a hard thing to put into words that it wasn't right Herrick was so happy.

Old Anne came into the room holding a new emerald-green dress in her arms from the tailor shop in South Morlaix. "It's time for you to get ready for tonight's banquet."

Gressa rushed to the window and pointed with her spy glasses. "They are building a new wall over there. Look!"

Old Anne set the gown on the bed before taking the glasses and seeing for herself. "I don't know what to make of it, princess." She turned her back to the window. "Perhaps tonight I'll see my sister and she will have answers."

And maybe I could talk to Manny. He would know why they're building a new wall.

Gressa allowed Old Anne to fix her hair for the evening. The tournament games were to begin the next morning, but that evening a great banquet was being held in the smaller meadow of South Morlaix. Only royalty and the competing knights and the appropriate servants would be present.

"This is the traditional style," Old Anne said as she twisted and tucked Gressa's hair. "The way we girls used to do our hair when we were part of one kingdom."

"So, I'll not only be making my debut at this tournament, but I'll be making a statement?"

"Only if you want to. I can style your hair in the usual way."

"I'd like to see the traditional way."

"As you wish."

The tugging and twisting continued. "Will I have to sit beside him?" Gressa asked. Her fingers trembled as she adjusted her skirts.

"I don't know. At some point, you'll have to."

Gressa pressed her lips together. "Maybe he will know the secret of the new wall."

∼

GRESSA DIDN'T HAVE to sit beside Nigel. The two kings were placed side by side, along with Ingrid, followed by the children arranged oldest to youngest. That left Gressa at the far end of the table with no one to talk to, since her brothers were all engrossed in a heated debate about where the best land would be for Axell to build his estate. They were all dividing up the lands according to the way they wanted. Did they learn nothing from what happened to the kingdom because of their father's quarrel with Simon?

To steal a glance at her betrothed, Gressa would have to lean too far forward and risk calling attention to herself. All day she had been so distracted by the strange wall going up that she hadn't had time to fret over her impending marriage. Now, alone at the end of the table, it was all she could think about. She absentmindedly watched the cupbearers taste the ale and sample the food set before the kings while imagining what life would be like with Nigel.

"A toast," said Herrick, standing and raising his silver goblet high in the air toward the two kings. "To old friendships. And new alliances."

The crowd hesitantly copied the toast, "Old friendships."

Herrick stood a second too long as he watched everyone drink to the toast. Gressa narrowed her eyes. What was he up to? When Herrick saw her watching him, he simply raised his goblet at her and sat down.

He did nothing unusual the entire night. Not once did he try to sneak away. Not once did he speak to anyone other than those at the high table. Not once did he arouse suspicion of any sort.

It was a strange night that had Gressa looking forward to its ending. For a banquet, the fellowship had been rather subdued.

No one was really talking. It was awkwardness all around and she felt like a statue at the end of the table.

She kept an eye out for Manny, but he was mysteriously missing, as was Sir Fletcher. Seeing Manny would have calmed her nerves. One thing made the night worthwhile, though. There, hovering near the shadows, were Old Anne and Abigail, deep in conversation, the food in front of them untouched. Abigail must have found a reason to be in the gathering. Such a clever woman would have news to pass on to Old Anne. If they put all their suspicions together, they might figure out what Herrick was up to.

CHAPTER 50

*T*he tournament had already seen sixteen jousts, and it was now time for Manny to help Sir Fletcher prepare for his first. South Morlaix was holding its own, not winning, but not dragging bottom either. Having never directly competed with the North, they were glad to have won some rounds. But the more experienced knights were getting ready to joust now, the king's sons among them.

Mindlessly, Manny set the plating over the gambeson padding. "Will you be fighting the Panther?" he asked.

"Not this first round, but I suspect it will be he and I in the end."

"What if…"

"Let's not dwell. My men are prepared. I have them stationed atop the wall and in strategic locations both on the tournament grounds and on our lands." Sir Fletcher motioned to their locations with a flick of his gaze. "If there is an attack, I believe we can hold them off. My only concern is that some of our people will be left in North Morlaix should we suddenly need to close off the tunnel in the wall." He nodded toward the piles of rock atop the Dividing Wall.

"There are enough foreigners here to stand as impartial

witnesses," said Manny. He helped the knight mount his horse. "Copello wouldn't be able to block our citizens from boarding ships to return home."

"No, but our people could be prevented from leaving in the first place. That's what the kings did when the kingdom was first divided."

"And why your mother and aunt were separated."

"Aunt Anne didn't have the funds to pay to be smuggled back across, and when we'd saved up enough for her, she'd found a new purpose and chose to stay."

"I'm glad she did."

Sir Fletcher snorted. "It's time to let that girl out of your mind. You had a fun season together, but your paths—never meant to cross—are diverging. The town is flooded with maidens come to watch the jousting. Take your pick."

But their paths did cross, and there had to be meaning in that. The walls opened up for them. No one else. Manny and Gressa could have simply been the catalyst for getting the kings to talk again, but his gut told him not to take his pick from among the other maidens. Not until Gressa was out of reach would he stop waiting.

Manny handed over the shield, and when Sir Fletcher bent close, he said quietly, "Have you noticed the knights from Copello pulling back when they could win their matches?"

He admitted he hadn't. His attention had been elsewhere.

"I may be imagining things, but one of the elder princes has been training in Copello. I wonder if he's been making deals over there. Get friendly with their squires. See what you can learn."

Manny smirked. "Permission to complain about you to them? A little bit of gossip loosens tongues."

"Fine. My reputation is untarnished. They won't believe you, anyway. Think you are a lazy sot instead."

Manny carried Sir Fletcher's lance out onto the field. When Sir Fletcher, atop his horse, trotted over to receive favor ribbons from the young women in the crowd, Manny watched the royal tent.

Gressa was sitting beside Nigel and there was a goodly space between them.

He said something, and she laughed. *Laughed.* Manny's stomach churned with jealousy, a terrible feeling when he had no claim on her. She didn't look at him once. He thought she might have at least liked him, even if they could never marry. But Nigel? Anyone but Nigel. It would be so much better if she were married to some far away duke so he didn't have to watch. There they sat in their royal garb, created in his father's shop. The privileges of royalty had never really bothered Manny before, not the way it bothered Hoxham, but today it was a pebble in his shoe.

The joust was over before Manny even realized it had started. Sir Fletcher's horse strutted by, bumping Manny in the shoulder.

"A knight is ever vigilant. He doesn't let the look of a lady distract him from the battle field." Sir Fletcher handed Manny his lance. "You didn't even see me take down one of those middle sons, did you?"

When Sir Fletcher's rounds were over, victorious in all of them, Manny stored his equipment, then wandered until he found a group of Copello squires. When he got close, they closed ranks. He was never any good at this. What would Hoxham do to wheedle his way in?

"Anyone for an arm wrestle?" He held up two coins from his pocket.

The tallest lad turned and grinned. "I'll take you on."

Manny sized him up and figured he could win. The quiet one sizing him up, on the other hand, would probably take all his money. So much for the sweets he'd planned to buy later.

A table was quickly found, and the two sat across from each other. Manny's arms were shorter, but these eager squires from Copello didn't know how strong his hands were. Few survived his grip for long. They had to pin him fast, or have the blood squeezed out of their fingers.

A third squire held their clasped hand, then lifted his hand off. "Go!"

A surprising pounding on the table ensued by the onlookers with their fists. A Copello tradition? They were a rowdy bunch, was all Manny was able to think before testing his opponent's mettle and realizing his initial assessment was correct. He could beat this opponent, and realized they were probably using this match to test his level.

"Have you been to the tournament here before?" He matched the force his opponent was exerting.

"Every year since I was old enough. You're from South Morlaix, eh? Aren't you afraid they'll kill you over here?"

"You know something I don't?" Manny applied enough pressure to tilt the angle to his advantage.

"There's talk."

"Oh yeah? What kind of talk?" Manny could end the contest here, but he held back, letting the squire think he was distracting him with his talk.

"The Panther has been trying to talk us into starting a war."

The rumors were partially true. It wasn't South Morlaix the Panther was riling up, but Copello.

"That mean you are here to start something?" Manny applied more pressure.

One of the squires watching laughed. "Are you joking? No other kingdom will come near here. A magic wall guarded by a mad fairy creature?" He shook his head. "We'll leave it to your people to figure out."

Manny could sense no guile in the answer, nor in the agreeing nods of the others, so he pressed hard and won the arm wrestle. The squire across from him flexed his hand.

"Quite a grip you've got there," he said.

Manny grinned. "Next?" he said. He was feeling generous now that he knew Copello had not taken the Panther's side. A few more pointed questions, and then he'd report back to Sir Fletcher.

CHAPTER 51

*A*t the second banquet, Gressa sat beside Nigel. No official announcement regarding their engagement had been made, and no one had told her when that would happen. So, there she dined in another of Manny's father's magnificent gowns, waiting to hear her future announced.

During the day, she had visited in the king's tent and questioned Nigel about the new wall. He didn't know why it was being built, just that King Simon had commanded it.

She also tested out what life would be like when she was married to him. She was pleasantly surprised that his table manners were impeccable, especially compared to Ulf's. However, he turned out to be painfully shy, and he lacked the sparkle that Manny had, although occasionally he could be funny.

When he did talk, he talked mostly about food production. He would make an excellent farmer if he weren't a prince. He gave her helpful tips on how to keep her herbs alive, and if that was what married life would be like, Gressa supposed her mother was right: there could be worse.

Her father stood to give another speech. When he rose, he wavered, as if rising too quickly. He grabbed onto the table with one hand before composing himself and continuing.

"There was a time when we were a united people. My child-hood companion Simon and I are glad to reunite once again in friendship and mutual interests. May this tournament be the first of many alliances." He glanced at Gressa before raising his goblet in a toast. "In fact, there is one such alliance it is time to tell you about." He forced a laugh.

Gressa's heart skipped a beat. This was it. But how did Father feel about it? He looked uneasy. She tried to catch her mother's eye, but her gaze was fixed on Father. Siguard? Axell? This didn't feel right.

"My daughter, Gressa, our precious pearl, has been pledged in matrimony to the prince of South Morlaix."

A stunned silence followed by cheers rose up from the crowd. Gressa smiled as was expected of her, and stole a glance at Nigel. He, too, was behaving in the expected way. He nodded at the people, waving his hand.

"They shall be married on the last day of the tournament, and you are all invited to celebrate with us."

At the end of the speech, Father's face grew pale and he fumbled getting back into his chair. Was he sorry for making the announcement? Even more puzzling was when he retired for the night shortly thereafter. He loved the circus, but the night's enter-tainment was still setting up their rings when he excused himself.

King Simon was not far behind, retiring to his own side of the kingdom.

Gressa watched him skirt around the juggler where Manny and Sir Fletcher were standing sentry. They turned to follow King Simon across to their side of the wall.

Gressa scrambled after him, not caring if Nigel was bothered by her sudden departure. "Manny, wait!"

Sir Fletcher nodded and continued after the king while Manny stood, staring somewhere over Gressa's head.

"I can't believe this is the first I've seen you. Even when Sir Fletcher was on the tournament green I didn't see you," she said.

"I was there. You must have been occupied."

Gressa noted Manny's coolness. Of course. The formal announcement had been given. But couldn't he, as her friend, be supportive? He had to know this wasn't what she wanted, exactly.

She slipped into her princess role, speaking more formally. "You and Sir Fletcher noticed the kings depart?"

"Yes, that is our job. We protect our king."

A spark lit within her. "I know what a knight does. I only want to know if you had any opinions as to why both our kings have retired early."

Manny gave her a hard look. "I would ask your brother."

Gressa had never felt defensive about her brother before, but she did now. "Why does everyone blame Herrick for every little thing that goes wrong in these kingdoms? I've been watching him and he has done nothing amiss."

Old Anne and Abigail walked by, arm in arm, whispering more tales. Gressa pointed them out. "He's made a way for families to reunite. For the shared tournament to take place." She faltered before pressing on. "And he's even made a better match for me than he had originally planned."

Manny bristled at this last comment. He bowed slightly. "That is a beautiful dress you are wearing. Good-eve, princess." Then he turned and strode off into the darkness.

Gressa's face burned. He complimented her on the dress his father had made for her, and then dismissed her. She was the princess. She was supposed to do the dismissing. She stopped herself. Why was she feeling this way? She never cared for protocol. But for Manny, she did care.

The Dividing Wall may be down, but Manny had put up his own walls. Of course, they should all still be suspicious of Herrick. Gressa, being optimistic, had focused on the good changes Herrick had made. She had been watching him, and he had been good. Too good. What was she missing?

Siguard had said the Trickster returned, and he always meant trouble. But when Herrick came from South Morlaix with the announcement of her betrothal, she had lost thought of him purchasing a poison. The look of the kings tonight brought it all back up again. Clearly, Herrick hadn't poisoned King Simon and Nigel at their first meeting, but what if he was doing so now? Now that he had easier access to them.

The food and drink were flowing freely at the banquets. Lots of people had a hand in the preparation and serving. It wouldn't be so obvious for Herrick to poison them now.

She should have told Axell her suspicions instead of Siguard. He would have searched Herrick's rooms, questioned him even.

She sought out the food tasters. If Herrick managed to poison the food or drink, they would be sick as well. A slow-acting poison.

"Old Anne! Abigail!" The townspeople moved aside as she rushed toward the sisters. "Do you know where the food tasters are?"

"There you are, child!" Old Anne hugged her sister before taking Gressa's elbow and leading her back to the North side. "I've just learned there is a new outbreak of the pestilence. We must get back to your quarters at once."

CHAPTER 52

King Simon was ill. Very ill. The prognosis was grim as the pestilence was working more rapidly than it had affected Manny's mother.

Manny paced outside the king's chamber with Nigel while Sir Fletcher sat with the doctor inside the king's chambers. He had a hard time looking at Nigel because every time he looked at him, he thought of Gressa and her laughing at something the prince had said. Manny didn't want to admit that Nigel had been improving as a human being as of late. He wasn't so sniveley and not completely selfish anymore.

"I'm sorry about your father," Manny said, meaning it. After witnessing his mother's pain, he knew what Nigel would be going through.

Nigel cleared his throat. His face was pale. Deathly so.

"Do you know what this business with the wall in the court-yard is about?" Manny had noticed the strange construction on his way into the castle. He and Sir Fletcher had been outside the castle walls on tournament business and had missed this oddity being built. He was concerned about his access to the meadow.

"Oh, that." Nigel waved his hand like it was inconsequential. "Father agreed to a reshaping of the wall boundaries. When the tournament hole is filled in, we will have extra footage for our meadow by pushing back the wall at that location. The North wanted more land within their castle walls. It was an exchange."

Manny didn't like what he was hearing. More of Herrick's machinations.

"Why did they want more land at this particular location? Didn't the king think it a strange request?"

Nigel drew himself taller. "They needed more room, and I secured the hand of the princess in the bargain. I'd say we came out ahead."

If Nigel thought being married to Gressa would extend his life, he was in for a surprise. On the one hand, he could give Nigel credit for thinking things through. However, he was still piddly Nigel if he believed a marriage would save him from the Panther. It would only bring the Panther more opportunity.

Manny chewed his lip to keep from lashing out at the prince. Of all the dim-witted trades to make. As soon as he had checked on the king, Manny planned to check on the meadow, to see if he could still access it.

The door opened, and the doctor left, patting Nigel's arm on the way out.

Manny and Nigel hesitated in the doorway. They could see the king through the anti-chamber. He lay on his four-poster bed, filmy curtains drawn on all sides so only his form could be seen. Sir Fletcher sat in a padded chair by the fireplace and a servant girl was wringing out wet strips of cloth to cool the king's fever.

Sir Fletcher immediately stood and bowed to Nigel. "Your father will not last the night. Are you prepared...to take over the crown?"

Nigel took a step back. With his trembling hand, he rubbed his forehead. "But, the Dividing Wall. It-it's open."

Sir Fletcher examined Nigel.

"The Panther," choked out Nigel in a gasping whisper. He backed away from Sir Fletcher until he was back in the hallway.

Ah, yes. The Panther has access through the wall and there has been no marriage yet. Manny ignored the simpering prince and turned to Sir Fletcher.

"Nigel tells me the Panther traded land, along with the princess's hand in marriage. The new wall is to open up more room on the North's side. We are to get more land in the meadow in exchange."

Sir Fletcher looked confused. "The king has said nothing of this."

"Because he knew you wouldn't approve," explained Nigel. He had slid down the wall and pulled his knees into his chest.

Sir Fletcher groaned. "He doesn't know the significance of this. We should have told him sooner." He signaled for them to enter the room.

"Isn't there a quarantine?" asked Nigel, rising to follow.

"No. The doctor is suspicious as to the source of the illness. It came on too fast to be the great pestilence, so he thinks it's a poison."

Sir Fletcher pulled back the bed curtains and dismissed the maid changing out the hot cloths on the king's forehead. "Sire, can you hear me?"

The king opened his eyes. They were mere slits, as if even the dim candle light hurt him.

"The wall. We mustn't make the trade of land."

King Simon licked his lips, trying to moisten them. "It is done."

"Then un-do it. We have not yet claimed our new land. Authorize me to tear down this new wall and we shall do it tonight. It's a trick by the Panther."

"How could an equal trade of land be a trick?" He fully closed his eyes. His breath was labored.

With a wary glance at Nigel, Sir Fletcher pressed on. "Manny found a hole in the wall within the upper bailey. It doesn't lead to North Morlaix as expected, but to a meadow. We think that is what the Panther wants. Perhaps something in that meadow."

The king forced his eyes open. His fingers, splayed across his belly, twitched toward Manny.

Manny stepped closer so the king could see him.

"What…is…. there?"

"A great meadow. And a tree with a brook running nearby." He left out the part about Gressa's hideaway.

The king closed his eyes again. His breath grew shallower.

"I should get the doctor," said Manny.

Sir Fletcher shook his head. "There is no more help for the king. King Simon has sent the doctor on to help the others who have been affected—the food taster, for one. The doctor is making up a special balsam."

"A balsam!" Why hadn't he thought of it sooner? Gressa had brought him that balsam for his mother and he had returned it to her in the meadow. "Excuse me, sire, but I have some medicine that might work, I'll—"

King Simon reached for Manny's arm and held on weakly. Round marks like those of the pestilence had already begun to form on the king's hand. His eyes opened. "No. There is no time. Death is at my heel. Stay here. Let me say what I should have said years ago."

The king's voice was barely a whisper, and Manny had to bend in close to hear it.

"Is Nigel here?"

Sir Fletcher hefted Nigel up by the arm-pits and hauled him over to the king's bed.

"Innocent boy. Forgive me for giving you burdens that are not yours." The king stopped talking and indicated he needed a drink.

Sir Fletcher held the cup to the king's lips. As he drank, water spilled out the sides of his mouth and spread on the silk pillow, leaving a dark, wet stain.

The king feebly reached for Nigel's hand, but the prince just stared at the sores forming and would not touch it.

"You are not…my flesh and blood son. You were born…to…a

sickly peasant woman. She died not long after coming into the palace. She offered...you to take Manny's place. To protect...my true heir."

Manny and Nigel looked at each other as the truth sunk in. Pauper and prince. Now prince and pauper.

Nigel sprang to life. "I don't have to be king?" The relief coming from him swirled through the room like a cool wind. "It's not me he's gonna kill? It's him?" Nigel pointed a finger at Manny. "You're sure? I'm no blood relation at all?"

King Simon shook his head. "I'm...sorry...both of you."

Nigel wiped his brow. "Thank you, Father. Er. Um. King Simon." Nigel looked ready to sprint out of the room, but he hung back for one more question. "Is there any left of my real family? How do I find them?"

"Ask your nursemaid. 'Twas all her idea."

Nigel nodded and, with one last look at Manny, ran out of the room.

Sir Fletcher, staring after him, said dryly, "He took the news quite well."

Manny, on the other hand was frozen, as immovable as the Dividing Wall once was. He and the king stared at one another.

"I did not know how else to protect you. Your mother...your mother had just died. You wouldn't stop crying. And the Panther!" The king closed his eyes and composed himself again. "Every day, he called out at the Dividing Wall. He called for your blood."

Manny didn't know what to think. He had always felt like he didn't belong in the tailor's shop, despite how well his parents treated him. But to come to find out he'd lost two mothers, and was about to lose his father before getting to know him, what was he supposed to do?

Just as his thoughts started to go toward anger over what he had lost, he remembered life with his family in the tailor shop. It had been a loving home. And they had been preparing him, in their reluctant way. The education. The training as a squire.

"Forgive...me?" The king's pallor was like the ashes in the hearth, and the rumbling in his breathing signaled that death was near.

Manny reached forward and held the king's hand, despite the sores. "Yes, my king. Father. I forgive you." What else was he to say? He could give the king peace now and work out his true feelings later.

The king gave a small smile. His eyes looked upon Manny with all the love and joy and pride that he had held back for seventeen years. The feeling overwhelmed Manny.

"The cross? Your mother's?" said the king.

Manny slipped his cross out from around his neck. "This one?" It was gold inlaid with blue lapis. "This was my mother's?" He had always thought the piece was made of fake gems. Now, he realized they were real.

The king nodded. "Last thing she...gave you. To remember her love." The king's hand went slack. He breathed a few more labored breaths, then the room went silent.

Sir Fletcher lifted a sheet about the king's head. He turned to Manny and bowed. "Your Highness."

$\mathcal{G}$ressa fought Old Anne the entire way up the turret to her chambers. Servants flew about the castle with hot water and cloths and garlic strings and any odd matter of remedy. Gressa wanted to be in the midst of it all, not secreted away. Her entire life had been secreted away and she was tired of being the Tower Princess.

"But I must get you to safety, miss. Once you're there, I'll go find answers for you." Old Anne's face was set. She was equally as stubborn as Gressa.

"Fine. Here I shall remain, and remain here I shall," she said, plunking down on her bed, with no intention of actually staying put. Old Anne had to know that about her.

"We'll make a plan as soon as we know what we are dealing with. Is that appropriate?"

Gressa nodded. She could wait ten minutes for Old Anne to find out what was going on.

A grating noise interrupted her thoughts, sending goosebumps up her arm. She pressed her nose against her window, trying to find the source. It was coming from the Dividing Wall. Why, Herrick's men were attacking the wall! And it was crumbling. The Dividing Wall within the courtyard was coming down.

The men of North Morlaix pitched ax strike after ax strike at the crumbling mortar. Herrick stood holding a torch high, supervising the whole thing. The firelight danced across his dark features.

But how? Year after year he had tried to *accidentally* harm the wall by throwing rocks and letting other heavy implements crash into the stones. What had changed?

They were able to break a hole in the wall near the tournament grounds because of cooperation, everyone had said so. But there was no way the South would have agreed to removing this portion of the wall, not so close to their inner keep.

Herrick had found a way. It was the meadow he was after. The magic inside. Gressa couldn't stay in her room. She had to stop Herrick, immediately. He couldn't take her meadow.

She met Old Anne running up the stairs. "Princess, it's worse than we thought."

At the same time, they said their news:

"Your father is dying," said Old Anne.

"Herrick is tearing down the wall," said Gressa.

They stared at each other. "My father is dying?" asked Gressa.

Old Anne cupped Gressa's face in her hands. "'Tis the pestilence. The doctor says there is nothing he can do."

Gressa shook her head. "It isn't the pestilence. It only looks like it. Herrick purchased a poison from the trickster, I'm sure of it now. I gave the antidote to Manny for his mother, but it was too late. I still have it." Her shoulders slumped. "It's in the meadow. I have to find a way past Herrick. Please don't stand in my way. I fear King Simon is already dead and therefore the peace treaty is over. Herrick can do as he pleases unless the people stop him."

"I'll come with you."

As soon as Gressa and Old Anne reached the courtyard, the men had already broken through. Herrick pushed aside all his brothers and fighting men and he alone was tearing through the wall. The noise had brought out a number of townspeople, both those concerned for their ailing king, and those curious about what the Panther was doing to the wall this time.

Finally, with sweat pouring off his face, he stepped back. The hole was large enough for a man to crawl through. He turned to retrieve his torch from his closest knight.

Gressa held her breath. Would the meadow be there, or would it be lost to her forever?

As he turned, his eyes locked on her.

"Care to join me, dear sister?" He waved her over. "Don't be shy. You can give me the grand tour. Show me what treasures lie within."

She took one step forward and her knees locked.

Herrick grabbed her and pushed her toward the hole. "You first."

Gressa climbed through, determined to run for her shelter—if it was there—and retrieve the antidote before Herrick could stop her. She fit easily through the hole. Herrick, with the torch and his larger bulk, struggled and took longer.

As soon as Gressa climbed through the hole she knew her meadow had not disappeared. The brook babbled merrily, as if unaware of the intrusion, and the breeze blew through the tree spreading its fresh fragrance. Using what little light the crescent moon cast, she stumbled forward. Herrick called out for her as she reached her shelter. He had made it through the hole.

Now, where was the vial? She felt around in the dark. She had to have it in the folds of her skirt by the time he got there. She searched through her pillows, her books, her drawing implements, dumping open all her boxes. Herrick was now at the door. His torch made his shadow as large as a monster as he loomed over her fragile lean-to.

"You cannot hide from me anymore, sister."

In a flash, the shelter was torn from the ground, leaving Gressa and her private world exposed to the torch light. She shrank back.

Herrick laughed. "Someone needs to teach you how to build a better shelter. Now, up with you. Show me what is so special about this place." He waved the torch in an arc around him. As he did so, the light glimmered against the vial near her pillows. Gressa scooped it up as she rose, tucking it into the folds of her skirt.

"This was the special part of the meadow. My own place, which you just tore apart."

Herrick, still in a jovial mood, only smiled. "You know of what I speak. The magic. Where is it? How does it work?"

"I don't know. I only came here to be alone." How was she going to get away from Herrick? She needed to get the medicine to father. And King Simon.

Herrick scoffed. "Don't you have enough alone time in your tower?"

"That's different. Here I was free." Herrick had stopped listening. He was too busy searching the meadow.

While he was preoccupied, she scuttled back through the wall and, ignoring all the inquisitive looks, raced to save her father.

$\mathcal{M}$anny was blocked from entering the Dividing Wall. He searched desperately to find the opening, but the stone was unyielding. Along with Sir Fletcher and several other knights, he tried to tear down the new wall King Simon had constructed, but could not remove a single stone. The magic that held fast the original Dividing Wall now held this new wall.

At the hole near the tournament, they found a new wall being hastily constructed by the North Morlaixers, knights guarding the hole with both armed men and hot oil to pour down on any who came too close. It seems friendly relations with the North were over.

"What next, sire?" asked Sir Fletcher. He had left King Simon to the ministrations of the doctor, who had returned in a hurry, minutes after the king's death. The doctor was to tell no one about the king's death until morning. Sir Fletcher would make the announcement, unfurling the death banner and announcing Manny's upcoming coronation at the same time. They couldn't find Nigel.

Manny leaned back, staring into the night sky. He was now the king, but no one save Sir Fletcher and Nigel knew. Manny's thoughts reeled. He needed to talk to his tailor father—not that he doubted King Simon's words—but to get answers. And, being the king of South Morlaix, he had to prepare for the Panther's attack, for that would be next. And Gressa. Sweet Gressa. He had to rescue her. It was likely King Jorvik was also dead by now.

Sir Fletcher shifted his weight. "Take all the time you need."

Manny looked over at him. "Did you know who I was?"

"I suspected you were someone important to the king. After all, he put you in training with me over his son—that is, Nigel. That caught my attention and my suspicion. My interest was piqued further when we were attacked in the woods."

"Do you think the Panther knows who I really am?" The thought chilled him.

Sir Fletcher shrugged. "It's possible, but I doubt it. All I can say for certain is that he knew you had been singled out and that was enough to do you harm early on, before you received your full training." He smiled, a rare sight. "You concerned him, and I'd not seen that before."

Manny turned his back on the wall. "How would you advise?"

"Attack him first. It's our only hope. We have not the force that he does, nor have we access to the power he has just secured for himself with moving the wall." Sir Fletcher continued to stare at Manny. "Do you know what new power he will have?"

"No. There was nothing beyond the wall but a tree and a brook. It was...peaceful."

After Manny sent Sir Fletcher on his way, he ran to the nursery tower. Taking a moment, he paused at the entrance to Nigel's chambers. To think that he slept here as a baby. That he should have spent all his days here. Manny patted the door frame and moved on. There would be time for mourning his lost years later. Now was the time for action.

He held his torch high in the nursery prepared for a sister that never came. If this was where Gressa entered the castle, surely this would be the way back to her side. There was so much he needed to tell her.

Manny paced the back wall, looking for the opening. This wall was even more solid than the one outside. He searched frantically to no avail. He made himself slow down. Look, but not look. Try to catch a shadow to lead him through. It was no use. There was no way through. Something had changed.

He would have to join the men crossing the divide by boat and risk attack out on the sea where the people of North Morlaix felt most at home. He felt sure all they needed to do was to capture the Panther to charge him with King Simon's murder. Then they would see how many true followers the Panther had.

As Manny left the room, his torchlight danced around the room and a shadow caught his eye. Without a second thought, he lunged toward the spot on the wall and stepped through to North Morlaix.

Immediately, he doused his torch and plunged the stairwell into darkness. He froze, listening. Based on the silence, he figured he was in a little-used corner of the castle. Thinking of the mirror image of South Morlaix, Manny hoped he had landed in Gressa's tower. Eagerly, he climbed the stairs, feeling his way along the cold stone walls. At the first door, he pressed his ear to the wood. Silence. He opened the door and paused. He heard no sounds of sleeping. Soft moonlight entered through the window and he could make out a small bed with its trundle pulled out for the night. Near the window stood two embroidery hoops.

He closed the door and went on. With each step, his muscles tensed further. He reviewed his weapons supply: a knife in each boot, dagger at his side. His light chain mail protection was quieter than the heavy metal Sir Fletcher wanted him to wear. Manny's plan was not to engage, but to sneak in, deliver a message, then lay low until the morning attack.

Where was everyone? Manny had been inside the castle of North Morlaix for a good twenty minutes and had yet to meet a soul. He had found several bedrooms, but they were all empty. He was beginning to expect the next door he opened to be a brightly lit room where he would be surrounded and taken prisoner. At least they wouldn't know who he really was. No one on this side of the wall could know he was the king.

Finally, he made his way to where he thought the king's chambers would be. A dangerous move, but he had to find out what was going on in this abandoned castle. No guards were stationed, and the door was open, letting out soft light. Manny eased forward and looked around the edge of the door.

King Jorvik lay on his bed, eyes closed, but visibly breathing. He was yet alive! At his side stood his wife, and Gressa crouched forward on a chair, her head on the bed. Behind her, a friar stood, head bowed. And Old Anne sat plaintively in a chair by the fire. Manny didn't mean to, but when he saw the king still alive, he gasped.

The friar lifted his head.

Before Manny could react, the friar had pinned him against the wall. Manny made a mental note to never turn his back on a friar.

"Who are you?"

"Why, that's Manny. From South Morlaix." Gressa tugged on the friar's arm. "Release him, Siguard, he'll do us no harm."

For several seconds Manny stared into Gressa's welcoming eyes. She looked well. No sign of the pestilence on her.

"What are you doing here? How is your king?"

"Dead." Manny's voice caught. He wanted to tell her he was the king's son, but not in front of her family.

Gressa's eyelashes fluttered. "I'm sorry. I had no way to get you the balsam. Herrick has changed the wall."

Manny nodded. "I crossed over…" He glanced at the friar and caught himself. "The way you did. The other way is gone."

"You must go back. He can't find you here. He's called off the tournament and has resealed the wall." She looked up at Manny with frightened eyes. "He has been to the meadow. He plans to discover the magic and use it against South Morlaix." She looked at her father and continued. "He tried to kill father, but failed. He will try again. We don't know what to do. We have to hide him."

Her face grew hopeful. "Would King Nigel permit us refuge in South Morlaix?"

What Gressa was asking was not part of Manny's plan. He studied the three faces looking at him and the pale face of the sleeping king. Manny did have the authority now to make such a decision.

"Yes. Your castle is deserted, so no one should see us if we move quickly. But can we get to a boat without being seen?"

The queen frowned as she rolled up the blankets under the king to create a stretcher. "We have no choice. All the knights are loyal to Herrick. The castle is deserted because everyone is examining the Dividing Wall."

Manny and Siguard grasped the rolled blanket near King Jorvik's head while Ingrid, Gressa, and Old Anne readied themselves to carry the blanket at his feet.

"Everyone, pull the blanket taut," Siguard said. "Now, lift."

King Jorvik was not a light man. Manny's trained muscles strained under the weight and the women struggled at their burden. They shuffled out the room and into the hall. Inch by inch they moved the king. As they stepped into the great hall, the doors banged open, and Herrick stood there with his arms outstretched as if claiming the space as his own. There was no place to hide.

Herrick's black gaze took in the king, still breathing, and his family members obviously trying to move him to hiding. He shook his head. "Not dead yet? Father, what does it take? Do you care so little about me and this kingdom that you cling to life needlessly?"

No one spoke.

The knights, coming in now behind Herrick, saw the king alive and many began to shift their feet uncomfortably.

"No wonder the magic is not coming to me. You are still alive." Herrick's hands clenched. He looked around the room as if deciding what to do next. He waved his hands. "Seize them all and put them in the dungeon until I decide what to do with them."

Several of his knights burst forth and grabbed the women. Manny and Siguard quickly but gently set the king down on the ground. Manny pulled his dagger, ready to fight, while Siguard took up a defensive position beside him. Having felt Siguard's strength, Manny was grateful for the support.

"Brothers," Siguard called out. "Our father is yet alive. Do not serve the Panther in this way. He is not our king but a traitor."

"Axell?" questioned Gressa, looking at the knight who pinned her arms behind her back. "Why are you doing this?"

"Hush, sister." He backed away with her, returning to the king's quarters. "You need not be a witness."

The knight holding the queen tried to drag her away, too, but she refused. "I am still your queen. I must stay with Jorvik." She fought him until he let her return to the king's side.

Manny concentrated on the fight in front of him. First, he had to save the king. Then, he would rescue Gressa.

Everyone drew their weapons and someone shoved a blade into Manny's hands. Some of the knights broke rank with the Panther and joined the protection around the king. Manny and Siguard fought hard to stay between the king and the Panther.

Together, they parried blow after blow from the Panther until Manny thought his arms would fall off from the strain. If he'd been fighting on his own, the Panther would have won by now.

Manny let his guard down for a second and the Panther's blade pierced his chain mail, cutting through to his flesh. Reflexively, Manny sucked in a breath and took a step back.

Then the knight Gressa had called Axell lunged into the fray, blocking another attack aimed at Manny.

"Thank you," said Manny, surprised.

He was wondering what happened to Gressa when she slipped in through another door and quietly made her way to her father. He wished she'd stayed where Axell had sent her, but seeing what she was doing, he understood. She was trying to keep her father alive.

The tide was turning against Herrick, and he was fuming. "It's only a matter of time. I will remember who was loyal to me!" He then noticed Gressa giving the king more medicine. He spun away from the fighting, lowering his weapon. He strode over to her and snatched the bottle. "What is this?"

"A balsam," she whispered.

Herrick stared at the bottle. It was the same amber glass vial with the emblem of a leaf on it that Gressa had given him to help his mother. That seemed like such a long time ago. So much had changed.

Again, Herrick looked around the room, as if he were figuring out a puzzle. The light from a torch glinted off Old Anne's necklace from where she stood bravely by the queen. He turned and gazed at the hilt of a knight's sword. The symbol swinging from the friar's belt. He looked at his feet, where there was a tile mosaic of a tree.

Manny cocked his head. The leaf symbol was even in North Morlaix.

Silently, Herrick turned and went out into the courtyard. Everyone followed to see what he was doing. He stopped at the door frame of the blacksmith's shop and brushed his fingers over a carving of a leaf in the wood.

"That cursed tree! It binds the kingdoms together and blocks me from what I want."

CHAPTER 55

*H*errick smashed his way into the blacksmith shop, grabbed an ax, and led a curious crowd toward the Dividing Wall.

Gressa's heart sunk. There was only one thing to do with an ax in the meadow. She raced after him, with Manny beside her. They maneuvered their way to the front of the crowd, but by the time they crawled through the tunnel, Herrick was lunging toward the tree with the ax high above his head.

The tree, which held such warm memories for Gressa, stood tall in its beauty. With the light of the torches illuminating its branches, it seemed to grow and fill the space in the meadow. Tiny pinpricks of light played in and out of the branches, like fireflies dancing. It was the prettiest sight Gressa had ever seen.

The first swing cut cleanly through one of the lower branches with a loud crack. The branch she had learned to climb on fell to the ground, and the tree groaned. Gressa echoed the groan deep in her throat. *No.*

Herrick chopped and chopped at the trunk, striking wound after wound into the tree and leaving deep white scars with each strike.

"No!" Gressa tried to run forward to stop him, but Manny held her back.

"You can't. Not now."

The tree was leaning, slowly falling, beyond saving. The tiny lights began to swarm around Herrick as if attacking him, yet Herrick continued to hack at the tree, his fierceness bringing it to the ground where he continued to slash even though his wild swings often missed and dug into the ground instead with deep thuds.

He tossed the dull ax aside and grabbed the closest torch and lit the tree on fire. A burst of heat flooded the area, and firelight danced on everyone's shocked faces.

Old Anne caught up with them and put her arm around Gressa. "A rowan tree," she whispered. "It was a rowan tree." She spoke louder. "A rowan tree!" She ran to the brook and began scooping up water and splashing it on the flames. "A rowan tree!"

Gressa and Manny stared at each other. They hadn't known. All the trees had died before they were born. If they'd had known, what would they have done differently? All this time she had a rowan berry in her pomander. If she'd only shown it to Old Anne, she might have learned the truth sooner. She could have made her own rowan balsam and not had to trade with the trickster.

Others followed Old Anne's lead and helped her scoop water.

The Panther backed away into the shadows, watching the townspeople try in vain to save the tree. It was futile work. The flames roared on, making it too hot to get close to the tree. Several buckets had been brought from town and so those who had been cupping water in their hands to douse the flames stepped back to make room. The buckets did little to help, either. Soon, all the townspeople gave up and watched their hope burn.

Manny pulled on Gressa's elbow, coaxing her to walk away from the sight. Reluctantly, she turned away, mourning the loss of the great tree.

A large figure moved in the shadows. "Papa?"

King Jorvik, propped up by Axell, had just come through the tunnel in the Dividing Wall.

"Is it true?" he asked. "Was that a rowan tree?"

Gressa nodded. "Are you all right?"

"I'll be fine, daughter. Thanks to your rowan balsam." He scanned the crowd. "Where is Herrick?"

Manny pointed into the darkness beyond the rowan tree, now burning embers. "Last I saw he was over there watching the tree burn."

King Jorvik looked over his shoulder at the men pouring out of the Dividing Wall. Knights from South Morlaix.

Gressa squeezed Manny's arm. "Axell was always on our side. He escorted me out of the great room so I could signal the South Morlaix knights. I bet you didn't know I could shoot a flaming arrow."

Manny laughed. "I'm not surprised in the least."

Sir Fletcher emerged from the tunnel, and then reached back to help someone else through. A gold crown glinted in the torchlight. Gressa caught her breath. *King Simon.* She looked at Manny, but he was already running to help his king.

"How are you alive?" asked Manny.

King Simon stood shakily to his feet, Sir Fletcher propping one arm and Manny getting under the other.

"It was Abigail. When Nigel left the castle, he went and got her. Somehow, he knew she could help. She had a rowan balsam."

"Amazing," whispered Gressa. Once again, she felt remorse for the tree. If she had only known what was plainly in front of her. She could have replenished everyone's supply.

"Axell," said King Jorvik. "Take a contingent and arrest Herrick and anyone loyal to him. Confine them to the dungeon where Siguard is waiting for them." Father turned to Gressa. "He said you told him your suspicions. I wish I had listened sooner."

"Thank you." Gressa nodded. She wished she'd been more persistent in her suspicions.

King Simon gestured for Sir Fletcher and his knights to assist.

"Father, come rest over here," said Manny, leading the king to the flat rock near the brook.

"Father?" asked Gressa. Why was the tailor's son calling the king of South Morlaix "Father?" She followed them to the brook where the crowd was thinning out. Some of the people had followed Axell and Sir Fletcher to watch them arrest the Panther, while others had gone on home after a long and tiring night.

King Jorvik, with an eye on his sons, joined them at the brook.

Manny settled King Simon, then turned to Gressa. "I was born in the castle to King Simon and Queen Margaret. When my mother died shortly after my birth, my father brought in another babe to take my place while I was sent to grow up with the tailor's family. He did it to protect me."

King Simon interjected, "I never should have done it. I feared the Panther would target Manny, and I couldn't bear losing him, too."

"Our quarrel didn't stop with us, eh, Simon?" said Jorvik. "But our kingdoms, the rowan trees, our families. We nearly destroyed everything."

Gressa didn't know what to think. She stared open-mouthed at Manny.

He held out a cross necklace he wore around his neck. "My mother gave me this before she died. I've had it all my life, but didn't know its significance until now."

"I know that cross." King Jorvik held out a shaky hand to touch it. "King Rorick gave us each one after the Battle of Five and Two. I also gave mine to one of my children."

Gressa, eyes lowered, touched the empty place at her neck where the cross used to be. When she looked up again, her father had pulled her necklace out of his robe and held it out to her. "I had word that the trickster was trying to trade a jewel cross necklace of great value. When I didn't see you wearing it any longer, I secured it once again."

Thrilled to have her necklace back, Gressa quickly put it on.

"I'm sorry, Father. I used it to buy the balsam from the trickster. He called it an antidote."

"The redeemed necklace was meant to be a wedding present for you."

In all the excitement Gressa had forgotten about her betrothal. "But Nigel is not the true prince. Does that mean my engagement is off?"

Manny cleared his throat. "Do you wish to end your betrothal to the prince of South Morlaix?" He bowed slightly, watching for her reaction.

She opened her eyes wide as she realized the implication, and what he was asking her. She shook her head. "I always keep my commitments. For the sake of the people in two kingdoms, I shall remain betrothed to the South Morlaixan prince."

He grinned, and swept her up to spin her around. This time, when he bent his lips to hers, she didn't push him away, rather, she clung tighter. Closing her eyes, she realized she was finally free. They all were. As she kissed him back, she tried to express how long she'd been wanting to be with him, Manny the tailor's son or Manny the prince, it didn't matter. He was her Manny.

EPILOGUE

*I*n a land not so far away, where the people are friendly and their hope is young, lies the kingdom of Morlaix. It is a famous land where people travel from afar to see the opening in the Dividing Wall and the secret meadow, secret no longer.

For it is in Kingdom Morlaix where a boy and a girl grew up on opposite sides of a Dividing Wall. Did I say grew up? I meant, fell in love. After all, they were both from Kingdom Morlaix.

Here the girl comes now, pushing a wheelbarrow weighed heavy with a rock. She has chosen it from her garden for its size and smooth texture, so the female woodlings tell me. They are besotted with her and rarely leave her alone, although she does not know it.

The rock is one that has been weathered by the sea, tossed and tumbled against other rocks until its sharp edges were worn off. On its surface, she has painted a tree in full spring bloom to mark the place where the last rowan tree grew, and where she and the boy met. A fateful event that changed not only their lives, but the entire kingdom.

The boy and the girl spend much time together. When walking through town, he peers into the alleyways and shadows looking for an old friend. He thought he'd seen him once, a shock of white-blond hair near the docks. He had. But the friend did not want to be found. The blond's future is uncertain, and we still watch him.

Meanwhile, the tailor, who himself paid a great price for the restoration of the kingdom, has begun work on a wedding dress for the princess. When the timing is right, there will be vows and a new family born.

We expect the celebration will take place in the meadow between the walls. As much as the prince and princess wanted to seal their secret place and keep it just for them, they decided to share it with the kingdom. A wise decision. A test passed.

King Jorvik, his lesson learned, announced wise son Axell to be his successor. He then confined the one named Herrick to the princess's old tower, complete with locks and two guards stationed at the door. Here, this son paces day and night at a window instead of a wall.

> *HIS ONLY VIEW IS OF HIS RIVAL KINGDOM:*
> *FREED OF THEIR FEAR, SADNESS, AND PALL.*
> *HIS LESSON IS NOT LEARNED;*
> *THEREFORE, HIS PUNISHMENT TRULY GALLS.*

King Simon, his lesson learned, has not recovered from his poisoning and will soon sing his final sing. When he does, the boy, Manny, will step into his destiny. He trains now with the one called Sir Fletcher. A knight of highest honor, whom I could not have chosen better myself.

The meadow remains a mystery—how can it exist, still between the walls? It draws the curious, and with them, increased trade with the countries which previously shunned Morlaix.

The wall was widened into a space large enough for a doorway and a corresponding door was opened on the South Morlaix side. The brook's waters were found to have healing properties—a happy consequence, folks assumed, from the rowan tree having grown nearby.

The princess draws closer now, and I must speak with her.

She pushes her wheelbarrow over the bumpy ground to the scorched mound where charred pieces remain. She finds a level patch, and, using all her strength, nestles the heavy rock onto it.

"What is this?" she says before I have a chance to speak.

A shoot of green pushes its way out of the blackened earth right in front of her eyes. She watches it grow into a respectable size, unfurling its green leaves. Rowan leaves.

"Oh! Look at you, brave thing," she says. "May you grow mightier than before."

She feels my presence and looks up from the sapling and into my eyes. Likely, I'm the strangest creature she's ever seen. I'm as tall as her waist, bearded, and covered in dirt from head to toe as I've just crawled out of the ground. A swarm of woodlings circle me, but she probably doesn't notice them. Nor does she notice the boy cutting across the meadow to join us.

She bows—impressive—then I nod and speak:

> *"I HAVE SEVERAL WORDS TO SAY, TOO.*
> *FIRST, HELLO AND GOOD MORN'.*
> *THE WOODLINGS WISH TO THANK YOU,*
> *AS FOR THIS GREAT PURPOSE, YOU WERE BORN.*
>
> *YOU HAVE DONE WHAT OTHERS COULD NOT.*
> *WHILE THEY SAW A WALL,*
> *IT WAS ANSWERS THAT YOU SOUGHT,*
> *AND BRINGING PEACE WAS YOUR CALL.*
>
> *OUR PEOPLE WILL RETURN*
> *IF WE ARE WELCOME HERE.*
> *THE LAND IS HEALING FROM THE BURN,*
> *WITH THE PEACE THAT YOU MADE CLEAR."*

At the end of my poem, I lift my hand and one of the tiny

woodlings lands on my palm. She had made a special request to reveal her presence.

As the princess watches, the speck grows and grows until the woodling is the size of an exceptionally large dragonfly, only, resembling a pixie.

The princess gasps and bends down for a closer look. My little woodling waves at her.

"Aren't you sweet," the princess says. "Such tiny feet. Oh! Are you the artist who drew on my tablet?"

My woodling jumps with glee.

> "*A YOUNG WOODLING YOU DO SEE,*
> *WE'LL MAKE OUR HOME IN THIS NEW TREE.*"

My gaze moves up over the princess's shoulder. She turns to see her prince, sweaty from morning exercises, standing behind her with a stunned expression on his face.

"I'm glad you came," she said. But when she turns around, we are gone from her view. Back to our silent, watching place.

"That explains a lot," the prince says. "I thought our kingdom was overrun by gnats, but they are tiny woodlings."

"They wanted us to find the meadow. To find each other." She smiles. "And this whole time, my brother thought he was the one in charge."

"Is that a rowan sapling?" the prince asks. He moves closer to her. "After that fire, I thought I'd never see another again." His arm circles her waist and he kisses her hair, above the ear. "Next to you, that's the best thing I've ever seen in Morlaix. North or South."

"It's our future," she says.

The tower princess is correct. This time, instead of leaving a hole, I left hope.

AUTHOR'S NOTE

The Tower Princess is the first in a new series I'm calling *The Lost Fairy Tales*. These tales are original stories, not retellings. Though, like all good fairy tales, they will draw from familiar tropes that make fairy tales fun to read.

DOWNLOAD A FREE FAIRY TALE

Go to ShonnaSlayton.com to sign up for updates and pick up your free story.

facebook.com/ShonnaSlaytonAuthor

twitter.com/ShonnaSlayton

instagram.com/shonna.slayton

ACKNOWLEDGMENTS

I've got a lovely team of beta readers who read through advance copies of this novel and gave me some wonderful advice. Thanks to Kristi Doyle, Sarah Chanis, Julie Ropelewski, LynnDell Watson, Shawna Shade, Olivia Farr, and Rebekah Slayton. It's so fun to work behind the scenes with you. (And also Stacy Abrams and Theresa M. Cole who read an even earlier rendition.) Additional thanks to Brandi Stewart, editor genie and bookseller extraordinaire, for a final pair of eyes on the story.

SPINDLE (PREVIEW)

PROLOGUE

Two servants filled the largest fireplace in the castle with wood while a small gathering anxiously watched on. Small bits of kindling and cotton on the bottom and larger pieces of dry hickory on top. It would be a fire that lit fast and burned hot. One of the servants bent down, striking the flint and setting the kindling aflame.

Aurora's face immediately warmed with the heat, and she allowed herself to hope. Her nightmare would soon be over.

"Thank you. Leave us, please," she said.

The servants exited, closing the solid wooden door behind them with an ominous *thud*.

Aurora reached for her fiancé's hand and gave it a squeeze. He kissed her forehead in response. *Such a courageous, patient man.* She turned to the fairies gathered in the shadows. They nodded encouragingly. They, too, had been waiting for this to end.

Careful not to prick her finger, Aurora took one last look at the item that had cursed her. Such an ordinary object, aside from the pretty scrollwork carved in the wood. No one would suspect the power it wielded—and that was the danger.

One of the fairies coughed, reminding her to continue.

"The end," Aurora said with finality, and tossed the spindle into the fire. No one else would ever go through the horrors she had. Still, she held her breath, fearful of what might happen. Were they standing too close? Would there be an explosion of magic? They waited.

Nothing.

Not a crackle, a sizzle, or a hiss.

Aurora bent down and peered into the flames. What she saw made her heart pound with fear. She'd thought her ordeal was over. Her hundred years of turmoil had ended, and she had found love with a prince who was eager to show her what she had missed while she was sleeping.

"Why doesn't it burn?" she demanded.

The good fairies gathered around. "I was afeared of this," said one. "The curse still lives. You will not be able to destroy it until it fulfills its intended purpose."

"Isodora will be furious," said another. "Her powers are wrapped up in this unfulfilled curse. We must hide it in a place where no young girl can ever find it again. For if a girl before her seventeenth birthday pricks her finger...."

"We cannot help her," said the third fairy. "She will die."

CHAPTER ONE

Briar walked the length of her spinning frames, keeping a close eye on the whirling threads. She'd been shut down more often than not today and tried to keep her mind off of her lost wages. It was Saturday, so they'd be ending early, giving her time to go home to the country and spend the night with her young siblings and their nanny.

All she did at the cotton mill, she did for those children.

Out of the corner of her eye, she saw several threads break on frame number four. Her heart sank. "Drat."

Quickly, she pulled the shipper handle on four and waited for the spinning to stop. With her other frames, she could easily fix a few threads that had turned thin while the machine was running, but not this frame. It had a mind of its own and would likely pinch her fingers if she tried.

She looked around for Henry. He worked in the machine shop and had a knack for fixing this persnickety frame. His boss allowed him to come up to the spinning room and doff for her, tweaking the frame each time to keep it running. Most doffers were children, their small hands the right size for slipping through the frames and removing the full bobbins and putting on new ones. Henry, despite being seventeen, didn't seem to mind helping her even though the other boys his age gave him a ribbing. He had been her first friend when she moved to town with her family, and a loyal one at that, so she was thankful for his help.

Briar set to work tying threads and straightening out bobbins.

"Can't leave you alone for a minute," called a voice close to her ear.

Henry. He had to yell above the roaring noise of a roomful of spinning frames. He reached out and pulled off a bobbin, then pointed. "This here is your problem. Something's wrong with this spindle and it sets the others off." He took out his tools and straightened the metal spindle.

Briar finished tying the last broken thread. "Can't you replace it?" she yelled back.

Henry shook his head. "Already have. Every one I put in here goes crooked." He grinned. "Besides, if I fix it for good, I won't get to see you every day."

Briar rolled her eyes, which only seemed to encourage him further.

With a wink, he pushed the bobbin cart ahead and began swapping out the full bobbins for empties. While he did that, Briar started up number four again, staying long enough to make sure all the threads caught and were spinning evenly before moving on to check her neglected frames.

When Henry finished doffing, he waved to catch her attention, signaling he was done. She lifted her chin and smiled her thanks. Then he tapped the edge of number four—the same spot every time—and was off.

The only person completely dependable in my life is Henry Prince.

Sure, Nanny was always available for the children, but that was only temporary. Stiff and unyielding as the spinning frames, Nanny had only agreed to help out for a year, ending at Briar's seventeenth birthday. After that, if Briar hadn't come up with a more permanent solution for the children, they'd be turned over to the orphan asylum in town that would put them on the orphan train sure as anything. No one would take three children all at once. They'd be split up and would never see one another again.

Until last week, Briar thought she'd found a permanent solution. But now, instead of planning for a summer wedding, she was scrambling for ways to earn more money to bring the children back into town with her and was finding it nigh impossible. No matter how hard she worked at the mill or how much extra piecework she took on, it would never be enough on her own. Wheeler—her former sweetheart—had spoiled everything when he changed his mind.

Finally, the overseer shut off the power to the frames and the day was over.

Briar raced out the door and down the outside stairs to the mill courtyard, getting jostled by the constant stream of operatives leaving the buildings.

There was her room-mate Mim coming down from the weaving room. Briar waved.

"Let's go, then," said Mim, straightening her new Sunday bonnet that she had saved up several weeks for.

Mim was a few years older than Briar, the fashion expert of their boardinghouse and the only blonde in the mix. She was a gem with a needle and had been teaching Briar how to smock little girls' dresses, adding pleats with colorful patterns to the bodice and sleeves.

Briar had also worn her best hat to work. Not a new hat. It

belonged to her mam, so it was dated but decent. She'd also risked wearing her best cotton dress, worried all day the hem would come away soaked in the grease that was liberally applied to the machines and often dripped onto the floors. They didn't have time to go back to the boardinghouse and change, if Briar were to make it home to the children before dark.

It was important she look presentable for where Mim was taking her: across town to where the wives of the mill executives lived and had their babies.

"You sure you want to do this?" Mim asked.

"Do what?" said Henry. He sidled up between them, his hands in his pockets.

"I'm looking for piecework," Briar said quietly.

He raised his eyebrows in surprise. "Don't you think you work hard enough at the mill?"

"You know why I have to take on more." It had been a long week and Briar was tired, more weary of soul than of body. She could push herself to work a little harder and, if nothing else, try to mask the hurt left in her heart.

"Let me—"

"No." Briar stopped him. Henry was the kind of guy who would give you the shirt off his back. "I can't. You can't. Your family needs what you bring in."

"Then let me walk with you."

Mim stopped. "You'll do no such thing." She looked him up and down as if to emphasize her point. He was covered in grease, wearing an old, torn pair of work trousers, and his shirt opened one button too many, on account of a button falling off and not being replaced.

Mim did have a point. It would be hard enough to impress these ladies that she could do the job neatly and cleanly without Henry hanging around in the background.

"Then I'll wait for you by the road to see you home. You *are* still going to the cottage tonight?" His forehead wrinkled in concern.

Briar nodded. She couldn't stay in town without telling the children first. They looked forward to her weekend visits. "Thanks, but you don't have to. Your mam will be worried."

"No, she won't. She'll know I'm with you." He turned and sauntered back toward the mill.

Mim snorted. "He doesn't know his mother, does he?"

Briar frowned, thinking of what she'd shared with her room-mates.

Henry had invited her to his house one day, not long after the children had moved in with Nanny. He was showing off, having never brought her there before. Their entire property was fenced off with ominous KEEP OUT signs posted everywhere, making Briar nervous from the start, even though she had already met his parents.

They had fed the chickens, petted the goats, and he was about to invite her into the house when his mother stood arms akimbo in the doorway. Her usual smile was gone, replaced by stern, set lips.

"Henry, may I speak with you inside, please?" she'd asked in a way that let Briar know she wasn't to follow. Trouble was, the window was open and Briar could hear everything.

"How could you bring her out here? What were you thinking?"

The white lace curtain in the window fluttered in the breeze. Briar stared at it, straining to hear more. As if of their own accord, her legs started forward, taking her closer.

"I'm sorry, Mama." His voice came out whisper-quiet.

"We don't know what causes a girl to be drawn to the spindle. You need to be careful who you bring here. The farm is not a place for a girl, especially a girl like Briar. Take her home now."

Henry had come out with a basket, the first of many that he would bring to the cottage filled with food from Mrs. Prince's garden. His grin faltered when he saw her so close to the house, but then he smiled wide and led her out of the yard. He never explained anything.

Nor did he ever invite her back.

From then on, Briar not only avoided the farm, she avoided Mrs. Prince, who seemed to have something against girls "like her." She couldn't figure out if Mrs. Prince was against spinner girls in general or *Irish* spinner girls in particular.

Briar wanted to tell Mrs. Prince it wasn't that she was drawn to the spindle, it was simply the only job she could get. Options were limited, which was why, with Mim's help, she was hoping these housewives would take the time to judge her by her work.

Mim rang the doorbell of the first house, a new, two-story brick structure surrounded by a manicured lawn and a dozen purplish-pink azalea bushes. Mrs. Chapman opened the front door. Dressed in a pretty green dress with a lace collar and puffed sleeves, she beamed at Mim.

"Have you finished already?"

Mim handed Mrs. Chapman the wrapped package. "Yes, ma'am. And please meet my room-mate, Briar Jenny. I've been teaching her, and she is ready to start taking on her own clients. Do you have another dress that needs smocking, or do you know of another mother wanting fancywork done?" Mim pulled out a sampler showcasing Briar's stitches.

Meanwhile, Briar stood silently under Mrs. Chapman's penetrating gaze. She stiffened as the woman's eyes roamed over Briar's auburn hair, her freckles.

Making judgments.

This wasn't going to work. Briar sensed it before Mim could.

There was no physical sign posted in the window, but Briar felt it in her being. She wasn't welcome here. NINA. *No Irish Need Apply.*

To continue reading, pick up your own copy of Sleeping Beauty's SPINDLE from your library or favorite bookseller.

WITHDRAWN